10679373

the man who got away

Books by Sumner Locke Elliott

The Man Who Got Away

Edens Lost

Some Doves and Pythons

Careful, He Might Hear You

the man who got away

by S U M N E R   L O C K E   E L L I O T T

Harper & Row, Publishers

New York, Evanston, San Francisco, London

FIRST EDITION

STANDARD BOOK NUMBER: 06–011183–6

LIBRARY OF CONGRESS CATALOG CARD NUMBER: 72-79706

Designed by Sidney Feinberg

For Tad

prologue

it was only

after a considerable time that Ruth began to think that George had been very long in the bathroom. Just when it began to occur to her she could never remember, never for the rest of her life was she able absolutely to recall. Only that there had been the continuous sound of the water runing into the washbasin and she, lying on the wicker chaise, reading and only half aware, soothed by words and water, conscious and not conscious, eventually became aware of a long sliver of time passing since he had said anything (had come to the bathroom door and asked her something she no longer remembered, never could recall it) and the water running, running, running . . .

His soapy razor lay on the marble-top sink and the hand towel beside it; the medicine cabinet mirror was slightly ajar, showing Ruth alone in the bathroom. Then she must have been so absorbed that she had not noticed him come out of the bathroom and cross the bedroom and go . . .

Not downstairs surely, for here were his clean shorts on the chair and his robe hanging behind the door and as she turned off the faucet she was prompted to do a childlike thing, to look behind the shower curtain.

Then had she drowsed? "George?" she asked the air. That had been it, then. She had unknowingly drowsed while he had dressed and gone downstairs or was in the little study which connected their bedroom with the hall.

Twenty to six, said his wristwatch on the dressing table.

She went downstairs.

She had no idea why she should have felt ill at ease with the way the late summer afternoon light lay on waxed floors, crisscrossed with moving shadows of branches, light falling silently on the white rugs and white chairs in the big empty (too white) drawing room and why, as she went now into the musty silent library, there should be an anxiety in her walk, almost a hurry, she who never bustled; no earthly reason why she should feel so washed with relief at the sight of him dangling in the deep shade in the hammock and, "There you are," she said smilingly, leaning over him.

But it was Andre Bouclez looking up at her lopsidedly and twisting around to find out did she want something, something he could do? No, she was looking for George, she said, and then to Charlotte Custis, sewing in the den: had George been downstairs? No? Not to her *knowledge,* Charlotte said without looking up. Then to Maiva, stuffing avocado in the kitchen. Had she seen Mr. Wood? Mr. Wood? Maiva was slow, Maiva needed a moment to figure out Mr. Wood; got him, liked him, the one who joked, the head of the house. But no, he had not been around, Maiva sighed, mincing tiny pink shrimp.

Both cars in the garage. The bicycles too.

As she went slowly down the path toward the swimming pool the word *prescience* came and went in her mind like a chord. She was noted for her cool. As far as anyone could remember never in her life had she reacted in alarm to anything other than spiders and it was generally agreed that she would remain cool under all circumstances including fire at sea. Her serenity, her unbreakability frequently chafed people; her warmth of reaction had been likened to the codfish but she never minded it when people said things in her hearing like Fatty Bronsen at an overcrowded and suffocating reception. "I'm so hot I'm *melt*ing. I've got to go and stand by Ruth Wood a minute." "Telling you good news," Andre Bouclez said, shrugging with exasperation, "is like pouring Napoleon brandy down the sink." This because she had not reacted sufficiently to George's having been given some award or other for a television documentary. But awards were not her *thing*, Ruth said, glad for George of course, but she had more regard for *re*ward.

"Oh, you lie in wait with those little saws of yours," Andre had said furiously because she had snubbed George's award; somehow lessened it.

And when she smiled because of her insufficiency to explain herself, it was mistaken for superiority.

Conversely, her insufficiency sometimes became her strength and buckler; it presented no alternative in a moment of indecision or panic, and where an adroit woman who saw possibilities of changing her fate might throw herself into feverish resistance, Ruth could only be still. Sometimes after she had been still long enough, events rearranged themselves for her satisfactorily.

George's Styrofoam armchair floated in the pool; little wavelets slupped at the steps.

Silently, turtlelike, Ruth let her mind move from suspicion to certainty that her prescience was correct.

That something unexplainable was happening; not unlike waking from a dream about snakes to find one coiled on the bed. The feeling was dreamlike and she would not let herself waken from it yet. It would be a while before she would be ready to say this or that might have happened. She was not yet going to admit to anything peculiar (she fixed her mind on George and he was right at this moment coming home along the path around the bay wearing his white duck pants and red sweater) because to admit it would introduce fact and fact would dictate action, doors would be flung open to her private rooms and enemies would swarm in to ransack her life.

She walked unhurriedly down to where the lawn ended in bayberry thickets overlooking the pebble beach and, looking down at the pathway, she thought she saw him a great way off; she willed it to be him and put a stop to this nonsense welling up in her. She saw him coming now, saw him striding along in his white pants, saw him turn into a saltbush, become a gull, fly off.

His absence was apparent. She could feel it, entering the house.

He is not here.

Before even going into the living room, He will not be there.

Turning on the first lamp of the evening, That's not his step in the hall.

"I've no idea where he went," her voice said coolly (hang on to your cool) and her hand went to play among her tangle of glass beads. Charlotte Custis and Andre Bouclez had begun to wonder. "Went out, I guess," Ruth said and looked squarely at them and they back at her. They had never liked her, with their fierce and often combative possessiveness of George; they could barely tolerate her and so they assaulted her with smiles and friendly winks and crinkled up their eyes at her in facial hypocrisies, calling her Ruthie, which she disliked, and emphasizing her redundancy whenever they had the chance, pointing out the needlessness of her by saying things to George like, "Oh, is *Ruthie* coming with us" and, "Oh, you brought *Ruthie*, how jolly."

Charlotte, with her fox terrier face wearing glasses, more than ever like a fox terrier in middle age, guarding George ("I'm Mr. Wood's *assistant*") from everyone she could; and Andre, who was weakly good-looking and very prone to break out in huffs without warning, was always slamming out through doors. Now for once they were in agreement, just a little worried.

Because where was George?

Then because they had nothing in common with Ruth except George they fell into an anxious silence punctuated only by pricking up their ears from time to time if they thought they heard a step, a cough outside, and from time to time Andre rushed out first the porch door and then the front door crying with relief that *here* he was at last.

And when the Tillotsens arrived, Ruth said calmly that George had gone out somewhere and when the Juliens arrived she said she guessed George had forgotten, for once, his guests, he was never so rude, as they all knew. She passed around smoked oysters and cheese and retained her cool and they discussed elm blight and the inferiority of local workmanship, the price of real estate, the deplorable conditions of certain back roads and the insolence of the boys at the check-out counters of the supermarkets and they passed their drinks back and forth in their hands so that there was the pretty tinkle of ice always in the background and the soothing hum of voices talking typical boneless summer conversation, the comforting reassurance of human voices discussing nothing very much in particular until this was all shattered in a second by a sudden cry and everyone, turning, saw that Charlotte Custis had overthrown or dropped her drink into the fireplace and that she was calling out that George was missing.

"George is *missing*," Charlotte said and her fox terrier face was drawn very tense and her eyes were dilated but not with fear, with anger, and she spit the words at Ruth.

"I mean missing. George is *missing*."

Yes, someone said, for Ruth had not moved, seemingly had not even heard Charlotte; her hand was playing with her glass beads.

"What I mean *is*," Charlotte said, "is this of any interest to anyone or do we all just go on sitting here or am I being *peculiar* in that I would think that perhaps somebody *ought* to be thinking of doing something or am I peculiar or something?"

Well?

That he might be lying at the bottom of a cliff? Smashed by hippies and/or hit-run drivers? What else? Abducted? Ruth spread her hands, trying to ward all this off, smiling her enigmatic smile, trying to evade them.

"I don't believe anything's happened," she said, which translated might mean she didn't believe anything could be done.

Whereupon Evelyn Tillotsen said, "Well, honey, you know best but, *honey*, it *is* nearly nine o'*clock*, Ruth, my God, I don't know about you but if it was *my* husband . . ."

"Excuse me," Ruth said and went into the kitchen to instruct Maiva they would not wait any longer for Mr. Wood, they would serve the buffet.

"Would you open the wine?" she said to Andre, who had slammed out of the living room.

The consensus was that George's absence (no one used the word *disappearance* until the next day) was not nearly as odd as was Ruth's behavior about it. Already, certain of the more eagerly cynical among them had begun to decide it was connected with a fatal disagreement. Perhaps even a permanent break, some might have thought hopefully.

Because Ruth Wood with her cool green eyes and cooler smile had never been liked so much as accepted, as pepper with salt, because of George and it was never so apparent as now here in her gloomy (God knows how he stands it) candle-lit dining room, the friends of George circling the buffet table while Ruth supervised in her chilly humorless way, saying to each in turn, Did you get rice, did you get chili; coconut and ginger? And there's Brie, she told them each in turn. Nothing was mentioned about George but the Brie, she told them, was local or at least from a local store called The Mousetrap and it was located just off the Montauk Highway on Whiting Lane. Do you know Whiting Lane? she asked them seriously. It was the second little street to the left after the main stoplight.

She asked them to believe this. She earnestly begged them to believe her about this one thing, that The Mousetrap existed. It might have been all she had left that she could actually prove.

Well, so they said, That's interesting, Ruth, we must look into it. Because it is always useful to have a couple of good cheese shops up one's sleeve.

What else could anyone do for the moment, she being the hostess, but suffer her relentless entertainment because she seemed unusually concerned with their needs and enjoyments, she pressed more food and wine on them and passed around hot rolls and relish trays until it began to seem like some ritual and, as she touched nothing herself, as though she were performing some last sacrament. She strained and pulled at the evening to keep it alive, she performed mouth-to-mouth resuscitation on the stone dead jollity; she tried to divert them with a long and unsatisfactory story about how she had tried to get an owl out of the guest room lavatory.

At ten twenty-five she was persuaded to let Jack Julien telephone the police.

So finally she allowed it to become fact.

She sat up dutifully half the night with Jack Julien (who

had stayed behind because Charlotte and Andre were in inflammatory conditions and it was clear they only were addling the brains of the police and a rein must be put on them) answering the questions put to her first by the squad car officers and later by the detectives. The questions seemed to her to be both bureaucratic and computerized. Even the description seemed unrelevant to George. She had not ever thought of herself as married to a male Caucasian aged forty-three with no visible marks or scars.

It seemed she was being required to take some tricky exam and if she could pass with a good average she would get not George back but a certificate.

Then had he been (tick off any or all of the following) nervous, tense, edgy, jittery, depressed, discouraged, sleepless, suicidal? A heavy drinker? Take any narcotics? Ever to her knowledge receive threats by mail or over the phone? Could he have been the victim of a blackmailer?

No, she said, no to everything. This was, she thought scornfully, the kind of nonsense that often went on in television series. She felt engulfed in clichés.

She looked at them coolly.

"You have something caught in your eyelash," she told the heavier of the two detectives. They were obviously suspicious of her cool; they slapped their notebooks against their knees and said that they would be in touch tomorrow, or today to be exact, said the heavier one. It was certain, their looks conveyed, that she knew more than she was telling.

Everything about Ruth's nature was calculated to give the impression of complicity whereas nothing could have been further from the truth, and if she refused to explain this it was because she knew it would be no use; she was unable to convince anyone she was not complex. The real truth was that she was simply one thing, herself, that her reactions and emotions were undecorated. Things happened or did not. Were either one thing or the other and because she merely said what she was thinking, people thought her quirky.

So friends of George (for she had none of her own), expecting to find a hollow-eyed woman exhausted from sleepless worry, were confused to be greeted by her untroubled manner. Her step was as brisk as always, her clothes meticulous, her hair in place, and she had the look of having enjoyed unbroken nights' sleep. She served them tea and asked solicitously about their children. Was Judith's foot better?

Only when they *had* to bring up the reason for their visits did she betray an occasional irritation.

"You see, if I *knew* something, what earthly reason would I have for holding it back?"

Then she would look out the window, silent for a while, and seeming discouraged about not being able to convince them this was so. And the friends, defeated, fell back now on the obvious conclusion that not only was she callous but that in their opinion Ruth even seemed perhaps relieved, even enjoying what was perhaps going to be her freedom. They cast back in their minds and none of them could recall a single time they had ever seen an openly affectionate exchange between George and Ruth. Come to think of it now, she always seemed just to *accompany* him around. Now, George was the direct opposite. Warm, sweet to everyone. "George just wouldn't *do* this," Charlotte Custis told everyone, anyone who was passing, even delivery boys, mailmen. "George is simply not capable of doing anything that would cause pain or anxiety to people he loves and so something terrible has *had* to happen." Charlotte had taken up the slack left by Ruth. Her face was bloated from weeping; she was half dazed with sedatives and often more than a little drunk. She swept everyone including very slight acquaintances into emotional embraces lasting for minutes until they often had to extricate themselves by force. She held gatherings in Ruth's drawing room where she often appeared to be on the verge of a serious breakdown, could not even get up to greet George's friends. Anyone not close to the situation would have taken Charlotte for the wife and Ruth for the paid assistant.

It was Charlotte who gave out the daily bulletins about the false leads that raised false hopes.

"We had a blow today," Charlotte would say. "For a minute we thought he'd been located. In Montreal."

"*I* didn't," Ruth said.

"Ruthie is a stoic," Charlotte said, narrow-eyed. "Alas, we don't all have Ruthie's strength."

In the sanctuary of her room Ruth often stared for long periods into the bathroom mirror as though, this being the last thing that had seen him, some trace of him might be left in the glass, as if some faint clue might be somewhere in or behind the glass. "Where are you?" she said aloud sometimes. "Where *are* you, where *are* you?" "Isn't she being simply *great* about it?" Charlotte or Andre would say. "Ruthie is a stoic."

Ruth felt that her stoicism or whatever it was did not extend to having Charlotte and Andre living with her indefinitely. One night she brought up the subject, she hoped tactfully, of their no longer prolonging this painful vigil together.

What? They lit up in alarm.

What? Leave her *alone?*

Walk out on Ruthie?

They tried to outdo each other about their duty to George's wife, about what George would want them to do under the circumstances, about their duty. But underneath Ruth read their panic and saw Charlotte alone in her glum walkup where a giant golliwog was her only mate in a field-sized bed and the walls were a seasick color and saw Andre Bouclez (correct name Aaron Burger) chained to a wiry and deathproof Jewish mother in a little fake brick house in Woodside, Queens. She saw that they were both on the edge of a precipice and imploring her not to push them off, not yet. She saw also that it was George who had left them there.

George had *left* them.

And something about their predicament, the fact that their lifeline was George, their only raison d'être gone, made Ruth all the more certain that their tinny optimism about George coming back was as hopeless as they were. George was not coming back. None of them would ever see George again. She was as certain of this as that she could see his empty Styrofoam chair bobbing in the swimming pool. Somehow Charlotte and Andre's desperate insistence on miracles made Ruth feel even more deprived.

They stood before her twisting their hands like children, pleading not to be sent away. She was not as strong as they thought.

"Stay then," Ruth said. "It's very considerate."

She sat between them at dinner. She might have been the floral centerpiece except when they asked her to pass the pepper grinder. She put up with their desperate illusion that there would be news, that George would walk in the door with plausible explanations. "You can't be with someone as close as we have been with George and not *know* there's a plausible reason," Andre said. "George had a plausible reason for everything he did."

Oh, did he? Ruth thought. They did not know George very well, then. They left lights on at night for George, left a door unlatched. But when Andre, who had begun appropriating little tasks, began with a straight-faced obsequy to lay a place for George at the head of the table, Ruth flared. She snatched up the knives and forks. "Don't be silly, Andre," she said and was surprised at the emotion in her voice. She said it would be like those crazy people who start talking aloud to the dead.

Andre said he thought it was a nice gesture (eyes spitting little tears, mouth working), a sweet touch; it would make it *seem* like George was coming.

"Please," Ruth said. She wanted to say, Please leave George alone, please leave him to *me*.

Andre flounced out.

Not only her house; they were appropriating her loss.

"A sen-si-tive hu-man be-ing," Charlotte was saying one day, pronouncing the words as if she were in a phonetics class. "George Wood was—*is* a sen-si-tive great hu-man be-ing."

Ruth had come into the den to find Charlotte, without asking, giving an interview for the local paper. "I knew you wouldn't mind, Ruth," Charlotte said hastily. "This is Mr. Phelps of the Easthampton *Sun*. Mr. Phelps, this is *Mrs.* Wood." The young reporter (and it was par for the course, Ruth thought, that even this most mysterious and dramatic event of George's life would be covered by only a cub reporter) gazed myopically at Charlotte and Ruth through finger-smeared glasses; his nails were bitten to the quick and he seemed resentful at having had to cover it at all; he groped uninterestedly around for facts and occasionally made a note with a blunt pencil (what was the name of the children's TV program George had created and produced? He thought his nine-year-old sister used to watch it). Mr. Phelps's condescending attitude suggested that he knew that George had pulled off this disappearance for publicity.

And supposing he had, Ruth thought, taking up her needlework to cover up the fact that she was in the room;

it had had almost no impact whatever, the barest mentions in the New York papers. No doubt Mr. Phelps's piece would begin, "Mystery surrounds . . ." and George would be referred to as "popular, well-known resident of . . ."

But not just a show for *children*. Charlotte was barking along in her shrill terrier's voice. " 'G and B Diddle' was not just talking animals and fiddle-faddle to amuse the kids; in fact the Nielsen ratings showed that only a fraction of the viewing audience was under the age of ten and our mail was mostly from professors, deans, historians."

Mr. Phelps glanced at Ruth.

"You can see why it went off," Ruth said, and Charlotte looked at her sharply and then at Mr. Phelps with an expression meant to indicate that grief had temporarily dislodged Ruth's balance. "We never played down to anyone," Charlotte said. "We were unique in the history of television, we preceded educational television, *our team* . . ." Charlotte talked a lot about the "team," we did this, we did that; Ruth, sewing, was not part of the team, never had been, she was indicated to the reporter as being merely a necessary concubine. The reporter not wanting to know any of this, and Charlotte, insisting on its being told, was creating another disservice to poor George. Charlotte was trying to *explain* George and this was something beyond her skills. How to explain George (even to someone anxious to know) without making him seem ridiculous, even slightly odd, was a feat better left untried. Trying to explain, for instance, what George meant by saying that a chair *resented* him (now Ruth looked over at the chair in question), which perhaps sounded pixieish but was meant in deadly seriousness. How could one say to a Mr. Phelps (whose deadly seriousness must be gauged by his nylon toupee, which looked as though it were a starling's nest that had dropped on him from a tree) that George could sense emotions in furniture.

If chairs could speak and not Charlotte, one might begin

to explain George. Not poor Charlotte, bereft, deserted like a spinster bride, with wide eyes appealing to Mr. Phelps to believe, please believe in the aura of this man.

"What kind of horror?" the reporter asked.

"Not horror, *aura*," Charlotte snapped. A kind of gift. It touched everyone he came in contact with even in the slightest way. If anything he gave too much of himself. He would give an arm or a leg.

And this was true, Ruth was thinking, stitching, hiding from Mr. Phelps's curious glances at her and seeing George giving away an arm, a leg and other bits and pieces of himself until finally nothing was left and he had *vanished*. But not in the way that Charlotte was describing it. That was not the way George did it and no one knew better than Ruth how it was done and she wanted desperately to interrupt and say, You are getting it all wrong, it never was this way. It was so much more subtle than that. But she had a lifetime record of not interrupting, never could seem to find the right opening to get in between a sentence or a phrase and by the time she did the statement had been made and finished and by her silence she had become party to it. And Charlotte was wound up by now, lighting cigarettes in a feverish manner and spewing out anything that came into her mind, any balderdash. "His *mother* . . ." she was saying. Oh, why drag *her* in, Ruth thought as old Mrs. Wood, resurrected, hove into view, old Jessica with her vinegary sweetness, that pillar of rectitude and a smile for everyone but living a life of secret vengeance (and wouldn't you like to know what *I* know, Ruth thought, looking at Charlotte's ecstatic face).

But this was too much, all this balls about the old bitch being a source of inspiration to George; she adored him and he her, they were *pals*. She was like a pal to him.

A pal? That blue-eyed blue-haired purveyor of cold consolation? A pal? That woman who came into a room like a draft, with her smile as hard as a saddle? Even her words of praise for anything seemed to be imprecations. Her compliments were handed to you like sprung mousetraps.

"So thank God she's dead," Charlotte was saying. "This would have absolutely killed her stone dead, absolutely. She worshiped him and vice versa."

Now Ruth remembered the day, not long after they were married, when old Jessica came to the apartment with two bone china cups (as cold looking as herself) to present to them; refused tea because tea would be a nuisance, "and I have a talent for knowing when I'm a nuisance," Jessica said and spread her forced niceness around her like porcupine quills. But there was something symbolic, Ruth had thought, in her handing over her precious bone china cups, perhaps signifying that she approved of Ruth and everyone knew that to obtain her approval was tantamount to a papal blessing and Ruth was pleased; Ruth, who was not accustomed to much approval, let alone acceptance, Ruth, who was a dumb captive inside herself, who was also outwardly cool, responded to something inwardly seeking in Jessica. In her guarded way Ruth tried to explain this to George, gathering herself together as she always had to do before making any pronouncement, holding up the cold white cups to the light as if she were examining the cold tissue and soul of old Jessica and saying, "She's very nice really, isn't she?" and saying she felt they'd get along, be friends, and then (and *then*—even now after all those years she could feel the moment in the marrow of her bones)— and *then* George said:

"There's something I ought to tell you about her."

And now to hear Charlotte bleating on about old Jessica and George was suddenly like a blasphemy, thought Ruth. But she couldn't speak. She was sworn to silence about what George had told her about his mother. It had never been mentioned again, even when Jessica died. But it had been a bond between them and sometimes it had comforted her to have this secret bit of him.

How she would have loved now to look up and say casually, "As a matter of fact they were lifetime enemies."

Instead she put aside her needlework and, getting up, crossed between them and opened the glass doors leading to the porch, letting in huge gusts of sea wind which sent the curtains ballooning to the ceiling and Mr. Phelps's constipated little notes flying around the room; glass pendules on the wall sconces tinkled and sang.

"I just thought I'd let a little of the hot air out of this room," Ruth said and then went out. She passed Andre in the hall, who began to say something, but she cut him dead. She was a thoroughly patient woman who had reached the end of patience. She was not about to put up much longer with being condescended to in her own house; with being bossed around by the bereaved friends and the "team" under the pretense of being comforted.

They ate at the kitchen table that night. "I'm sick of being on ceremony when there's nothing to be on ceremony *about*," she told them and they agreed too quickly that of course she was right and anyway they were not guests, they were "family," they said soothingly. So they were not going to be easily budged. Ruth took hold of invisible reins and moved ahead of them. Workmen arrived to drain and cover the swimming pool. She closed off the big drafty drawing room to save on heat. She became busy with Maiva, clearing out this closet and that as if she were looking for old skeletons; a wild spasm of activity took hold of her so that no one saw her except in passing, bearing a big pitcher and basin from one room to another and most often not answering anything said to her. Up and downstairs she went, tirelessly changing rooms around (her aims were not always entirely clear), switching furniture from one room to another, closing down a guest room here, a sunroom there (it now became evident the house had always been too big for a childless couple) but, she being in continual movement, Charlotte and Andre were unable to catch her and so bobbed uselessly in her wake like buoys.

When the day came that she began to put George's things in the attic while they stared resentfully, unbelieving, as she and Maiva piled up the well-remembered suits, the slacks, the sports jackets, shoes, ties, blazers, they knew they were licked.

"You certainly are *sure*, aren't you?" Charlotte said. "Is that *all* he means to you?" Andre asked.

They packed.

They wouldn't allow Ruth to drive them to the train; they wanted no favors from her, a woman without feelings; they called the local taxi and Andre carried out the bags without looking back. It occurred to Ruth that the last thing she would ever see of him was his very unfortunate walk, like a sissy camel.

Charlotte stood in the front hall pulling little black gloves over her paws; she was more than ever terrier-looking. She had prepared her parting shot.

"Whatever happened, in *some* ways he's probably better off," Charlotte said.

Ruth sat in the den for a long time and thought about that. Ideas always filtered to her very slowly, which accounted for her silences. She was thinking about Charlotte's parting shot and about whether it might have hit the mark, not in the way Charlotte intended it but in a deeper and broader sense. She was thinking about the dark pools that had lain between her and George that she knew not to ripple, not disturb; those long silences of his and the (strange now to think of this) times he appeared to disappear literally into the furniture or the brickwork. "If you don't want someone to notice you in a restaurant just make your mind a blank," George said once and then went on to prove it, as someone he didn't want to run into passed right by their table serenely unaware.

Supposing in one of those dark silences, curious withdrawals, George had made up his mind to escape? (Now George brought down his fist on a table. She saw him. "This is as *far* as I'll go," George had said. She remembered that. But when? Why?)

She climbed the lonely stairs in the now (except for devoted Maiva) empty house. She went into her bathroom and looked into the mirror where he had been shaving on the last afternoon and tried to picture George looking at George and saying that this was as far as he would go. Was that the moment he had decided on his own evaporation? Glancing out at the sky, she caught sight of five wild swans escaping south and fancied for a moment one of them was George because it was the kind of thought he would have liked. He was fond of telling about how when Isak Dinesen died a wild swan had suddenly appeared on a marsh nearby. And who *knows?* George had said. It would have been very characteristic of her, Isak Dinesen, to transmigrate into a swan, both lovely and gothic.

And once he said he often wished you could get right away from people sometimes; wouldn't it be great if you could do as they do in movie cartoons, draw a little door with a doorknob and then open the little door and go through it.

What did—

"Are you all right up there, Mrs. Wood, honey?"

"Yes, Maiva."

"Is there somethin' I can get you, dear?"

—mean by that? Was he trying to prepare her?

She sat for ages, it seemed, hours on end, doing nothing but watch the creeping up of winter tides and sometimes putting on a scarf, walking along the bay. She had begun to assimilate her despair so that she could now wake up in the mornings without the sickening jolt of What is it? What has happened?—sleep-forgotten shock (someone had opened a little paper door and gone through it forever)—and she had begun to think of it less as a calamity than as something to be quietly accepted. She was determined to accept it; she had made up her mind not to try to alter this condition that had been forced upon her.

It had to be faced and performed alone and she was conscious of being watched all the time by Maiva, who may have started to think Ruth's mind was loose judging by all the questions she asked (You all right? You look strange a bit; you OK, honey? You had a good cry yet?), and of being followed around by this dear well-meaning puffing wheezing good and faithful servant.

Ruth felt she should not have to be watched.

She had to break it to Maiva as gently as breaking an egg.

"Oh, dear Lord God," Maiva said. "Oh, you mustn't think about the money. I'll stay on workin' for you, Mrs. Wood; oh, Lord God, never mind about the salary, honey, if that's what's been bothering you."

But, Ruth explained, she didn't *need* live-in help when there was virtually nothing to do but scratch up her own meals and make one bed and—

"Oh, God!" Maiva rocked and wailed and threw herself into a kitchen chair and wept with the shock, the surprise of Ruth's cruelty to her. She beseeched, she implored to no avail; Mrs. Wood was a cucumber.

"You're goin' to be *all alone*," Maiva threatened.

"I've been all alone all my life," Ruth told her. Felt sorry she had picked up Maiva's easy cue. The statement, though indisputable, sounded stilted when spoken aloud.

"Dear Lord God forgive you," Maiva said a few days later from a taxi window.

Ruth let the gardener go. He was darkly resentful. He had spent several years working on the rose garden alone.

"It'll all go to brambles in no time," he said. Brambles, Ruth said, would suit her down to the ground.

Her mother drove down for the day.

Ruth lighted a fire in the den and they sat across from each other. Her mother smoked a great deal. She had beautiful tapering prayerlike hands that might have been painted by Giotto. She was richly attractive and, now approaching seventy, unchanged in all the time Ruth could remember, even to the style of her hair, which she wore in a thirtyish bob and which held currents of its natural red in it. She was dressed in wintry blue. She had the look of someone on whom, in a lifetime, no drop of rain has ever fallen. She had the air of someone who is escorted to waiting cars under umbrellas held over her. She said she'd have a very dry sherry.

She said, "Lots of my friends have asked about you and whether to call you and so forth and I tell them no, I don't think you want to be troubled with a lot of calls when there's nothing you can say anyhow."

"Yes."

"What? Yes, you *would?*"

"No. Yes, I wouldn't."

"That's what I thought. Did Gaylord's do those curtains for you?"

"Yes."

"Funny. They usually do a good job and you wouldn't think *any*body could go wrong with velvet but they have, haven't they?"

"Yes."

"Of course I'm dubious of velvet in a small room anyway. Is that mirror new?"

"No."

"Don't remember it."

"Used to be in the upstairs study."

"Ah, yes? It's *good*, I think. *Looks* good. Italian?"

"French, I think. Or Italian. I don't know for sure."

"Nice. Oh, don't put on that huge log just for me, I'm not staying."

"*I* am," Ruth said.

"What?"

"Nothing. I just said I *was*, that's all."

After a silence:

"You don't *look* too bad, considering. Are you sleeping all right and so forth?"

"Yes."

"Eating all right?"

"Can I refill that for you?"

"No, no, I don't want any more. It's a very *buttery* sherry, isn't it? Are you sure it's dry?"

"I don't know; I never drink sherry."

"Oh, it's all right, not bad really. Did I tell you Hetty Sheldon's coming round the Cape with me?"

"No, I don't think— The Cape?"

"Well, I told you I was going round the Cape this winter, I know I did."

"I think perhaps you did. I just can't *quite* remember the —when it was."

"Valparaiso and so forth."

"Oh, Cape *Horn*."

"Well, you didn't think I meant we were going to sail around Cape *Cod*, did you?"

"I wondered."

Her mother laughed. "That's funny," and Ruth laughed too at her own stupidity.

"I'm frankly not looking forward to it much but at my age you've got to do it while you still can and so forth. It may well be the last big trip I'll have." Her mother paused and Ruth knew she had hoped to be contradicted; people had been contradicting her mother charmingly ever since Ruth was a child.

Then her mother said, "What are you going to *do?*"

"In what way do you mean?"

"I mean just what are you going to do?"

The question raised both terror and impotency and Ruth put her hands up to her head as though a moth had flown into her hair.

"What's there to do? I don't understand you. Is there something I'm supposed to do? Do what, *what?*"

Her mother said nothing and let her fidget and wriggle, so that she looked a fool; after all, it was a logical and clear question. So her mother looked for a while out the glass doors to the garden blowing wild; running to brambles.

"There's one thing you ought to think about when the time comes and that's having him declared legally dead."

"*Legally dead,*" Ruth said. "What a ridiculous phrase."

"It's only the legal term."

"I know but how pompous, *pat*ronizing. As if you could be *il*legally dead. As if you could be dug up and *fined* for being illegally dead." Ruth was suffused with laughter because George would have so appreciated the idea of being exhumed and fined and for a moment George seemed so near she felt she could reach out and touch him and a sob bubbled up in the middle of her laughter and became a hiccup.

"I don't see," her mother said, "that it's exactly hilarious."

"I can tell you who thought up a pompous asinine term like that," Ruth said. "You can bet your bottom dollar it was a *living* person." Her mother was staring at her now. Outbursts from her were so unusual. "Anyway, why should I do such a thing?"

"Just in case."

"In case of *what?*"

"Suppose you wanted to marry again."

"I don't expect that'll happen."

"Well, you didn't expect *this* to happen, did you? And I believe you have to wait seven years anyway so how do you know how you'll feel then?"

"Are you about ready for lunch?"

"Any time you say. I want to kill two birds and run in on Gina Glover while I'm here. Ruth, are you letting your hair grow?"

"Yes. See. I *am* doing something."

After her mother left, she went upstairs and lay down on the bed and fell asleep (which was becoming a habit with her; these long assuaging sleeps took a large bite out of the day) and dreamed of her brother Tony, whom she had idolized, and who had been killed near Bastogne in the last days of the European campaign when Ruth was still in her teens. In her dream she was walking with Tony under spreading dark trees near their childhood home in Butley, Connecticut, and Tony had his arm around her waist and was, as always, being attentive and sweet and the peculiar thing was, like all her dreams of Tony, even as she clung to his arm she knew he was long ago dead and she knew everything that had happened to her up until this moment, knew this was a dream, and then just as Tony had prevented her from slipping into a crevice and turned his dear face to her to say something very tender and comforting to her, he changed, as people do so maddeningly in dreams, into somebody else and she saw that the man who was bending toward her under the dark trees of this wish fulfillment was not Tony but Archer Hurst, and Archer was saying something pretty filthy and she pushed him away with her weak paper hands but he seemed like an iron door and twisted her up against him; Archer, oversexed, over good-looking, said, Don't be so cool, Ruth, don't be silly, after all I'm your brother—but in the kiss she managed to shake herself free and awoke, tossing under the eiderdown.

Archer.

She never was able to dream of George, not once since it had happened had she dreamed of George, and here was Archer coming easily and fluidly, sexually into the wandering subconscious. But Archer *was* a direct link to George and that evening while having her long slow second drink before she put on the TV dinner she suddenly was possessed with the idea of speaking to Archer and finding a Beverly Hills number in an old address book in her desk, she called and seemed to astonish whoever answered by asking if Mr. Hurst was there; following some covering up of receivers and muffled talk, a woman (an ex-wife?) asked Ruth sharply who was calling him and then said with the grace of a subway guard that "you might reach him at this number," which, after so many rings she almost gave up, was announced as being the Somethingorother Motel Gardens (now, too late because she was being connected to cabin 17, Ruth remembered someone saying somewhere that poor old Archer had been having a rough time of it lately and all he'd been doing was quickie Westerns made in Spain) and a girl's voice said hello, a colorless voice that suggested white eyelashes and eyebrows, said who was it and wait a minute she'd see if he was there, he may have gone out, and then finally Archer must have grabbed the phone because there he was, the stag voice, cock of the walk voice.

"For God's sake, for God's sake," Archer said after she had repeated her name several times and then her maiden name, "Ruth *Carver*."

"How'd you know I'd be here?" Archer asked. "I just got in from Yugoslavia day before yesterday and I'm leaving

for Germany day after tomorrow so this is the craziest thing
that you'd know I'd be here. How did you know? Did you
speak to Miriam? She usually only passes on my number if
she thinks it's someone I owe money to."

After Archer had told her about the picture he'd made
in Yugoslavia right down to the name of the unknown
director and then all about the one he was going to make in
Germany right down to the name of the unknown director,
Ruth said, "Archer, have you heard about George?"

The pause was so long she almost said, "Hello, are you still
there?" when Archer cleared his throat in a professional way
and said yes, he had known because there had been a
small piece about it in the Hollywood *Daily Variety* just
before he left for Yugoslavia. Archer conveyed the impression that he thought it was an unfortunate choice of subject
for Ruth to have brought up; almost as if he were now
waiting for her to apologize for bringing up such a personal
matter (not personal to Ruth but to *him*, George's close close
buddy; again Ruth had nothing to do with it) and anyway
Archer was conditioned to living in a sort of sunlamp land
where there shall be no night, no want, no woe; Archer had
long been conditioned by the Hollywood dictum that you
never speak of failure or disaster for there is no such thing
and in any case, someone important might be listening.
Then Archer's voice took on a curiously warning tone.
"Remember this isn't a private line, we're on a switch-
board here."

"I wasn't going to say anything personal."

Did he think she might be going to mention his age?
She had already begun to regret this call.

"I was thinking of *you*, not me," he said.

"I don't have any dark secret to tell you. I wish I had."

"I'd have called you," he said, "if I'd known where to
reach you."

"I'm at home."

"Oh? Really? I naturally thought you'd be somewhere you wouldn't be inundated with phone calls day and night."

"I haven't been inundated with phone calls for a long time now."

"Well, how *are* you anyway? Are you holding up OK?"

"Oh, yes, on the whole."

"Good girl. Do they have any—um—leads?"

"No. They—"

Someone must have just then burst into Archer's cabin; shouts and what sounded like shots and angry voices; a girl screamed that she was innocent, innocent.

"What's happening?" Ruth asked.

"It's just the television," Archer said and told someone to turn that damn thing down and the voices subsided. Funnily, the shots and screams seemed more plausible than this conversation with Archer.

"Sorry," Archer said. "What were you saying?"

"Never mind."

"What?"

"I've forgotten."

"What a crazy thing though."

"Yes."

"I guess he got through the crack," Archer said.

"What crack?"

"Oh, it's just an expression he used—you know, one of his jokes. He used to say when he was put out about something or someone was bugging him—he used to say that one day he'd get through the crack."

"Oh."

"That's all."

And that seemed to be that, Archer seemed to suggest, and, in a long pause, that it was time to let him go but Ruth hung onto this connection with George.

"Anyway," Archer said—he was being very super-nice-off-the-screen-natural-as-you-or-me—"Anyway, I'm glad to hear you're OK and holding up. You keep that up now, Ruth."

"Oh, I'm not going into a decline or anything."

"Course you're not. One thing about you, you've always had a lot of cool. I don't know of anyone else could've taken a thing like this better, I honestly mean that, girlie."

Girlie. It brought him back immediately to her, the ever-ready smile, the ever-ready wink, very fast arm around you, girlie.

"Wish I could be of some help but I don't know any more than what I read in . . ."

Archer's comfort.

Don't cry over *George,* girlie, it isn't worth it, Archer told her, finding her in tears behind the raincoats in the cloak-room. Cheer up, Ruthie, girlie, Archer would tell her when she straggled miserably behind the others at picnics with her mournful secret. In the days of their youth she had been in perpetual mourning because she knew George Wood would never be hers. Ah, now, girlie, Archer would say, appearing with a glass of punch for her and a made-to-order embrace, and she would dry her eyes, grateful for his comfort even though she knew it was as ready made as pancake mix.

But that was all long ago and Archer was no longer the dispenser of comfort, Archer was now trying like hell to get her off the phone.

"Wish I could be of some help, girlie, but as I say—and I'm in a hell of a rush, leaving for Germany. . . ."

"I didn't call you for any particular reason. I was sitting here and I was thinking about you and me and George and Clytie Bundock and the Holly and Ivy Players and I thought I'd like to call you up."

"Ah, yes."

"That's all."

"Very very very nice."

"No other reason."

"Really really really sweet."

"My God," she said suddenly. "He loved you."

There was a long silence from his end.

"I believe out of everybody, he loved you the most."

A long expressive silence. She wondered if they'd been cut off.

Then his voice came back to her like buckshot.

"I know that, Ruth."

Said nothing more and somehow, jolted at apparently making a gaffe, she got off the phone in a flurry of little empty wishes of good luck. "Keep well," she said in a schoolgirlish voice.

"Bye-bye, Ruth," Archer said.

She felt as snubbed as a schoolgirl watching everyone else drive off to a picnic. She felt as she used to as a young girl around Archer and George and their friends, intensely left out. There was something clubby about George and Archer as if they spoke some kind of sign language. There was something very hurtful in the calm, sort of superior way Archer had said, "I guess he got through the crack," as though Archer had expected something of the sort to happen and was mildly surprised she would put a call through to the West Coast to tell him.

Ruth sat and ate her TV dinner and felt excluded right down to her bones. The house seemed huge and empty; he was more missing than ever to her now, yet he seemed to be everywhere around her.

"What?" she asked the air. "What was I not supposed to know?"

But had he been there, she knew that her question would have been answered with some sweet compliment on her dress or the way she had done her hair; she had not been allowed to know George and Archer had just as much as told her so.

Well, it was just another thing now to put up in the attic with all George's things.

"Wouldn't you rather come *home?*" her mother asked from Connecticut.

No, she said. She could not give any valid reason why she chose to stay on in the big cold empty house except that vaguely she felt she was waiting for something; ought to be here for something.

So she hibernated, slept on into the winter.

She was sound asleep when the doorbell rang.

It took a while to penetrate her consciousness that the buzzing was the front doorbell; the doorbell had not rung for so long she couldn't at first identify the noise. Then she got off the bed, trembling with alarm, trying to find her shoes, still in a half dream state, hair all matted from sleeping, blustered downstairs looking like the madwoman they very likely expected to find these days.

It was a very ordinary-looking woman standing at the door, so very suburban-looking, wearing a blanket-gray wool coat and sensible matron shoes, that Ruth supposed she was very likely one of the local summer domestics who sometimes hunted for odd-jobbing in the off season, laundry, ironing, and surely it was going to say so on the card she held out.

But the card read: *Mrs. M. Gorse. Psychoneurologist. Readings, analysis, etc.*

"No," Ruth said, handing back the card. "I'm not interested."

But Mrs. Gorse refused to take back the card and said something in a low voice that was lost in a gust of wind. Mrs. Gorse, putting up her arm to defend her eyes against wind and leaves, said something about a husband.

"I didn't quite catch . . ." Ruth said with the door open only a crack, trying to be as uncivil as possible.

Mrs. Gorse combed her gray hair with fingers and clung onto her very large handbag for support against the terrible weather and people's unkindnesses. She put out an arm to steady herself against the brick portico.

"I just wondered," Mrs. Gorse said, "if you knew that your husband had been coming to me."

For sessions.

Hypnosis and something that sounded like "infused contemplation."

Mrs. Gorse followed Ruth to the kitchen. She had a slightly deferential manner, like that of domestics of another generation. She waited until Ruth said to please sit down and then she only sat perched on the edge of the kitchen chair as if to oblige it. She opened her capacious black handbag and searched inside it (would she bring out toads? newts?) for tissues because she said she had the sniffles.

She also said she had put Mr. Wood "under" several times.

Mrs. Gorse said this in a quiet polite tone as if she had said she didn't want to boast but she really had a way with corned beef. She was so very housewifely. She had children and a husband who was an electrician, she told Ruth. She also had peculiar eyes. They were a lightish milky gray color. Ruth tried to avoid looking directly into Mrs. Gorse's eyes. Mrs. Gorse was a bit of a legend, of course. It all came back to Ruth now, snips and snaps of conversations at parties. She'd heard jokes and arguments about this woman who was jestingly referred to as the witch of Watermill, all going in and out one ear because who in a lifetime would have expected her to be sitting in your own kitchen full of secrets about your own husband? There were those who made fun of her as an outrageous charlatan and there were others who swore she was a natural, an honest hypnotist with clairvoyant talents. Somebody or other Ruth knew had gone to her to be cured of smoking through hypnotic suggestion.

Mrs. Gorse seemed reluctant to talk about her mystic powers. "I only try to help people who have problems. Well, let's say I try to put them into a state where they can solve their own problems."

"What problem? What did he come to you about?"

"I take it you didn't know, then?"

"No."

"Well . . ." Mrs. Gorse ran a finger along the edge of the kitchen table. "Mrs. Wood, I have to tell you that I make it a rule never to discuss what a client might say. . . ."

"Oh, but to *me* . . ."

Ruth could feel her heart thumping at this new strange thing. Mrs. Gorse was sympathetic but immovable. She would not discuss anything a client said during "sessions" or why a client had come to her. Sorry, but "in my method you have to start by getting their confidence in you or you won't get anywhere if they think you're untrustworthy."

"But you could tell me what the problem was, surely," Ruth said. "I mean it wasn't just to . . . stop smoking . . . something like that—trivial?"

"Mrs. Wood, we don't say trivial. I mean it might seem trivial to you, you see, but it isn't to the person coming for help—so we never say trivial."

Again she ran her finger the length of the kitchen table.

"I suppose I could tell you this. He didn't know what his problem was and he wanted to find out."

"And did he?"

"He might have been beginning to but I advised him to stop."

"Oh? Why?"

"There are some people hypnosis is not right for. It's dangerous for some people."

"Was it dangerous for him?"

"I think so," Mrs. Gorse said placidly. "I told him I would recommend he go to an analyst. Even with people who've been in analysis sometimes hypnosis is dangerous." Mrs. Gorse sighed contentedly. "He is extremely sensitive to memory and I thought—well, I thought he was in too much of a hurry. You see, bringing to light certain events of your past can be . . . like a shock. In *analysis* it's done to a time-table and he wanted to go into self-hypnosis far too soon, I thought. I told him that."

"Did he go into it? What did he . . . ?"

"I really can't tell you any more than that, really I can't."

"Well, but . . . was it anything to do with *me*?"

Mrs. Gorse caressed the table and then looked directly at Ruth with her milky eyes.

"I wouldn't say so."

"You don't have to be kind. I'd *rather* know."

"The little we went, I wouldn't say *you* figured in it at all."

Mrs. Gorse stood up, reluctant to part with the kitchen table. "That's been scrubbed for years, hasn't it? I don't think there's anything nicer than an old scrubbed table."

"Well, I hope that you have good news about him soon," Mrs. Gorse said at the front door.

"Wait just a minute." Ruth hung onto Mrs. Gorse by her coat as she stepped out into the wind. "What were you going to tell me?"

"That was all."

"No. Just now. You were going to tell me something and then stopped."

"You're quite acute," Mrs. Gorse said. "You'd make a good subject."

"What was it?"

Mrs. Gorse twisted the straps of her handbag. Well, it wasn't anything much, she said. Well, most people came to her to help them to quit something: smoking, overeating, procrastination and so on. Well, Mr. Wood had said a strange thing the first time he came. "He said, 'I want to quit being myself.' "

Mrs. Gorse walked away, shielding her head against the wind.

Silence.

The silence in the house was almost visible, textured; it lay on the air like smoke. Now and then the grocery boy stamped in and out of the kitchen and broke the stillness but once the van drove away the silence returned. No one rang the doorbell. Dust gathered on the telephone. Her cool had put people off and they were relieved to be rid of her with good excuse. Occasionally she found it had advanced into a new month without her knowledge. Once in a while she actually stirred herself to make plans. She would sell the house and move into an apartment, move back to New York. The plans withered even as she made them; just walking from one room to another, her resolve vanished. One of the reasons she avoided looking at calendars was that she didn't want to be aware of when it would be a year since he had gone away, which it would be soon.

Then one afternoon the telephone rang.

She was in the garden cutting back some of the honey-suckle vines that had begun choking the roses when she was startled by the ringing of the telephone.

Startled because it was now so rare. But also as she went indoors, taking off her gardening gloves, because she was shaken with the feeling that it was news of him; without any doubt the telephone had a shrill insistency, a come-quick ring to it, so much so that she let it ring several more times to quieten her heartbeats with several deep breaths before she picked it up.

"Hello."

And now whose voice?

But to her disappointment it was a child with a wrong number. Or it seemed to be a child. Ruth could make no sense of the voice, coming through the static, perhaps long distance.

"Who did you want?" she asked. "What number are you calling?"

The indistinct babbling continued. "Who is it?" she asked once more.

After a little while she hung up.

part one

it was like

turning a corner and coming face to face with yourself.

Coming toward you and you not being in the least surprised. So one might take one's own arm and proceed down the street with oneself, interested in what oneself had to say and had been doing lately. The insight into oneself was piercing. It was euphoric and yet detached. It was like the satisfaction of talking to yourself out loud in the way that solitary people do, chatting away by the hour informing themselves of what they already know, which is ridiculous and at the same time innately natural because part of the self listens and there is no listener more rapt.

Now I am the listener, George thought, now I am the watcher. Now I am the self I've been talking to all my life. Now I'm the self I discussed things with, argued with, agreed with, conspired with.

It was the most curious exaltation, unlike anything he had ever known. Like being high without alcohol or pot, feeling the freedom and elation but being in control. Emotionless, as one might watch oneself being emotional on a film taken at some earlier time.

As being handed an old snapshot and saying in surprise, Why, when was this taken? Who took it? Who are these people with me? Where were we and what were we doing? Was I really there that summer? But here is the proof in Kodachrome and there you are with your arm around some forgotten person or some now dead person and you could never have imagined that you owned such a sweater with reindeer stitched across it, what a ghastly sweater, how godawful, one says, but this pretended scorn is sophistical, the pain is from looking at the younger self.

But this feeling, this floating along being absolutely aware of oneself, was not painful.

"Safe," George said. "Safe as if I were in a snapshot." George thought that this safety was what produced the feeling of ecstasy, of joy. This self could not be touched, injured, irritated, elated, hurt, hung over, uneasy. . . . Yet there was, around the edges of his brightness, a rim of dark. He was not prepared yet to examine it but he knew it was there just on the edge of his circle of happiness. It had to do with the fact that he still as yet was not sure what had happened. "I seem," George explained to himself, "to have opened a door and gone through it and I guess that was what I intended."

He was remembering what Mesker had said (Mesker, the Viennese parapsychologist, who had conducted the auto-hypnotic experiments at Hay University and to whom George had gone mainly because Mrs. Gorse had warned him not to; had said don't go to anyone like Mesker, you're too receptive).

What Mesker had said about being wary of the auto-hypnosis tests without a doctor being present; what Mesker likened to the Sorcerer's Apprentice knowing enough to make the broom fetch the pail of water but not enough to stop it proliferating until an endless parade of brooms brought endless pails of water. As people who have been on a bad LSD trip may find themselves suddenly reexperiencing it without dosage; just crossing the street they are suddenly back among nightmares, stepping on snakes. So, Mesker said, osmotic self-induced hypnotic therapy, the reliving of events, can with certain people (and he'd looked at George severely) begin to reoccur without them inducing it. There had been a graduate student of psychology who agreed to undergo hypnosis only under the supervision of a resident analyst and who, after only one deep hypnosis session, had two days later suddenly reentered the experience and thrown himself in front of a truck. "You are ultrasensitive to memory," Mesker said. Muriel Gorse in Watermill had said the same thing: "I wouldn't hanky about with it if I were you."

At first there had been only little flicks of déjà vu. Only those little psychic tics known to everyone where for a second or two the feeling is overwhelming that all this has happened before. Like light flicking on and off, see it and it is gone; the beam of the lighthouse sweeps the dark garden and for a second every tree and bush is outlined and then is blackness again.

He had seen the snow outside his office window, snow whirling around the clock on the Paramount Building. But it was July and when he looked up again he saw only the hot gritty air. But he had seen the snow. For ten seconds on a blistering July morning he had seen the snow whirling through Times Square and he had been no more surprised than if he had nodded off for a moment and dreamed it (but he was not asleep; he had looked up and seen the snow, looked away, looked up again to find it gone). Indeed the only way to describe these quick lapses into memory was that they were like deep short sleeps, the nodding off in the armchair, the sudden deep catnap on the train, head bobbing over the newspaper or lolling drunkenly against the windowpane and bringing instant bright dreaming. The catnap dreams that expand very rapidly in the subconscious and are like those Japanese paper flowers that expand in water; so whole series of events pass vividly in that cold timeless country of dreams: you pass into love, cross seas, marry and divorce over long long periods of time until, shaken awake by a jolt, by a grinding of wheels and brakes, you find you have only been asleep between Speonk and Westhampton. That was what it was like and like seeing the snow it was on him and gone before he knew it.

Then there was the occurrence of Maiva and the big dog.

The thing was, like falling asleep you were never conscious of when it began. He had been in the den reading poor old Dudley Rivers' script and depressed as hell about it (was there a connection here? George wondered) when coming up out of deep concentration and finding his attention drawn to look out of the window, he saw Maiva carrying a tray of lunch things down to the pool and at the moment of seeing her George felt the familiarity of the scene as strongly as if it had nudged him, he felt his skin tighten with the total predictability that in a moment or two a huge dog would appear and overwhelm Maiva and almost with a feeling of exhilaration, like being on mescaline, he saw, as Maiva sashayed, swayed like a ship across the lawn, a huge woolly dog had broken through the privet hedge that separated their house from the Nelsons'; Gloria, the big woolly Saint Bernard, a great hairy rug in motion, had capered loose and into their garden and delightedly across to Maiva and reared up on her as tall as she was, perhaps taller, and Maiva, terrified, had dropped the tray (and in a minute she would go down on the lawn with Gloria teasing and licking her, unable to convey by anything less than assault her complete delight and love) and now Maiva was over on her back and screaming for help, for someone to come take this dog off of her, oh, please, please come, Mrs. Wood, as George ran out on the terrace and the whole scene disappeared behind the high hydrangeas and then he came running across an entirely empty lawn but there was no Maiva lying on her back and no great Gloria leaping all over her. He went slowly back toward the house and because this kind of recurrence was new to him then, went into the kitchen where Maiva was peeling something and said, "Maiva, has that dog been after you again?" "Which dog?" Maiva always had to be reminded of anything that happened longer than five minutes ago. Big Gloria from next door, George said. He thought he just saw her in the garden annoying Maiva. And Maiva looked a little changed by memory and said, "No, Mr. Wood, not since last month. That was last month you mean."

So he could not have seen it. It was autosuggestion, it was the photographed memory.

Then smack in the middle of dinner at the Tillotsens' (and again he had been feeling depressed as hell and that again seemed to be the kickoff to these little slipbacks) he had withdrawn into himself to rest a minute from the exhaustingly tedious conversation, had thought of nothing, nothing, and was off in a trance for a moment and then, looking at Evelyn Tillotsen's hand resting beside spoons on the table, had noticed something odd had happened to it. The scar was gone. He looked again to make sure. But then glancing up through candles saw that nothing else had changed, the same six people sat around the table saying the same tedious things and yet Evelyn Tillotsen's deep red scar was gone but now he saw she was wearing not black velvet but a dark red brocade and glancing across at Ruth that she was in a dull silver dress that she had not worn in as long as he could remember and he felt his skin gathered tightly all over his body with the knowledge that he was living for a second or two in some moment before Evelyn Tillotsen burned her hand, which had been over a year ago. They all sat around the table in the past and George could not remember the exact evening or moment in it except it was the moment Ruth in her silver dress picked a tangerine from the bowl; so if it could be tabulated and filed, it would be such and such a date of such and such a year at the exact moment that Ruth picked a tangerine from a dish and it would be that for all eternity; time being turned back a million times and Ruth Wood a million times picking a tangerine.

Then the vision shook and quivered like water and as if a burp were coming, "Excuse me," George said and passed his napkin over his mouth and was sweating because there lay Evelyn Tillotsen's hand with the deep scar and the ugly diamond ring she wore the size of an ice rink and there they all were, sitting around the table exactly as they had been a few seconds (minutes? how long had he been "away"?) before, Evelyn back in her mossy black velvet; it had been like a quick cut, a flashback in a film in which he'd traveled back and forth without having been missed. Or had he been noticed? He thought perhaps Ruth was aware of something, that maybe she was looking at him inquiringly, but then Ruth had been looking at him inquiringly since they were in their teens, Ruth habitually looked at him with some mute question and he often felt that if she ever asked it, God help him, it would be exceedingly shattering, it might be the truth of him. He thought about confiding to her that something extremely out of the ordinary was happening to him but it was not only difficult to explain but impossible to even begin such a confession to Ruth; Ruth was chilly and pragmatic, Ruth was like a very large pane of cold clear glass and that was about *all* she was (looking now at her turned-away very beautiful empty face) emotionally and that was not her fault, that was her asset, the main reason he had married her, for this very suspension in emotion, this undemanding, unforaging, uncurious nature of hers; her range of emotion was as flat as a field. It was certainly impossible to imagine himself

saying, Look, I'm not having a psychological crack-up but
I have been playing around with certain tricks and methods
of self-hypnosis and trancelike states of memory and relaxa-
tion all of which you would say is hokery-pokery but, dear,
listen, the human brain has more than twelve billion cells
and the possible intercellular combinations between them are
as incalculable as is the infinity of connections we can make
instantly with the past, with every breathing second of our
lives which has been recorded and stored forever, all those
trillions of minutes there on tape ready for instant replays
and so you cannot dispute what is possible, not all your
earthly common sense can disprove anything that I'm experiencing because the fact remains I'm proving I can do it because lately I seem to be . . .

Only at the last moment had he said something to Ruth. He
had come naked out of the bathroom and said, "I feel
very strange, I feel everything's going backward," but she
did not raise her head from the book she was reading and
anyway he had left it too late, it was entirely too late, all
the warnings about the Sorcerer's Apprentice chain reaction,
all the warnings about his too bright receptivity and consciousness, because already around Ruth lying on the wicker
chaise the room was building itself trunks of trees and even as
he called to her sharply, called *Ruth*, her face was beginning
to be blotted out with green moss and leaves and in the last
moments she was Botticelli-like, she was Primavera, her face
breaking out in flowers, disappearing into leaves, all fronds
curling, disappearing into greenery like the wall behind her,
the bedroom wall sprouting with deer antlers and ferns and
he was standing on a wooded pathway outside the
    Old Butley Arms Inn.
    But it was like turning a corner and coming face to face
with yourself and not being in the least surprised.
    Safe, George said to himself, safe as if I were in a snap-

shot and yet only a moment before, standing in the bathroom, shaving, he had seen that terrible vision of himself in the mirror, empty, having missed the boat, the bus, the point, all wet, having accomplished nothing, honestly nothing, because of having put too much energy into it, hopelessly achieving nothing because of his stubborn pursuit, his inability to let things just happen, the years and years of what Dr. Mesker had called his "overtry," wrestling to make something of himself or to try to create something (which even when he did only caused shrugs) so why all the trouble anyway? Why all this activity to try to impress people and why bother to pick up the slack of their failures for them, why bother to help pick up the conversation when it flagged because of a feeling of duty and to praise fools and flatter the ugly and kiss the unloved? And for all your pains to end up looking in the mirror and seeing you were now empty. So the swimmer fighting upstream against the tide finally tires, relaxes, floats, gets carried back in the tide, back, why bother, sky and water is all there is, the body floats serenely as it is meant to, back.

And with no effort at all you drifted on to reach yesterday and the day before and the month before and just as sounds, once made, stay somewhere in atmosphere eternally, you would be doing and saying whatever you had been at that time, like now walking up the steps into the old Butley Arms Inn with its classic eighteenth-century windows and with the deer antlers over the front door and now he was being impelled into the big dark hall with its random floors and the big grandfather clock that always stood by the stairs with a tick-pause-tock and instantly he smelled the past, the smell of cedar and floor polish and sweet potpourri; no different from when he used to be brought here for a treat to have Sunday dinner after church and he half expected Mr. or Mrs. McMicking to come out from the little dark office next

to the reception desk which still had the gold-framed paint-
ing of the first Fulton steamboat hanging over it. Only the
McMickings had gone years ago to what they had called
their "reward," long before whoever came next had turned
the lovely old oak taproom into a bar and wouldn't the Mc-
Mickings have cried out to see what had been done to it in
terms of phony Currier and Ives wallpaper and pink plastic
stools and heartbreaking arrangements of plastic flowers and
ferns and glass ashtrays stamped with a picture of sheep and
the legend *Please Ewes Me*. But nothing else had changed
in all the years since he had been here. There was no one at
the desk, nobody in the little writing room, and as yet he
was not able to remember what he had been doing here
whenever it had happened, the slipback was so rapid that he
felt disoriented, like a parachutist bumped to earth, rolling
over and now standing up to take his bearings; there he was
now in the old speckled hall mirror and he saw he was wearing his Sherlock Holmes cap with the flaps and his yellowish
tweed coat and pale blue muffler so it had to have been
winter at this moment and probably not too long ago; last
winter? He looked no different to himself in the glass. When
he took off his Sherlock Holmes cap (which women told him
he looked cute in, adorable) he saw he was just as gray at
the temples, just as thinning on top and his big mustache as
brown and luxuriant as ever (and that, women told him,
was so sexy, that mustache); his clever, crooked face gazed
back at him quizzically, sardonic today, sardonic mood,
frowning, obviously bothered about something; clearly the
reason he was hesitating, dawdling around in this public
hallway, was that something unpleasant lay just ahead and he
was postponing it as long as possible (he was wise to his
tricks and methods and long mirror-gazing was one of them;
it was not so much vanity as an assurance that he was still
there that he sought for himself in mirrors in public hall-

ways) and now he saw he was leaning forward and grinning as if to admire his teeth, of which he could not help but be proud; almost everyone mentioned his teeth sooner or later; they gave him his dazzling smile which he was exercising now, perhaps in rehearsal for the thing or person he was about to meet; there he was with his unbalanced face, his deeply cleft chin, his soft eyes and his great smile, and he remained smiling at himself until a waiter carrying a tray of drinks whisked suddenly out of the bar and said, "The young lady's in the dining room, sir," and held open the dining room door for George.

The young lady?

He went into the dining room looking rueful.

She was sitting in a dazzling sunny alcove reading the menu; she was in attractive tobacco color pants and a yellow sweater.

Coming through all the snowy tables to her.

Pretty, pretty, oh, God, yes, pretty and nice girl.

"Did you find them?" she was asking without looking up from the menu.

Apparently he had her gloves in his hand, little brown gloves.

"They were just at the bottom of the steps," he was saying.

"Oh, good," she was saying. "They're ostrich, or supposed to be ostrich."

"They were just about to bury themselves in the sand," he was saying and apparently not happy about this weak joke, not happy about something. He was sighing, sitting down.

"Well," Gwenda said, "listen, they have Yankee bean soup, do you want that to start?" She had laid her hand down on his sleeve and was plucking at it with her clean sharp nails. "Or what? The New England clam chowder?"

She began reading aloud from the menu and she had a way about doing everything which was very dedicated and serious. She read the menu as she would the *Aeneid* and leaving nothing out, she read right through from appetizer to dessert and then, shaking her head prettily so her long silky hair fell about all over her shoulders, said what did he feel like, was obliging, would, if he wanted, read the menu to him again from top to bottom. There was something rather Asian in her disposition, something that smacked of breaking open rare jars of frankincense or myrrh over his feet. There was also something very subtle but deliberate that she conveyed in the way she bent slightly toward him and touched him, the admission to everyone that he was her lover and that she had a justifiable conceit about it.

Just so free and wonderful, he remembered as the scene vividly came back. Just so delightful that he wanted to go out and come in again and do it all differently now, come across the dining room with outstretched arms and not sidling in, avoiding what he took to be curious glances as he had just seen himself do. And full of sighs for some reason. What sighs? What for?

But she was free and wonderful, she was not beholden to God or man, this blond twenty-three-year-old ordering his lunch for him. She was not constrained to be anything she was not just because this was a public dining room full of stuffy New England types and so all the time that she read to him about chicken Newcastle and brisket of lamb she caressed his hand and then, looking up at the waitress (who was all starched out in a Puritan bonnet), she rested her head on his shoulder while she considered the beefsteak and kidney pie and, "I'll have that and he'll have the lamb," she said and handed back the menu and then let her head continue to rest on his shoulder. And now what? And *now* he would have been flattered and tender and let her stay there resting in the crook of his arm. Instead of which he saw that he had been intensely fidgety and that instead of letting the moment happen, as she was doing, just letting everyone think whatever the hell they wanted, he saw that every bit of his concentration had been focused on the hat at the next table and it was quite clear to him that he was not enjoying this joyful girl leaning in the crook of his arm like a sweet bird, but he was wriggling in squeamish awareness that this Butley, Connecticut, lady, spooning soup into her prudish mouth, was listening to them.

"Did you find out there's no shower?" Gwenda asked in her clear voice. "What'd you do? Did you take the tub? It takes about five minutes to fill up."

"Yes," George said and then, "Lovely day," to the Butley lady and then saw himself shift so Gwenda could no longer rest against him, so she must sit up straight beside him on the window seat and make as though there were nothing between them whatever; and yet this was the girl that at three o'clock that morning he had panted and raved and sweated over and said, among other poetic fancies, that she was the cave of his heart.

The Puritan waitress offered a bread basket as if it contained stones. "Oh, popovers," Gwenda said. She had been easily delighted, he was remembering, "Do you know that we can't *get* popovers in New York?"

"Butter, butter," she said. "Lots and lots of butter."

I remember now that things will happen, George thought. I will leave her.

Outwardly, though, he was protesting their having installed Musak in the dining room, all this early Yankee pewter candlesticks and Musak. "Imagine them adding insult to imagery," he said.

"Do you think they'll have Musak in hell?" she asked. "I imagine they'll have Musak all over hell and no way to turn it off and nothing to read but Holiday Inn brochures. Are you nervous?"

"No, no."

"You keep looking around so I think something is concerning you."

"What would I be concerned about? At my age there is very little left to be either curious or concerned about." But then he said into her left ear, "There appears to be a certain amount of interest in us among the DAR present."

"We're of great interest," she said and looked down at his hand. "At least, you are of great interest to *me*."

"Adorable girl, I know but I know *not* why."

Later on she walked ahead of him through the dining room pulling on her ostrich gloves and looking very young and demure in her slacks and her neat little tasseled loafers, something so reassuring about those neat loafers; she could easily have been his daughter and he adopted her with a look to the heads turning and swept the whole room, a proud-father look as they went out the door, and felt a good deal better until the saturnine-looking manager at the reception desk said, "Afternoon, Mr. and Mrs. Wander," and smirked as though to say, And if you really *are*, then I am Gunga Din.

True, as he caught sight of them in the big greenish mirror they looked mismatched as she pulled on her woolen cap (Gwenda McCracken, *that* was her name, it came back to him now) and he put on his deerstalker; they looked profoundly unmarried, anyone could tell, this serious older-minded girl and this naïve younger-minded roué; roué was what he was beginning to be; he looked lined and fatigued and full of all kinds of inner concern whereas she looked unlined and as unconcerned as a marble bird. And he remembered even as he admired her that he would very shortly, on this very afternoon and somewhat callously, abandon her.

She had taken his arm, she jogged up and down beside him, her long silky hair blew across his face. "Wander is an odd kind of a name," she said as she jogged across the drive to where he'd parked his car half hidden under a spruce tree. "Why an odd name like Wander?"

"I guess I thought the odder the name the more likely to be believed."

"Why does it matter about being believed?"

"I have my little quirks, Puritan streaks."

"But Wander, what made you think of it?"

"It came into my mind. Plonk."

"It's subconscious wishing. You wish to *wander*."

He had looked sharply at her as if she had discovered something; he had not yet begun to imagine himself vanishing; he had not yet begun to ponder the idea of stepping through a little paper door and yet she had seen the seeds of it in him; she was (had been) remarkably preceptive.

What a strange afternoon. Even the weather had changed, brilliant one minute and threatening the next, black and gold, gold and black as they drove into Butley township around the statue of Ethan Allen. Under these threatening pitch-black skies, a winter sun pricked its way through, went in and out again, its piercing gold making the church spires stand out against the blackness. Coming back into Butley for the first time in so many years, the town had seemed to have hastily been put together when they had news that he was coming back; like a movie set with all the pieces marked and stored somewhere until news of his imminent arrival and quickly hauled out and put together in a few minutes: Hatcher's department store and the same old dummies in print dresses in the window that had surely been there when old Jessica took him in to buy a cheap serge blazer and next to that Rodman's Cake Shop and then Jack the barber's (three chairs, no waiting) and the Mary Elizabeth Tearoom and Jonas' Liquor Store, which never once had been patronized by his family; and next to that the quaint colonial-style movie theater (advertising BRUTALITY, BESTIALITY NOW THRU FRI.), which had used to be rented out six times a year to Mrs. Nona Holly for the productions of the Holly and Ivy Players and where he'd first tasted the wine of success, coming on between Archer and Clytie to cries of Author, Author on the opening night of his own original drama (the hand-printed posters had read in bold red letters that *the Holly and Ivy Players proudly present for two nights only: George Wood's original drama* A Pomegranate for Judas, *starring Archer Hurst and Clytie Bundock; directed by the author* and then—it could have been an indication of things to come —a heavy rain had washed all the names away in the night except for Archer's). Now he skimmed past the movie house and the public library and past the old Dutch house which used to be Mrs. Mendoza's boardinghouse where Archer had once lived and out onto Shady Lane Road toward Butley School because Gwenda had heard how lovely and New Englandish it was, every bit as good as Kent, and because it was where George had gone to school. He was driving now very fast along the road toward the school and the bell tower appeared, the graceful fieldstone tower thrust up through the bare trees (he could imagine the tolling bell); they could see the little running figures on the soccer field, the well-remembered winter Saturday scene.

Instead of crossing the bridge over the reservoir he turned sharply up a hill and into the cemetery, stopping the car wildly only a foot away from a family mausoleum, and said, "Mind if we stop off here a minute? I'd just like to look in on Mother," and got out and started walking quickly through the Presbyterian section. Looking back once, he saw she was following him in that obedient-daughter way of hers and when cold drops of rain began he'd turned and said to her to get back to the car, sweetie, not to come on, he didn't want her to get wet. "But I'd like to if you don't mind," she said and, Oh, mind, mind, he had said falsely as if grateful but then had plunged ahead in the rain, boorishly not waiting for her, and had tramped on through the cemetery, tight-lipped and wondering what he had come for until a sign read that he was now in the Catholic section so somehow he had missed his way and now had to turn back, embarrassed to have to admit to Gwenda that somehow he had mislaid the grave, sorry, and she had said in her nice way that so many graves look alike *any*one can mislay one, Gwenda said, the rain running down her face like tears, she walking along beside him as they went up and down, hunting and bending over tombs to read names while George had grown more and more furious with himself, muttering that he could have sworn it was somewhere near this lilac tree; and blundering up and down, a worse thing happened: they had come across poor Clytie Bundock's grave. Only of course he had not mentioned the fact and anyway what could Clytie Bundock possibly mean to Gwenda? Except as a span from one end of his life to the other and that (he had realized, somewhat surprised) they were alike in some ways and "*Boxer* Wood?" Gwenda had asked. She had found it for him and was standing in front of the twin marble slabs, one old and lichened, the other newer, the older one reading Harold Edward Wood and the newer reading Jessica Boxer Wood. Born. Died. He had never been able to think what to put on her gravestone. Beloved wife of, mother of? With her vinegary sweetness and her sharp barbs and her carefully guarded secret (which had certainly taken a lot out of her, worn her down until at the end she was as transparent as a thin sliver of soap) so that she would likely have said to him, "Why don't you just put on it 'Least Said, Soonest Mended'" and then given that crusty little laugh of hers which so put people off her.

So he had stood there with Gwenda slightly behind him staring down at the family plot, and certainly had no idea why. Then as a watery sun came out, he saw that he had really been testing to see if he could feel any emotion over the woman buried here, he had been trying to squeeze out at least one tear of regret but that nothing had come; he was standing there just as empty and devoid of feeling as it was possible to be but putting on a very serious, indrawn look for the benefit of Gwenda and then he had turned and taken her arm and walked away silently, all the way out of the cemetery and back to the car without a word.

And he'd begun to realize about this time that Gwenda had seen through this little bit of playacting, begun to understand that this child could not be hoodwinked, and so he was pondering on this when—what had happened next? A sudden shock? Waiting on the corner of Reservoir Road for the only traffic light in Butley to change, glancing beside him he saw, in another car waiting for the light to change, Ruth's mother.

Come exactly at this moment to this intersection. Kitty Carver, the only still living person in Butley who knew him, an example of the joke his personal fates or Norns liked to play on him; Kitty Carver sitting behind the wheel of her station wagon when she ought to be in Stockholm or Rothenburg or Melbourne; she whom you couldn't keep home, who only came home to plan her next excursion, was here beside him waiting for what must be the slowest-changing stoplight in America and looking like a woman admiral, looking very like her dead son Tony, and George felt his face flaming (had she or had she not seen him?) not because of the fear that she would be racing home to telephone Ruth but because she would not. He knew she would not. Not even if she caught him in flagrante delicto. There was a demilitarized zone between him and Kitty concerning Ruth.

Just the same when the light finally changed he let Kitty get ahead and stay ahead until he saw her turn off onto the road that led to her big ugly house while he kept on the old road into New York State, where right away the houses had a less attractive look, not as well kept. They had the pinched look of one-time tenant farming rather than the affluent look of the Connecticut houses.

New Forks was as dispiriting as ever, the unpainted shops on Main Street and the old disused railroad depot. They passed quickly through the shopping center, unchanged since his boyhood, except the movie theater was now boarded up and for rent; and then on to Prize Road, which could only take a prize for the most weeds and the most broken paling fences in the county, and pulled up outside the gate of his family house.

"Here's where I lived."

She'd said she wanted to see it. Now they sat and stared without saying anything at the uncurtained windows. At the birds' nests in the eaves of the verandas. Someone years ago had inadvisedly painted the house pink and it had now faded to a stale turnip.

"It looks deserted," Gwenda said. It had an unlived in look about it.

"Let's see," he said. They pushed open a rotting gate. The front yard was deep in weeds and debris. They peered through a window. But there was furniture. So somebody lived here.

"The living room," George said. He had begun to smell the past; the past had an actual smell like certain ferns. "The kitchen," he said and they peered in through grimy glass.

It was easy for him now to knit the past and present, hooding his eyes with his hands to see better into the dark kitchen and simultaneously being his baby self in his high chair and strenuously beating an egg to pulp with his spoon. What was it Mama called his egg? His goo-goo, and peering through the dirty glass George saw clearly through to this back-then moment, saw Mama stroke his bald head while she crooned, "Where's a goo-goo for the bitsy boy-boy?" He could see Jessica Boxer Wood stroking his little bald head. "Ungle, gubb, goodly, gug," he said, which would make crystal sense to him at the time even though not understood by others. "Bunniddy booge," he said, dribbling egg and spit, lovely, and wetting his other end. "Spooooooge," he said and imagine if he could have looked up *then* and seem *himself* outside the kitchen window looking in at him? George had conjured up a vision. George was always good at conjuring up visions and this one had been startling. He had joined the two ends of his life in a loop. He saw the baby look up and see him. He waved to the baby and made a face at the baby through the glass. Oh, horror. The baby dropped the spoon, the baby shrieked, up flew the tiny arms to beat the air, boiling red went the tiny face, into convulsions, the baby screamed and screamed. Enough to make any baby scream, the knowledge he had bestowed on this baby. The sight of *himself* at the window, as he was going to *become*. Worse than the most hideous eyes-gouged-out Dracula bloody bogeyman, this horrible sight; ahhhhhhhh, the baby screamed and pointed. That *thing* looking in. I am going to become *that?*

"Oh, the past, I can smell the past," George had said, turning away with a genuine groan, and had put his arms tight around Gwenda and hung onto her until the horrible imagined moment had passed; the vision of the baby had appalled him for some reason. And he knew the vision of the baby would return. None of us escapes his baby self and now . . .

"Hold onto me a minute," George said and then, "Oh, dearest girl, I don't know, I don't know."

"Don't know what?" She was young.

"*Anything.*"

And they were standing there, arms looped around each

other and simply holding each other like children playing post office, and then suddenly the kitchen door flew open and a woman asked sharply, "You looking for someone?"

How he'd hated being surprised like this in what had been his own kitchen garden by this rude stranger and he saw that he had overreacted and extricated himself from Gwenda rather as though he didn't know her and said, No, no, sorry, didn't mean to trespass. I used to live in this house once.

"You one of the Tarrants?"

"No. Wood."

"We bought from Mrs. Tarrant. I don't remember any Woods."

"We've largely died out," he said and stalked back to the car; he was still shuddering from the vision of the baby in there and with the terrifying thought that he and the baby could be joined by a span or ribbon of time.

"Did it hurt?" Gwenda asked. "All this revisiting?"

"No, no."

But the day was spoiled not only by the weather, there was the color of disappointment about it and she knew it too. He could tell by the way she walked upstairs ahead of him when they got back to the inn and in the room she said:

"The main difference between you and me is that you're a moralist and I'm not."

"Oh, come now."

"Yes, it's true."

"No no."

"You are kind of ashamed about this, about me, about being in Butley with me."

"Oh, no no."

"I always know when you say no no like that it's your way of being nice and getting out of saying what you mean at the same time."

"Oh, no *no*."

"I wish you would say that you're miserable."

"But I'm not. Why would you want me to be?"

"Not want you to be—want you to admit it, then I'd have something to go on."

"Something to *go* on? You haven't anything to go on?"

What a strange girl she was, flat heels, long hair, daughterish one minute and the next being the older one, she was gentle as a dove and sharp-beaked as a sea gull, and it was at this point that he had begun to pick at the candlewick bedspread. It was at this moment that he had begun to be nervous about her.

"You have the better of me," he said.

"I wish that I did," she said. "I wish that I had something of you. I don't know what to do."

"What has brought all this on?"

She had made a helpless little gesture, all the time staring out the window at the fading light.

"You care about people and I don't," she said.

"Oh, now, you care about people, dear girl. . . ."

"You care about people's *approval*'s what I mean."

"Oh, not as much as you might think."

"Oh, I've watched you *watching* to see what effect you're having; to see if you're being approved. You have to—desperately for some reason—be approved and—"

She could read him like a book and it was disturbing hearing all this from a girl he hadn't meant to let get this close to him and he automatically pressed his knees close together as though to conceal and protect his private parts.

"—and you see I couldn't give a cent, not one cent about what anyone thinks about me and I wish you didn't either because I think people who are always watching other people to see what other people are thinking about them get all mixed up and get to trying to be something or other to please the other person and that's the principal reason I don't ever want to get married. I'd be scared that I would be trying all the time to be a wife and not a person."

She squatted, putting her elbows on his knees and looking up at him, and so he put his hand against her face.

He said, "And now tell me what's brought this on and what I've done to upset you."

"Oh, you haven't upset me," she said. She stroked his leg and again he pressed his knees closer together. "That hasn't anything to do with what I'm saying."

He had let her tread water, not flung her a word of help.

She said, "I think people go around looking for reasons too much, I think *you* do all the time—look for reasons why you do things, even why you think you ought to love somebody or go to bed with somebody. It's got something to do with you thinking you *ought* to do something or other—that's what I mean about I'd rather you told me you were miserable than pretend—do the *nice* thing because you're a moralist and I'm not. So call me an immoralist if you like but I don't want to find reasons. Do you see?"

So all he did for her was nod.

"I don't want to love anyone *because* of anything. There shouldn't have to be a reason."

She was quiet for a time and then said, "What I'm trying to say is I hope to God you don't ever find a *reason* to love *me.*"

Then she got up and said, "Do you know what I think I'll do? I think I'll go for a little walk."

"All right," he said.

"Just a short one."

"OK."

"OK, OK?"

"OK. Wrap up though," he said.

She pulled on her woolen cap, her ostrich gloves. She came over and lightly kissed him on the lips.

"Byeeee," she said.

"Byeeee," he said.

And when she had closed the door he walked quickly around the room a few times and then took his suitcase out of the closet and tossed in his pajamas, his bathroom kit, his—

But no, no. No, George thought, surely it wasn't this way, not the moment she went out surely.

Surely he had sat down and had long dark difficult thoughts about her. Surely he had sat, almost groaning that once again he had unintentionally brought about real love and attachment and then, weighing one kind of cruelty against another, had finally come to the painful decision. He would have sworn to it in court, he had wrestled with himself, suffered and whistled through his teeth in pain.

Yes, he was whistling. But he was throwing things into the suitcase, then on with his topcoat and his deerstalker and hurrying downstairs and into the little writing room and, "Dear," he had written (feeling "Dear Gwenda" was altogether too cold, that was for letting the maid go). "Dear," he wrote, "I have found a reason for loving you: you read me like a book. But God help me, I can't stand being read. George." Then he had added as a postscript, "I am not going to use Dudley's script so it will be suicide time again and he will need you badly." Then, crowning touch, he put in the bus fare, closed and sealed the envelope, on which he wrote "Mrs. Wander," and he had felt this was the better way, this piece of calculated cruelty was far less cruel than letting it run on, even a little longer, even the rest of the weekend longer. Stab her, he had decided upstairs, stab her quickly through the heart as one would put a bullet through the head of the fallen horse.

And paid the bill and muttered about an urgent message he'd just received (by pigeon? Morse code? asked the clerk's eyebrows) and would you give this to my wife when . . .

Shock treatment. She would be stunned by it and the shock would help her to get over him more quickly so it was more humane this way. The only way.

Had driven away feeling almost like Sydney Carton and that was all, that was the end of it. . . .

Now, he thought, the reliving of this bit of my life is surely over and like the other times there will be a little snap, a jerk in the subconscious and I will be . . . suddenly emerge perhaps in my bathroom, the mirror steamed over, clearing to show my face looking back at me slightly startled because this all may have only been a few seconds like it was seeing Maiva, the maid, and the big dog from next door, seeing Evelyn Tillotsen's hand without the scar and knowing only a few seconds had gone by while I was away.

But this time the turnpike continued on and now in this state of additional dimension he saw that just as one may drive along a turnpike and at the same time be thinking of another place and see it *also,* saw Gwenda returning to the Butley Arms Inn and being handed his note and this was not something he had thought of, imagined later, this was happening in parallel time; at this moment as he was driving along the turnpike she was coming into the inn and it was so bright that the stitching in her coat was visible and she took the note and leaned on the stair rail reading it and she was as calm as if she had only been given expected news, put it in her pocket and then, by gum, she was standing by the postcard rack, she was swiveling it around and looking at postcards; she seemed disconsolate but she was looking at *postcards!* Not hurrying upstairs to hurl herself down in the empty room on their connubial bed and weep and throw herself this way and that crying out, Oh, George, George. She'd seemed to pocket the news as simply a confirmation, with a sigh that sadly she had been right. She'd gone out for a walk simply to give him the opportunity to skedaddle without long scenes and painful excuses; she read him like a book and she had read him all along.

So it hadn't been any heroic or generous gesture on his part; it had been hers. Her gesture, this quiet intelligent girl who called herself an immoralist; she had the character, not he. Oh, Christ. George winced, bent over the wheel flying to New York. He'd been gently set free; she had been much wiser than he. It had been love on her part but he had no love left in him, was all dried up like a withered lemon when it came to love and could only approximate its gestures now and Gwenda McCracken had known this all along and still had loved him, which was entirely too generous (and she was to be the very last of a long line of people who had been entirely too generous).

And if I am going back, really going back in a continuous sequence, he thought, my God, this thing just now was nothing, *nothing* compared to what I will have to see in the further past.

Let me *out*, he said aloud to himself, willing himself to be out of the car, to break the

the turnpike blurred and narrowed.

"I thought you'd prefer a nice quiet little place," he said. He was obviously trying to warm someone up, encourage someone who was

Going down steps. No memory of this. What? When?

Oh, La Torte on East Forty-ninth Street, one of his places where he was comfortable and known, but the slipback was so sharp, like a turning point in a dream when one is transported to Africa in a wink. So for a few seconds he seemed to be in limbo. The woman passed under the door lamp. She and the restaurant were quickly building into substance out of colored bits and pieces that he had put away and then he saw he was with Alice Hurst, Archer's first wife. Why this night?

He couldn't pinpoint the exact date. Only that this had been quite some time before Gwenda and the Butley weekend.

And here was old Madame waddling forward. "Ah, Monsieur Wood." "Good evening, Madame," George said and something about her being a welcome sight and that this was Mrs. Hurst, a visitor from California.

Taking off their coats, "And how is your good wife, monsieur?"

"She is in Easthampton."

"Ah, good evening, Gerard," he said to the waiter. He was trying to create the atmosphere of ease and comfort for Alice Hurst so that eventually she might like something or be pleased about something, a breadstick even. She had the same pained look she had had as she came out of the elevator. They had not seen each other for years.

"Do you think you *have* to?" Ruth had asked and he had said, "Oh, poor Alice, she's got nobody now."

"Never a breath of air," Alice was saying, "in New York restaurants and if there *is* you'd rather not breathe it." She would have a vodka martini, Alice said. She was too dressed up for just a simple old-friends evening; she had on a sort of lamé suit, metal it looked like, perhaps the only chance she had had of wearing it. Perhaps she was genuinely pleased and excited to be taken out. Her son was gone off somewhere driving a truck for revenge, she had no idea where, she had told George in the taxi, last heard from months ago from Butte, Montana.

She read the menu as though it were a list of those who were to go to the gas chamber. She had never had charm and was unaware of the fact, couldn't understand why she raised hackles and ruffled feathers. Now she took forever ordering, frowning at the menu. No, she wouldn't like this, wouldn't care for that, not the vol-au-vent. Gerard explained six dishes. Gerard sighed. George smiled and smiled and smiled.

Reluctantly she would have the beef Wellington then. "The food at the hotel," Alice said. "I think they run it through the laundromat."

Beautiful little *moules* were offered by Madame with the drinks. Alice shuddered.

Already, he remembered, he was feeling tired and they'd hardly begun.

"Are you still doing that documentary program?" she asked.

"It's now called 'Studio 21.' "

"Is it on that educational network?"

"Right."

"I get that channel so badly. I'm in Malibu."

"You ought to get cable TV, you get all those added—"

"Oh, what's the good of it? Everything's so rotten anyway."

"Have one of Madame's homemade brioches."

"It's—no, no, I never touch bread—it's painful to have to look at that channel so I never get to see any of your work— oh, except I did see the Disraeli thing you did."

"Er—"

"Which I thought was excellent, George, excellent, and that's a compliment coming from me."

"I know it is."

"Who does *not* throw compliments around as I don't have to remind you. You remember how Archer would never let me go to a preview of any of his pictures; he said it wasn't worth being exposed to Alice's terrible white scorn. My white scorn, he always called it; why white and not black I cannot imagine except he's a sickening bigot. Anyway I liked your Disraeli and I should have written you about it."

"Well, you're most kind, Alice. Actually it was Parnell."

"Was it?"

"Parnell not Disraeli, but thank you anyway."

"Whoever it was I liked it. I can't drink this, they've put lemon peel in it."

"Didn't you want lemon peel?"

"I can't stand lemon peel but everywhere you go in New York they never stop giving you lemon peel. They have some sort of *thing* about it."

"Gerard, would you bring madame another vodka martini on the rocks but without the lemon peel."

"Oui, Monsieur Wood."

Alice said, "And don't let him just take the lemon peel out and pour it into another glass because I can always tell."

"Madame wants a completely *new* drink, Gerard."

"Oui, Monsieur Wood."

"Never trust a French waiter, especially in New *York*," Alice said and she seemed to have thought she'd said something both wise and witty; she was a faultless example of being one's own worst enemy; poor lonely Alice, she had aged perceptively and she was telling George how depressing it was to see how her New York friends had aged so; she included him without saying so. She was dispiriting, stifling. So why had he been sitting here, smiling at her over the wine list? It had not been true what he said to Ruth, that he was sorry for her; you couldn't be sorry for Alice longer than five minutes. So why was he sitting here, nodding and agreeing with her (he had observed to himself when she came out of the elevator that her shoes were an instant giveaway, they were very cruel-looking with black moiré tongues; what cruel shoes, he had thought, skeptical, like her), and then it had come over him in a flash why he was here; he was getting satisfaction out of the fact that Archer had left her, it gave him a kind of gratification, and sharp as a tack she seemed to catch his thought, so fast that he almost started.

"Did you know," Alice said, "that he had left Miriam?"

Now it was Alice getting satisfaction.

"He's living with some little *hat check* girl."

"I had heard that he had left Miriam."

And now here was her new drink; naturally also came their *escargots,* which she would now let go cold while she sipped her drink.

"Do you ever hear from him?"

"No."

"Not ever?"

"Not ever, not in blue moons, haven't."

"I thought," she said, "that you heard from Archer all the time."

"Not *ever,*" George said.

"Why?"

Well, he told Alice (he speared an *escargot,* fancying that it was her heart), he'd hurt Archer's feelings (but went around in circles virtually explaining nothing to her; he was unused to letting people into this sacred arena; even after all these years his heart was sore when he thought about it). But, he said resignedly, these things have a way of burning themselves out, these friendships have a way of wearing out (he felt the soreness in his heart after all these years; his eyes pricked). He said to her, pettishly, "Well, *you* know Archer always picked up and dropped people at will. I think it astounded him to be the one to be *dropped.*"

There was something oddly wooden in the stare she was giving him, sipping her drink.

"Drink all right?" he asked.

The wooden stare continued to bore into him, as though she were trying to hypnotize him.

"Peculiar," she said in a very low voice.

"What is?"

"I am," she said. "I am feeling suddenly very peculiar."

She had put aside her drink, she had clenched her fist

against her forehead in a melodramatic gesture reminiscent of Modjeska.

"I am feeling ill," she said.

"My dear," he said, "sit back a moment and relax." She had indeed become an ashy color. "Try a sip of water," he said, genuinely concerned for her, he had thought.

But saw now that already he had been annoyed, squirming around because oh, God, this was absolutely typical of Alice and in one of his own special restaurants where they knew him and here she was going to be ill all over the floor.

"Was it the lemon peel?"

She shook her head. "I don't know what's come over me," she said; her lips were a little blue.

"Look," he said, "hadn't you better . . . it's just there by the stairs, that door there."

She had risen and for some reason turned toward the wall and was now fumbling with a net curtain that hung behind the table.

"I'm caught," she said.

"I don't understand. What?"

"I am caught," she said. Sure enough a metal button on her cuff had become enmeshed in the fabric.

Only she in the world could have arranged it.

"See if you can get it," she said.

But the fabric was made of tiny loops threaded together and trying to free the button became like intricate crochetwork; just as you slipped one loop free, another folded over.

"Keep calm," George said but she was looped fast.

"I am caught on this thing," Alice announced angrily to the restaurant. "Somebody come."

Beads of sweat had broken out on her forehead.

"Hang on," he said. "I've almost got it, I think; lift your arm up a bit."

"Be quick."

"I'm trying."

"I may be going to pass out."

"Put your head down, dear; no, you're not going to pass out, you'll be OK. Madame, Madame, can you get some scissors or something—she's caught in this drape."

"Ah, no, monsieur—don't tear if you please; this is imported."

"Alice, can you slip out of the jacket and then—"

"No, I'm not wearing any bra."

He and Madame and Gerard were all arms and thumbs at once with Alice leaning on him and beginning to make strange noises. Then Alice pushed them all away and with an effort tore the button off her dress and, snatching up a napkin to her face, ran.

"No harm done," George said and smiled as Madame said it was *incroyable.* "Just *un peu malade,*" George said to the waiter and Madame but pondering what effect continuous scorn could have on the spleen and liver; and that Archer's expression was exactly on the nose, that Alice's was a terrible white scorn and that inwardly she was radioactive with it; even when they were young she had walked with a peacock step and a slightly condescending smile for everyone. She could pooh-pooh anything, Alice Gibbs could, belittling was almost a talent with her; so to tell her you had won the Nobel would be to have her ask, Oh, were they still giving that out? and sometimes she caused people to break out in rage and scream at her that such and such was a *fact* that they had seen and experienced themselves and after that she was more peacock than ever and they only felt fools for having given way to anger. And Archer (the thought had broken over George like an unexpected wave from behind) had never been a cause for skepticism, he had only been cause for wonder and spoiled beyond belief by everyone, so Archer had been astonished when Alice regarded him with her white scorn and pooh-poohed him and he had become fascinated by her and had to win her and . . .

And, George thought now for the first time, he and Archer married similar women, women who disliked each other but were similar. Alice with her scorn and Ruth with her cool.

"Feeling better?" George asked and pulled out her chair for her. Alice had been crying. She shook her head. "A little food will put you right." The beef Wellington was being wheeled up. "Look how pretty," he said.

Tears ran down Alice's face.

"*Must go*," she said.

She got up and ran through the restaurant in her ugly shoes as though she were being pursued by muggers. Heads turned; inwardly George cursed her and signed for the un-eaten dinner; alas, the wine had already been opened.

She asked to be driven around Central Park and in the dark as they drove under the dark trees she said:

"All New York taxis smell like old men's shoes."

It was apparently going to be her only remark until they got back to her hotel and she got scornfully out of the cab, refusing the arm of the commissionaire with a grimace.

"Come up, George, will you?"

"No, Alice."

"Yes, come up, will you?"

"But you're not feeling well."

"Come up."

Up in her hotel room they drank bitter black coffee inasmuch as room service neglected to send up any cream. "And fifty dollars a day for this dream of old Williamsburg," Alice said. She lay on the bed and her face was an oddly yellow color.

"Why are you sitting way over there?" she demanded.

"I'm just here in the chair."

"You seem miles and miles away. Come and sit here." She moved her legs to make room for him on the bed. Surely not, he thought. "When I think about it," she said now, out of the blue, "I have been giving, giving, giving all my life."

Now he remembered what she was about to lead up to, nothing to do with sex and yet maybe in a subtle way very much to do with sex and because of her genius for putting down, maybe she was stealthily getting out her implements for castration . . . now he remembered what she was leading up to. He had been afraid of what might be coming. But how undignified he looked now (she had made him move on purpose, even the move was a put-down) squatting on her bed, not quite enough room so he had to lean sideways on one elbow and to make the thing complete he'd caressed one of her feet. . . . "Giving, giving, or else giving *in*, which is the same thing," she said. She had begun a lament about her life with Archer Hurst; of how he could not be satisfied no matter what she did, no matter what new tricks she learned, what new humiliations in the sack (watching to see his reaction to that so he merely stroked her foot and looked sorry), giving, giving, giving in to Archer, always hoping he'd be satisfied for a time; the huge house in Bel Air they couldn't afford to staff, the airplane to test her nerves the way he flew, he flew like a deranged bat, then the racing cars, the speedboats (the joy of killing oneself is orgiastic, she said) and finally the child she managed to have at last and nearly died having, but none of these things were any more than toys and diversions he quickly tired of.

"Giving, giving, giving," Alice said, "until there wasn't any more of me left to give."

"Poor Alice," he said. He held her foot because he couldn't think how to let it go. It felt like a lukewarm potato.

"Except the one thing he craved was the one thing I *refused* to give him."

"What's that?"

"You ought to know."

This was dangerous, their talking about Archer. He could see he was very rigid.

"You certainly ought to know. Worship."

"Yes."

"Worship. Everybody fall down at the sound of the flute and the sackbut and worship him."

"Ahhh, yes."

"Monster," she cried out. "Monster."

George let go of her foot and she yanked it up under her.

"Monster," Alice said and her face was suffused with love, only he had not noticed it at the time. Only now in the new dimension he saw how dangerous she was. She was spoiling like uneaten food in the heat, her scorn was working away in her like maggots.

She lay back on the pillows; her hair had come loose a bit and her eyes were very black, boring into him. Then she said, "And you never hear from him?"

"No."

"Did something happen between you and Archer that day at the school?"

"At the school? What school?"

"Butley. The day when we all had the accidental running into each other, the day Archer and I both arrived to see Michael not knowing the other was coming and it turned out later the little bastard planned it to see which one of us would be the most embarrassed."

"Michael did?"

"Yes, the bastard. He's off somewhere in Montana driving a truck, the little scum, did I tell you?"

"Yes, you told me, Alice."

"Why are you sitting up like that so stiff and proper?"

"Would you like me to lie down?"

"No; don't be smart, just tell me what happened between you and Archer. What put him in such a rage?"

"He wasn't in a rage."

"I thought he was in a rage when we saw him later in the teashop those dykes run for the parents to have tea and sympathy with their devoted sons."

"No," he said. "And, Alice, love, I'm going to have to say good night."

"You are a liar, George, you are a sweet liar; you would lie your ass off to save a friend, wouldn't you?"

"Not true."

"Anyway, you don't tell people necessarily the truth, you tell them what they want to hear. I've seen you doing it."

She was smiling, dangerous, beady-eyed with the excitement of criticizing him (she must have disliked and resented him all these years, poor Alice), so he put an end to her gusto by leaning down and brushing her forehead with his big mustache.

"Good night, Alice," he said. "Good-bye, dear, have a good trip back, get home safe."

"Do you know *why* I got sick in the restaurant?"

"The strong garlicky smell of *escargots*—"

"George, do you know why I got sick in the restaurant?"

"Why?"

"I suddenly solved something."

"Did you?"

He knew in a flash, something he must have intimated, given away; he also knew she must be ignored, otherwise she would pursue it to the end, perhaps demand to know certain facts; well, she would never get anything out of him. He put on the look of a mildly bewildered pope, raising hands to heaven and rolling his eyes, miming that he could not in the world think what she was talking about. He went to the door and saw in the mirror she had got off the bed and was following him.

"I suddenly solved something about you."

She was stepping from one rose to another on the carpet with her peacock walk. "Something I never thought of, George."

And what a smile he had given her, arctic.

"Well!" Hearty, evasive.

"Yes, *well* is *right*."

"You must tell me about it someday"—anything to stop her preening and peacocking it all over him for whatever revenge she wanted, so he pushed her up against the Williamsburg dresser and gave her a hard concrete kiss on the mouth and at the same time a similar hard push into her stone woman's parts and then out into the corridor and nothing more to remember of this night or why it had recurred and waiting for the lighted corridors with the tiny chandeliers to dissolve and ringing urgently for the elevator but no, it wasn't quite over, she had come out of the room and leaning on the door said:

"Oh, give my best to Ruth, will you?"

"Yes, course."

"Funny Ruth should have got you in the end."

Just rang and rang for the elevator.

"I wonder if Ruth has solved it too."

To his disgust he saw that, perhaps in relief, just as he stepped into the elevator he had blown her a kiss, only a social gesture of course but humiliating in the general sense, seeing that he detested Alice, had always detested

very quickly.

In a terrific hurry. Hurrying upstairs in a dingy dim-lit-hallway fourth-floor walkup, this was months and months, no, a year ago, long ago this summer suit he was wearing had gone to the Easthampton Thrift Shop and if so then the whole experience was being experienced in jumps. He was receding

back into his own life with no choice of events; it was holus-
bolus. It was a bit frightening not knowing where he was
likely to emerge next, like being on a train traveling through
mountain ranges and plunging into and out of long dark
tunnels, emerging, peering from the window to orient himself
and finding he had come out of a different and unexpected
side of the mountain, so where was the expected view of the
chalet, where was the waterfall? But they had been passed
by, they were not relevant to his journey. He had set himself
a goal; he wanted to examine his life, to find the heart of his
life and see if he could then find an explanation of himself
and so, pulsations being set in motion, chasms bridged, there
now could be no selectivity, no lingering in the gardens of
his mind where he had enjoyed the fierce pleasures that were
not germane (panting up the last flight of stairs to Dudley's)
to the central plan. He was a passenger. He had no more
control over this journey than he had physical control over
his heart missing a beat.

It was inevitability spelled backward.

A young, pretty girl opened the door.

"I'm George Wood," he heard himself explain. "Someone
phoned."

"I phoned," she said.

"Is he . . ."

She had put her finger on her lips and indicated the room
behind her. But Dudley was not dead. Dudley was sitting in
the cracked leather armchair and looking like the sad young
King Edward perpetually about to make the abdication
speech, Dudley, very English, a type almost extinct, continuously saddened by today's standards, shocked at bad
manners, dismayed at shoddy workmanship, standing to attention for the national anthem (and finding it was not going
to be played), forever young-looking flag lieutenant bravely
going after the *Graf Spee*, getting up to offer a lady the chair,

atavistic, almost gone from sight, a relic like home rule and
jars of Indian chutney, blue-eyed and pink-cheekedly so
unduly sensitive it was as though he suffered constantly from
a kind of white sunburn which would make him wince if he
were touched.

Both Dudley's wrists were bound in adhesive tape.

"Tripped and fell on a glass ashtray," Dudley said.

"Nasty things, those big ashtrays."

Because you never said the truth to Dudley, you said
what Dudley would want to hear (now who just had or was
later to accuse him of that?) and you weighed out the truth
in delicate little scales to be sure of how much Dudley could
take.

You held your drink rather than drank it because Dudley's
whiskey could have been used to remove varnish.

Dudley sitting in the famous cracked leather armchair and
the pretty young girl who had answered the door and who
obviously knew every trick and turn of him sat on a low
wooden stool beside him.

"This is Miss McCracken," Dudley said.

"Hello," George said.

The pretty girl just nodded; her eyes seldom left Dudley.
From time to time she struck a kitchen match and held it to
his cigarette. Lucky for him, Dudley said, Miss McCracken
came to return a book and found him in time, bits of ashtray
in his wounds.

All around him on little tables and on dusty bureaus and
on the windowsill, all around Dudley were photographs of the
famous; surrounding Dudley in their frames but no longer in
person and in varying stages of yellowing time, some ob-
solescent, some now dead, saying, Dudley dear, saying My
dear Dudley, from yours very sincerely, always with my love,
Elsie, Noel, Vivien, Dolores, Myrna, John, Maggie. Archer
Hurst had written in his bold attention-getting hand, "To

my dear Dud," but Dudley was insulated against possible hidden meanings.

"Dear of you to drop in, old thing," Dudley said.

"No no."

"Fearfully kind."

"ESP," Miss McCracken said, perhaps warningly.

Dudley said something to Miss McCracken about creese and chackers. Dudley was quite a bit drunk.

"Yes, cheese and crackers," the girl said.

"No no," George said. Not Dudley's cheese and crackers. Brave of Dudley in a way, Dudley the last one left on the burning boat, all alone in whatever he was all alone in, taking the razor. And yet it should have been me, George had thought, I am the one who has thought about doing it. He found himself annoyed with Dudley for bungling it but Dudley did everything half-assedly. Yet, he kept thinking, Dudley is brave, Dudley is braver than me.

Miss McCracken brought grayish cheese and two withered apples.

"Ah, delicious, thank you, how awf'ly nice you are, dear. Do dig in, George. Last of the Fortnum's some old chum sent."

If God was with them, it would not remind him of something. But God was not with them.

Dudley said, "I was thinking about the poor bloody musical comedy actor . . ."

George and Miss McCracken focused their full attention on him because he was sensitive about being paid attention to and if interrupted would stop and say that no, it wasn't important, not really funny anyway, and look so wounded, so like sad King Edward, that you could not forgive yourself.

"This poor bloody musical comedy actor in London I used to know, getting old you see, not working, do you see, and who was down to playing in—this is true, you see, this is not a story—he was down to playing *Good Night, Vienna* in Walthamstowe. . . ." Dudley paused. "Do you *know* about *Good Night, Vienna?*"

"No," George said.

"No," Miss McCracken said.

"Ah, well, you have to know about *Good Night, Vienna,* you see, or there's no point. Well, *Good Night, Vienna's* the most frightful old draggy ancient musical comedy, that was first done just after the war, World War *One,* that is—anyway it's the most ghastly piece of ancient old *Student Prince* moth-eaten claptrap ever put together and in fact I doubt that it was any good even when it was new if it ever was, it's so awful. But anyway—don't let me get off the point; I'm always getting off the point—"

"No you're not," Miss McCracken said.

"Well, anyway, to cut a long story short because it's bloody boring but it's rather touching, d'you see? Anyway, this poor old washed-up musical comedy star is playing *Good Night, Vienna* in Walthamstowe. . . ."

Dudley paused, seemed to expect something of them.

"D'you know about Walthamstowe?"

George and the girl shook their heads.

Dudley sighed. "Well, there's no point unless you know about Walthamstowe." Dudley seemed piqued. "Walthamstowe's a rather awful dreary suburb of London and it's sort of the last stop for an actor before rock bottom, d'you see. So the point *is,* it's bad enough to be playing Walthamstowe but to be playing *Good Night, Vienna* in Walthamstowe is the abolutely bloody *nadir.* So this poor bugger's having a drink in a pub and in comes a pal he knows and the pal sees that the poor bugger's looking most frightfully down in the mouth and buys him a drink and says, 'How are things,' and he says, 'Only fairish,' and the pal says, 'What are you doing?' and he says, 'I'm doing *Good Night, Vienna* in Walthamstowe,' and the pal doesn't know what to say to *that*, that being the bloody bottom, so he fiddles around and finally he says, 'Oh. Well, how's it going?' and the old musical comedy coot thinks for a bit. . . ." Here Dudley paused and thought for a bit to show the old actor.

"And finally the old musical comedy coot says, 'Oh, well. I s'pose it's going about as well as *Good Night, Walthamstowe* would go in *Vienna*.'"

So they laughed, George and the girl, because it was kind of touching.

Then Dudley put his bandaged hands up to his face and began to cry. Like everything he did, Dudley cried delicately, hiding behind his hands and sounding like a boy soprano having hiccups.

Nothing to do but wait for it to pass, knowing Dudley would hate to be touched. One must pretend to be unaware.

"Is it still raining out?" Miss McCracken asked, which was exactly right of her.

"No, it's stopped," George informed her and they kept their eyes away from the gasping man in the chair and looked at each other. They were joined in knowing exactly what not to do and suddenly George found he had begun to be interested in Miss McCracken with her soft hair and serene dove face.

"Why do we ask that—is it raining *out?*" She smiled. She was delectable, she was like a very nice attractive daughter in her tartan skirt and long socks. "As if it could be raining *in*." It occurred to George he would like to run his hand up the back of her neck under that soft fall of hair.

"Sorry," Dudley said, muffled.

"Oh, no no."

"Sorry. Disgusting display."

"Hell, you are with friends."

Miss McCracken had taken a comb to her hair as if she

had caught his thought and curled up there on the stool, her young knees were like two smooth green pears.

"Oh, God," Dudley gasped and had another slight spasm of tears.

They waited.

"Suddenly," Dudley said, coming out of mist and spray looking like the Duke of Windsor, "suddenly it came over me that was my whole mistaken life—my whole *plight* in a tunshell. In a nutshell. You see, in *England* I wouldn't have to *explain* that story, d'you see, you'd have begun to laugh right off at the beginning."

"I might not have," Miss McCracken said, passing the comb through her lustrous blond hair, clicking with electricity.

"Gwenda," said Dudley. "Do me the favor of not chiming in with little nice falsenesses."

Miss McCracken looked at George and a message passed between them. For a moment then the room shrank, diminished with them, with the furnishings, as a television picture shrinks, diminishes as it is turned off. Then it sprang back to its full shape again. It had been because George had experienced such a thrill of happiness from Miss McCracken's look. It was all coming back to him now (this was the evening when he and Gwenda had met and they owed it all to poor old Dudley's bungled suicide) and he saw that in his elation at the thought of Gwenda, so sure was he that Gwenda and he were going to embark on an affair that he could hardly contain his joy. He camouflaged it with concern for Dudley. He made a big-man fist and twisted it against Dudley's jaw.

"Snap out of it, dear old cock," George said.

"I'm lost, George. I'm abs'lyf'cking lost."

"No no."

"Stuck. Stuck. Stuck."

"No no."

"Can't go back to England. Can't work here. Stuck like a pig in a lub of tard, a tub of lard."

"Well, but—"

"I'm a funny man when—"

"You *are* a funny man and that's what I was going—"

"Shut up, please, and let me finish. I'm a funny man when it comes to things like Walthamstowe and Harrods and so on but I can't seem to be funny about Brooklyn or the Mets or Girl Scout cookies. I'm in the middle, George, I'm in the asshole of limbo and I'm never going to get going again."

Dudley pressed his hands to his forehead and valiantly fought down sobs. The decent young flag lieutenant carrying the wreath to the Cenotaph on Armistice Day, blue eyes blurred but upper lip stiff.

Dudley Rivers had written, long long ago, only dimly remembered now in the Burns Mantle collections, a feathery play of charm and wit in which unreal people circled a sliver of plot in elegant epigrams and beautiful clothes. A famous English star had played in it as Casals would on a cello. It ran for two years in London. Then it was brought intact to New York, where it ran for a little longer than two years. Dudley and his then wife Lenore came over for two weeks for the opening; for the wining and dining. Eight months later, reduced to a chain-smoking-skeleton by homesickness, Lenore sailed back to London. Dudley remained. Dudley wrote nothing more.

"You can *still* be funny," George said, noticing the way Miss McCracken's breasts moved this and that way as she combed her hair. She was a mermaid, a siren. "You're in a rut, Dudley, you're just in a rut, that's all," George said.

"My bridges all are burned, nowhere to go," Dudley sang.

"Let me tell you," George said (remembering he had made it up as he went along), "what I came here to tell you about, what I have in mind."

"Because of my love affair with—"

"I wish you'd listen to Mr. Wood," Gwenda said.

"Because of my love affair with the unkind, putrid, pol-luted, notaxi, overtaxed bloody city of N'York. New York."

"He doesn't even like to go to New Jersey," Gwenda said.

"Atsit in a tunshell. Two days away, all that freshair and can't wait to get back to the dogcrap and you come out of the tunnel on Thirty-fourth Street and oh, the relief. There it is. *There* it *is*. D'you know the feeling? You feel relieved because it's all still there, all that noise and litter and bloody awful and marvelous and nowhere else like it on earth. I'm like—you see—I'm like one of those young men—let's say I *used* to be like one of those young men in those awful South Sea islands plays, *White Cargo*—before your time. Always a young doctor very spruce in white suits comes out to the islands all very humanitarian and there's this old wreck of a drunk who says to him, 'Don't stay too long, go home before the islands *get* you,' but he stays and he startsa drink a bit and then a bit more and then he startsa stop shaving and gets himself a Tonkinese girl, much silk and many bangles, Tondelayo like mush silk 'n' many bangles and they say, 'You must go home onna next boat or else,' and he says, 'Next year, next year,' and fin'lly he's the outcast of the islands, crazy now and making beads and crap to sell for bottle of gin. That's *me*. Just can't leave, d'you see, can't leave. It's terrible and you know it's terrible. Papers full of nightmares every day and everyone with six locks on their door and then one afternoon you're walking down Fifth Avenue in the fall, one of those late October afternoons and there's a kind of light, a kind of mauvish blue light you only get in New York, and you look up and it comes over you suddenly, everything soaring up into the sky, the steeples on Saint Patrick's and the RCA tower and the birds flying up there in the clouds and you want to lift your arms up to it and say, 'Oh, yes—yes, *yes*.'"

Dudley had lifted up his arms.

George then had touched Dudley gently and said something about writing a script, would Dudley consider doing a script for a show they were thinking of doing on "Studio 21" (making it up out of whole cloth), something about the alien in the city with a witty ironic look to it as only Dudley could do it.

They probably would never do it but give Dudley hope, pay Dudley out of his own pocket if necessary. Somebody had to rally around, someone always had had to rally around Dudley.

He got up to leave now because he couldn't take any more; Dudley muttering about knowing who your friends are and asking George please to forgive this godawful display, could George forgive him? But it's you who owe *me*, George thought, if only you knew.

"Good night, old bean," George had said.

"T'rifically kind; *bless* you."

"Is this your umbrella?" Gwenda asked and at the door she said in a whisper, "Thank you."

They touched hands.

"And listen, thanks for all the things you didn't say." As George started downstairs she leaned over the stair rail and said softly, "It's the things you *didn't* say that I appreciated, Mr. Wood." That nice girl. Well, perhaps it was meant, them meeting through Dudley. Long ago he had done Dudley an enormous favor (not so much the favor itself but in the nobility of not telling Dudley; in the discipline of never having said to Dudley in the middle of one of his marathon stories, Listen, you boozy, boring, self-pitying attention-getter, shut up for a change and listen to what *I* have to tell you) and now maybe, just maybe he would take Miss McCracken in exchange.

He had begun to whistle.

Then as he opened the grimy front door onto the street, the

word *failure* occurred in his mind as if someone had spoken into his ear. Not *his* failure, Dudley's. It was not so much Miss McCracken that had pleased him as Dudley's failure. He saw himself standing there on the sidewalk with one arm raised to hail a taxi, looking pleased. The details of this event were growing hazy at the edges, the taxi was coming in slow motion, the look on his face was a shock to him, the look was so pleasant and beneficent—friend hailing taxi, having come to the aid of friend in trouble—when all the time he had been thinking *failure* and had found the word sweet as honey; Dudley's suicide attempt had succored him. Dudley owed him nothing; it was *he* who owed Dudley.

Over the years of their friendship, every time he had been depressed about what his career might have been he had automatically thought about poor Dudley's utter failure. But Dudley has done so much worse, he had thought and just like taking aspirin, the pain of his own failure quickly disappeared. Even this evening he had capitalized on it. Why, when Ruth had come running in and said to get on the phone quickly some girl was calling and Dudley Rivers had tried to do it, he had hurried to the phone saying he was not surprised. "Mind you, I'm not a bit surprised," he had told Ruth and had felt a little spasm of thrill as he picked up the phone. But he had not admitted it to himself.

What now shocked George immensely, watching himself standing on the curb in the lights of the taxi coming down Eleventh Street, was the look on his own face. He had been innocent, sincerely convinced of his friendship; a blissful look in the lights of the taxi which had blurred his eyes, now blurred the street in the sudden downpour of rain, deafening rain

the lights were right in his eyes, not rain, applause, and he seemed very startled by all this attention; the spotlight had been turned on their table and George had suddenly leaned over and squeezed Ruth, which seemed to surprise her slightly, though it was hard to tell with Ruth, with her lack of response. But his attention must have wandered during the endlessly long boring speeches of acceptance and the heavy-handed humor of various MCs and comings and goings of celebrities with mounds, simply mounds of false hair and false jewels and false remarks about every person coming on to accept or present a prize as being a wonderful, wonderful human being whom it was their privilege to know, and in between staggeringly awful jokes which received roars of insincere laughter and undertones of bitchery that could be overheard at nearby tables (and Charlotte Custis, George's assistant, his man-girl Friday, was clasping her hands together in prayer), it was in this moment, a flash, a roar, that George had been caught napping, his mind straying, while someone had said that whoever would now read out the nominees for the best hour-long documentary and suddenly confused by the spotlight and the applause he had got up and started down the long aisle to the dais in the explosion of this sudden success, recognition at last, broken into a run with his eagerness (and because the distance was so great— they had a bad table, way, way at the back among producers of little-known children's shows), and was almost to the dais where a woman wearing tons of jewelry was holding out the fake-silver laurel wreath when he saw the fat little bald man trotting down the aisle just ahead of him, saw the fat little man stop to clutch at someone's outstretched hand and then bob down to kiss another fat man and only then, oh, God, only then to realize he was romping down the aisle behind the real winner and that not only were there buzzings and titterings but that he was also making a spectacle of himself on screens all over America and so he grabbed the little fat man and began pumping his hand in congratulation, as though he had torn down the aisle for this purpose, and the little fat man muttered something like, Screw off, buster, and then in the thankful darkness, mopping his streaming face, making his way back ignominiously up the aisle with faces turned up at him, grinning like gargoyles at his gaffe, had finally reached his table.

"I guess you might call me the runner-up," he had said, and everyone had laughed, everyone except Ruth, who looked sideways into him in that sharp way of hers, and Charlotte Custis, who was not prepared to leave well enough alone and had to come around and kneel by his chair and clutch at his sleeve and say, "But you are still the best, you are the *best,* do you hear?" She kept on tugging at his arm; what a boring, doting nuisance she was, she *would* make the Matterhorn out of his molehill, but she was so feverishly loyal to him (he patted her little dog face), so miserably plain, bereft of anything but her job with him on the program so that, "Thank you, dear Charlotte, dear *thing,*" he said. "You are the *best,* did you hear me?" Charlotte's face was a river by now. "Who cares for their cheap acco*lades.*" Charlotte fell over on her side.

So then again it had been necessary to take her home to her mustard-colored apartment where all she had for company was a giant golliwog. She tried several times to get her thin arms around George's neck and pressed her bony unfertile self against him. "Now, Charlotte," George said, but wondering why he was always cast as the comforter, why no one comforted him. "What incenses me"—Charlotte could not leave it alone—"is that *talent* like yours is passed over, passed over and always will be." So thus comforted by Charlotte, unable to find a taxi, he walked the nineteen blocks home in a sogging rain. I am a loser, George thought, through and through. Tonight no comparisons with other losers brought any sense of comfort.

Ruth was sitting in the drawing room and something about her incurable calm (her feet together, she was simply waiting for him) brought out a hidden little boy in him, wanting to blubber. "This is as far as I will go," he cried out and brought his fist down on a table so fiercely that the lamp shook. Ruth nodded and he realized she probably thought he meant he was fed up with people like Charlotte and Dudley who got drunk and maudlin. Everything had boiled up in him: his losing the puny award and being sportsmanlike about it, about everything, his being good-natured George, his age, his thinning hair, his not having been capable of giving Ruth children, his second-rate talent.

But what he had meant was that he knew he would go no further, never get anywhere, this was as far as he would ever go.

Maybe this was the moment the wish was born, to get through the crack; the words themselves may have announced his intention to some distant Norn as "This is as far as I'll go." (A lighted train compartment and a faceless guard looked in the window to say this was the last stop.) He felt giddy for a second because a lighted train compartment had super-imposed itself in the drawing room; the train jerked and started shunting backward; he swayed with it for a second and then the living room returned, quaking, and was still.

Ruth sat as she usually did, waiting. Ruth often seemed to be waiting for something, like a distant telephone to ring. She still had not taken off her evening coat or gloves and she sat there with her evening bag on her lap like a guest.

"Why are you sitting there in your coat?" George asked irritably, and only then did she seem to be aware of it. She arose and took off her coat with slow graceful movements.

"Are you sorry you married me?"

He was stunned that he had said it. Had he really spat it

out at her like that? All because he was stung over losing this piffling prize?

Ruth began peeling off her long white gloves as though she were removing her own skin and she seemed entirely absorbed by taking off her gloves but he knew she was turning the question over in her mind in her cool unhurried way; she was seeking a full and fair answer. Ruth weighed every question. What are your five favorite books? Are you sorry you married George?

Then, "Noooooo," she said. It started low and unsurely, an oboe note, but it grew in conviction, she drew the word out in a long musical note. "Noooooo," she said.

She rose and threw away her gloves in a sudden quick movement of having found her answer without any doubt. Then she turned around and fixed her full attention on him.

"No," Ruth said.

"I didn't mean to—" George began.

"I'm only sorry that—"

"Beg your pardon, you go on."

"What?"

"You said?"

They both looked at their fingernails for a few seconds.

"What?" George asked. Ruth had sometimes to be nudged forward or they would be here all night while she thought it out.

"I am only sorry," Ruth said, "that you are unhappy. I can't stop you from making yourself unhappy."

"I'm not so unhappy," he had said, denying her elbow room. He could see himself sitting there denying her her point of view.

Ruth said, "I think—I wish you would stop trying to impress—"

"Oh, I don't give a canary's shit about the prize, Ruth."

"I wish you could get over trying to impress."

"Who?"

"Thinking you have to outdo."

"Who? Who?"

He was daring her to speak the name and then he could be truly angry and attack her and in the noise and dust of battle the truth could escape unnoticed.

"John Citadel." Ruth said it calmly.

So now up he flew, whirling around her, a big man in a fury, and being deliberately bullying, big mustache all spit, chin jutting at her, arms flailing (that was how he was seeing himself as though he were looking in at them through the dark window), and saying first of all he was surprised she would break the pact they had never to mention the name of John Citadel and then secondly that she was so wrong it was—he was wordless; there was no word for how wrong she was. All the time he was circling around her, nodding his beak down at her like an angry bird, and all the time Ruth stood there and gazed at one spot in the carpet, while he seethed and boiled around her until he felt her point had been nullified. The truth was this, he said, he could not remember when John Citadel had last crossed his mind. Not for years, he said.

Then sat down, exhausted.

But of course now he could see he'd lost. Everything had been a dead giveaway.

Then at last Ruth said, "How do you feel about an omelet?"

Well, an omelet was inspired. She was inspired. He had eaten practically nothing at the awards dinner. But he had to punish her for her insight.

"No," he said. "I'm not hungry, thanks."

Ruth had picked up her cloak and bag and gone into the bedroom and he had sat there pretending to look at the evening paper, temper abating, now trying to think of ways to atone for his outburst; making amends was never easy for him except with strangers, not something he could do in cold blood, simply walk into the bedroom and say, I'm sorry, I'm a bad-tempered sonofabitch; even if you *did* get me very pissed off I had no right to say. . . . He could only sidle into apologies, directing her attention to something funny or curious in the paper (there was nothing funny or curious in the paper tonight, not even any interesting or amusing person had died) or else remember to tell her something trivial, for their easiest conversation was always trivial. But there was nothing, his mind was a blank. He stood at the dark window looking out into the blackness and wished a fire could break out in the apartment building opposite so he could call her to come look at it.

"Look," Ruth said. She had come back into the room behind him.

She carried two glass goblets, one amber with a thickly ornamented escutcheon, the other a plain dark luminous red. They from time to time picked up goblets they saw in a vague sense of collecting something. It gave them the fantasy of purpose. "I found these in a little shop on Third," Ruth said.

"Oh, show," he said and she gave him the amber glass and he held it up to the light. "Oh, nice," he said.

"Think it's Bavarian," Ruth said. "The man said he *thought* Bavarian because there's a boar if you notice—see the boar?"

"Aha."

"And the other one I just got for the red."

"Oh, the red's terrific, Ruth, hold it up. Oh, yes."

"See it's a very *red* red, *wine* red."

"Oh, it's terrific, sweetheart."

There they stood. Each holding an empty goblet. And

any more than you can trust closing your eyes in sleep that you won't dream, how could you expect any guarantee where you would be next? Seconds after sleep you could be in a nightmare, no escape, and so he felt frightened not having any choice where next he would appear; things simply re-occurred, some partly remembered, some wholly forgotten (once emerging in total darkness in a gloriously orgiastic but totally unremembered sex experience so bountiful it was like an enormous three-dimensional wet dream but whom was he with?); and occasionally very frightened, so dimly aware of how the journey got started he tried to beat feebly on the door of his consciousness and say, No more, no further back, I want to return, I really am only in my own bathroom all the while this is going on and I want to be back there, so stop this; *no more*, he bellowed, but it was no louder than the sigh of someone who dreams he is bellowing, and as he fought back against this stream it was only a baby strug-gling, no stronger than a sleeping baby who dreams of fighting immense forces, moving with tiny feeble fists against down pillows, so now he was drawn on, drawn back kneeling with their faces pressed into the unpleasant smell of varnished wood and whose funeral was this now, whose funeral was he at? There were several funerals of some importance going all the way back to

"and," the voice said as impersonally as if this were a taped, recorded funeral service, which would be no more insulting, George was thinking, and he glanced at Ruth kneeling next to him, her eyes closed dutifully, but possibly she could be going over the laundry list in her mind. And, the voice asked Almighty God, look with infinite grace upon the soul of thy daughter Jessica. So it was old Jessica Wood in the closed casket and on his left Charlotte Custis wept copiously and as continuously as a tap that had been left running and yet as far as George could remember Charlotte had met his mother at the most twice.

George turned his head and saw that Andre Bouclez, his

music director, was across the aisle. Andre looked back at him and formed a word soundlessly that could have been *prunes*. There were a few ancients from New Forks to speed old Jessica on her way here in the F. C. Rutter Funeral Home.

Back before (he felt his bare lip) he had a mustache; before he had a mustache was when he thought he had less to hide from.

Outside the chapel the locals stood, blown together by a chill wind, his mother's friends from around New Forks, the old, the halt, the lame.

"So nice," George said, passing a hand among them. "Do so appreciate. . . ."

"I'm Miss McLean," one of them said. She presented an aged hand in a lobster pink nylon glove and hung on. "So nice of you," George was saying in his reverent-son-bearing-loss manner but this withered old thing was not to be shaken off. "I'm Mabel McLean," she said, her whiskered lips with bright lipstick peeling back over her gray dentures. "You were just a little boy when I first knew you." She hung onto his arm, spidery. "I'm Bob McLean's sister." This would have made an awkward moment then. *Mr.* McLean, as he was always known, the suitor who came around calling, nice-looking, highly polished shoes, calling on his mother, and it had got as far as her wearing his ring for a while. So this would have been awkward, meeting Miss McLean. George saw what he had done to end it. A dazzling smile and he turned his back completely on old Miss McLean and said to Charlotte and Andre, who were standing there waiting as usual for his orders, "Where's the car? Where's Ruth?" But the old crone had clutched his other arm now. Ridiculous plastic cherries bobbed around her hat. "I knew *Mary* too." Nobody could know the feeling of dismay and nausea that name brought on; it was worse than when people talked

about John Citadel. He made no further pretense of politeness, just glared at the withered old face clustered in gray
ringlets.

"I knew *Mary* too," she said, giving a wink to show there
was something between them that no one else here knew;
quite obscene she was, winking away under her cherries,
disgusting, something lewd about her wink almost as though
she intended an indecent proposal to him. She would be
well over seventy.

"Poor old Jess," she said. "She never had much reward, did
she?"

George had continued to stare icily at her. "She certainly
lived for *you*, didn't she?" She squinted up into his face.
"You couldn't have wished for a more wonderful mother,
did you know that?"

"*Very*," George had said, "scum of you to—nice of you to
come." He gave his hand. Instantly she grabbed it, he could
not shake her off; he began to look around desperately but
Charlotte and Andre had gone to find the car.

"I lost my brother, you know," Miss McLean said ac-
cusingly as if George were directly responsible. "I lost my
dear old Bob, you know, seven years ago."

"I'm sorry," he said.

"I've no one now," Mabel McLean said. There was just the
hint of the blackmailer about her. "And now Jessica, now
your dear old mother is gone too."

"Good-bye, Miss McLean."

"She certainly loved you. She sacrificed a lot in her life
for you, do you know that? She would have done anything
in the whole wide world for you, George, did you know that?"

"Yes, yes." George was sweating in the cold wind. What
did she want?

He made a motion toward where the hearse was appearing
but Miss McLean skipped in front of him in an anile pirouette.

"Don't run away yet," she said, squinting up at him; there was a ghastly coquettishness about her.

"I'm the only one left who knew them *all*," she said. She left one with nothing to reply to.

"The only one of those boys and girls from long ago, poor old Jess, poor Hal, poor Mary and poor old Bob, who *all*— now listen to me—wanted to do their best for you."

"Ah, me."

"Lucky boy, lucky boy."

"I was?"

"Lucky, lucky to be loved like that, did you know? Not everyone is as lucky, my dear. They made a lot of sacrifices for you, Georgy Wood, including my brother, as you *may* remember."

And he'd stood there just taking it from the old crone with a simpering smile.

"Now listen a minute. I know you're trying to get rid of me—"

"Oh, no *no*."

"But I came today to say how do you do to you in respect for the past, my dear, whether you care about those people or not now you're top of the tree—"

"Oh, please."

"Wherever you are. But I'm representing a lot of people who cared for you *including* my brother, who was fond of you no matter what you did; he never held any grudge. He was still fond of you."

Oh, the fondness of Mr. McLean in his highly polished shoes. How many years it had taken to be able to forget the kindness of Mr. McLean.

So now he knew what she'd come for, the mincing old puss, she'd come for revenge (so she swung her purse, she smirked) and she'd gotten it. She'd come to remind him of the kindness of her brother. Well, it had been her brother who had in all kindness given George certain facts about himself.

"Like a father," Miss McLean said and took hold of a button on his coat and twisted it as if he were a television set she was going to turn off.

It was at this point he'd realized he'd begun to feel a bit sick because it was obscene, her closeness was obscene, all her dirty inferences. Because from what she'd implied, she had to *know*. She knew all about him.

"George."

But Ruth had come, Ruth had come like a blessing. She steered him away as if he were a lost child.

In the car Ruth said, "Who was that creature?"

"It was a Miss McLean," George started but felt his throat thicken as though he was going to throw up. They followed the hearse for some time until he was able to speak.

"She knew Mary," he said.

Shifted, flicked instantly to his carrying flowers down the corridor in the private hospital where he had to come as often as he could to see the old dying woman who couldn't get it done, God help her, tried to, tried her best to die but having been stubbornly persistent all her life about living, couldn't change; her constitution was not physically or psychically rehearsed for collapse.

Putting his head around the screen, "Anyone for tennis," he said because nothing better came to him and because it was necessary to be as lighthearted as possible about the fact that she had not died yet and Nurse Fickett, as she always did, clapped hands and said, "Oh, petty pie, here's your big boy." Nurse Pickett had tied a blue bow in Jessica's hair. He bent over and kissed the old cheek; she smelled of death and lavender. "Goodness gracious me," squeaked Nurse Fickett (she had been with the case from the start on the day shift; she was one of the family by now), "what pretty carnations; look what he's brought you, honey cake, all the way from New York City because you can't get anything as good around here. Oh, we're going to sit up now, aren't we? Doesn't she look pretty as a picture, Mr. George? How about her hair ribbon? Oh, she's the belle of the sixth floor, there's not a doubt about it."

Old Jessica had spoken through this gush something they had missed.

"What, cutie pie?"

"Shoot if you must this old gray head," Jessica said.

"Oh, she'll be the *death* of me, the *death* of me," said Nurse Fickett, squeaking out to put the flowers in water.

"I wish that were true," Jessica said to Nurse Fickett's vanishing ass.

Now they had again to get through the visit. It had never been an easy mother-son relationship (perhaps that was why it was always easier for him to refer to her as Jessica rather than Mother; Mama was unthinkable) and already her eyes were wandering to the window, her thin hands were pulling at the hospital-tight sheet, and George was (he could see himself now) sitting forward too eagerly. "Dear," he was saying, "I spoke to the matron about the desserts, about you saying you just can't eat the desserts they serve. . . ."

"Oh, I eat anything that's put in front of me," she said. "I'm not fussy."

"About so many custards."

"Ahh."

"Has there been any improvement, dear?"

"Improvement in what?"

"In the desserts? Have they been cutting down on the custards?"

"Oh, yes, yes, they've got me on tapioca now."

Gave him that blue cold smile of hers.

"She had a little peach tart with her lunch today," Nurse Fickett said, whisking in with the flowers in a vase, squeaking around on the rubber floor. "Tell your big boy how you had a little peach tart for lunch."

"I had a little peach tart for lunch," Jessica told him, her head rocking from side to side on the pillow, hoping to die.

"She's no trouble at all," Nurse Fickett said. "She's my *pet*."

"Fancy *that* now," Jessica told George.

"I only wish some of the others were as easy to please as her."

"Fancy *that*," Jessica said to George. "Fancy being difficult when all you have to do is lie here and be waited on hand and foot and the days go by like greased lightning."

"She's just as good as gold to the whole staff, Mr. George, she's just adorable and that's all there is to it." Nurse Fickett pounded the pillows around Jessica furiously, pumped her up into a higher position. "Comfy now? Do you think Mr. George would like a cup of coffee?"

"Well, I really don't know; perhaps you ought to ask *him*."

"No, thank you, nurse."

"Okey-dokey then, I know you've got loads to tell each other but don't let her get tired, now. She has to save her strength, you know."

"For what?" Jessica asked.

"I'll pop in later," Nurse Fickett said.

"Oh, *good*."

There they were, left.

George gazed at the bottles on the bedside table, Jessica gazed at the wall. Neither of them knew that this was the last visit. Otherwise he would have got down on his knees by the bed and (or would he have? would he have?) begged her to believe how pitiably sorry he was, clasped her old hands (but would he have? she despised any display between them, cold-shouldered him with her porcupine smiles), kissed her old hands and pleaded with her for God's sake to believe that he was sorry about everything, about how rottenly he had behaved to her all his life; now in their last few minutes in life surely he could have made one effort to repine, to touch her cold gray heart.

Oh, the sadness of old people dying alone in hospital rooms at the mercy of cheerful nurses.

Oh, the punishment of remembering what we did not say to them before the end. George was reliving every detail of the scene, the way the sunlight came falling across her bed and touched her thin old wedding ring, felt deeply emotional at witnessing this, the last twenty-six minutes they would have together; this would be his last sight of her (and he heard himself telling his mother that Ruth had found two little end tables for the den "at the antique place you suggested"; driving back to New York after their last visit they had stopped by and there in a back room under piles of junk were these two little rosewood tables which were the very things that Ruth had been hunting for fruitlessly, just perfect and dirt cheap into the bargain).

"Well," his mother said after a while, "I'm glad to have been of some service," and then the next few minutes had been occupied by him insisting, though she denied it, that the sun was hurting her eyes and by fiddling around with the venetian blind and managing to convert the room into a more depressing grayness. "Oh, that's *fine*," she said resignedly.

"And have you had some visitors?" he was asking. "Has anyone been in?"

"Oh, yes. Mabel McLean. I forget what day. She brought *those*." She had looked with hatred at the withering gladioli.

"Oh, that's nice," he had said. "Well, that was thoughtful."

"Oh, *very* thoughtful of her. I have to remember that no matter how she bores me, she has to take three buses to get here."

"Oh, I see," he said. "Well, well." Looked around for inspiration. "Oh, listen, did they fix the television?"

"Hmmmmmm?"

"Did they fix the television? You said the double images were making you seasick."

"Well, I don't know. I think someone came and jiggled around with it to absolutely no avail. They all have green faces no matter what you turn on but—oh, well, I'd rather put up with green faces than be a nuisance."

"Ah, don't say that, don't be silly now, dear."

"Oh, it doesn't matter."

"It *does* matter. I should certainly think it matters with what we're paying that—I just mean you certainly ought to have decent—"

"Oh, I don't want any fuss."

"They promised me they were going to have it fixed and I'm going to see that they do."

He had gone on and on about it, playing the concerned son, but she had not seemed too convinced with his performance and when he petered out she said suddenly, "Ha ha."

"You are too nice with them," he had said lamely.

"Am I? *Am* I, do you think?"

"Yes, dear."

"Well, well," she said and looked at the ceiling. "You should know. That's something you're an expert on, being nice to people." Half sweet, half mocking, and leaving him to decide which. He had forgotten the enigmatic little remark she had made about his niceness to people; it had dropped into the limbo of wherever everything is stored that is said to us between the cradle and the grave; he had forgotten it or rather it had been obliterated because, this being the last day and the last ten minutes or so of the last day, then the shocking thing was about to happen and he had remembered only the shocking thing Jessica had done at the very last which had been like a small firework going off unexpectedly in a dark church and temporarily blinding one so that closing the eyes, the flash lingers on and on photographed on the retina; thus George had forgotten this slightly earlier scene that now he was witnessing as so outwardly misleading, perhaps as their entire relationship had been from the time he was born, utterly misleading from the outside so strangers glancing in the door now of room 604 might have gone on their way commenting favorably on George, keeping vigil by the bedside of his mother, her gaze resting on him, so close as people that wearying conversation is not needed between them, harmony flowing between them, her life ebbing gently away and (shame on him, for actually at this moment he had been thinking this and almost feeling the warmth of imagined admiration) saying, What a nice man, did you see him, such a nice guy sitting with his mother; you could tell just by looking that they have the closest mother-son relationship, just by the way he sat by the bed and by the way she looked back at him; something about that man, anyone can see right off he is nice nice *nice*.

Not for long though this self-congratulatory image of sweet old mom and darling son. Interrupted by Nurse Fickett in white rubber-soled wedgies squeaking around the screen bearing a glass of pinkish liquid which must now be swallowed. Then to see the relief shining on his face, the alacrity of jumping up so Nurse Fickett could get around the bed, of reaching for his overcoat and hat and saying in the most regretful tones that honestly he had better think about getting back because now it was almost four and by the time and considering the traffic on a Friday, et cetera, the usual eroded burned-out excuses one uses to be gone from the sick and the dying.

So he bent and kissed the old face, murmuring such foolishness as that she was to take it easy and look after herself now, take it easy, he had crooned into her ear, and she had said something indistinct that had sounded like "anyway escape you," this blurred remark not recorded from memory but which had sounded like "anyway escape *you*" and in reply to it he had said something (fancy this being the last sentence he would address to her in her life) facetious such as she must get fit, get into shape for her championship matches at Forest Hills, and he was a hoot and a howl, Nurse Fickett informed him, he would have them in danger of splitting their sides, she warned Jessica, and gave her the spoon and Jessica had raised up in bed, mouth full of pink medicine, gorge rising and unable to say another word, had fumbled among the pile of books on the bedside table. So what did she want? Nurse Fickett swished around to assist. Which one? This one? This? His mother had taken the oldish-looking volume and without another word had thrust it into his hands and with a gesture repelled him from her.

By the reception desk and saying casually good afternoon to the nurse on duty, glanced casually to see what book she had given him.

The poems of John Citadel.

Next he was outside and leaning against a tree for support. He was standing in a cold blinding wind that made his eyes run so that he was blinking and wiping his eyes with the back of one hand and trying to believe through the water what his eyes were reading. Two nurses passing must have glanced at this weeping man, crushed against a tree. Nothing but a usual sight here; somebody in some ward had just died.

On every page, between the lines and stanzas, scattered through the lyric beauty of John Citadel's glistening dactyls, which opened flower within flower, Jessica had written in her small rounded penciled hand obscenities. She could not have done it in the heat of passion for not only was the handwriting as careful and composed as it would be in a casual note of thanks but the reeking invective had been scrupulously created to scan and to rhyme in contrapuntal and hideous parody of John Citadel's verse; on and on ran the bawdy parody, every *i* dotted, every comma observed; page after page the pornographic mockery exactly matched in meter and with dreadful sense the exquisite printed lines so that it became a chant, a rhythmic ode for two voices, sacred and profane, a black mass intoned against a psalm; the deliberateness of it was fiendish, the calculation of it was ice cold, the filth of it arose like a stench from these pages of frangible beauty. At the end she had neatly written her name, Jessica Boxer Wood, and the date on which she had completed this long and arduous work.

The night nurse had found her gone shortly after seven that evening and she was smiling, they told George on the telephone, there was such a peaceful smile on her— He cut them off, cut in saying he would call tomorrow about the arrangements, and hung up.

He had no doubt whatever that she had been smiling.

"I want you to read it," he said to Ruth, "because you're one of the only people who know the whole truth," and Ruth took the John Citadel book and began to read it in her marvelously cool impassive way without so much as a lifted eyebrow; turning the pages slowly, she read Jessica's subterranean creation as solemnly as though it were a new translation of the *Metamorphoses* (and he never thanked her or showed the slightest appreciation for her doing this, for her truly sensible attitude toward the horror, and most of all for the crisp accurate assessment of it that he remembered she would now make) and she got up and walked with it to the fireplace and said over her shoulder casually, "You don't want this any more, do you?" and without waiting for an answer, dropped it into the fire and poked at the wood around it so that the John Citadel book, with its graffiti explanations of what had been going on in the mire of

Jessica Wood's soul, all went up the chimney, and then Ruth said, "I guess she was aiming to kill two birds with one stone, as she might say herself."

"The reason we never get what we want," Ruth said, "is because it isn't there." This was so non sequitur of her; she was not given to non sequiturs, and George turned to say, "What?" and for a few seconds everything was dotted as in a pointillist picture, as if Seurat had painted them into a summer lunch scene; they were sitting across from each other under a striped umbrella; acres of clipped lawn greened away toward a big house. Ruth had on a wide straw hat with ribbons.

"Why?" he asked.

"Just suddenly occurred to me."

"But why? I mean we were talking about the girl in *L'Avventura*."

"Yes. Why were we talking about *her?*"

"I don't know."

"I don't know either."

"But I don't get the connection."

"She disappeared on that island and they never found her."

"Well, so . . . explain."

"I feel like that sometimes. That I've never been found."

"Never been found? How?"

"Never been *found*."

"How?"

"I mean as if the person I *am* has never been seen by *any-body*."

"Well, everybody hides *something* of himself."

"No, that's not what I mean at all. It's much more subtle than that." She gave a little shudder. "It's awful."

"Well, darling, I can't pretend you're being very clear."

"Not being clear is part of it. Even if I *could* be clear you wouldn't understand. Even us sitting here talking about it

isn't clear. It's like somebody once said, '*I* am saying something to you but *you* are hearing what I say.'"

"But not what you mean, huh?"

"You know what I mean but it's not the same as I mean."

"How can it not be the same if I know what you mean?"

"Because"—Ruth glanced at the table—"it's like that
salt cellar. I see it and you see it but we don't see the same
salt cellar."

"In a way, maybe not . . ."

"If I pick it up and use it, it's my salt cellar, but when I
pass it to you and you use it, it's *your* salt cellar."

"But we could describe it the same."

"Oh, we could describe it exactly the same but it's not.
The minute I hand it to you it becomes your salt cellar,
which is something quite different from mine."

"I don't really understand."

"It can't be explained."

She was noncommittal behind sunglasses but there was an
urgency, unusual for her, a desperation about something. She
picked up a fork, jabbed at lettuce, swallowed. Something
was plainly bugging her. He put his hand on her arm and
started to say something about her hat being a triumph—

Suddenly she went on quite loudly, "I resent everything
that's lost all the time between people. I *resent* what happens
when we pass the salt cellar from one to another, when my
idea of it stops and yours begins because"—here she again
stopped and gazed toward her mother's house, searching for
something behind the sun-glinting windows where she had
been so long imprisoned as a child—"because it's the same as
when you try to pass on an emotion to someone; you say,
'I love you' or 'I hate you' but what you *meant* is transposed—
kerplunk—into what *they* mean by 'I love you' or 'I hate
you,' as quite distinct from *your* meaning."

"But is true to *them*."

"Not the same thing."

"Does it matter?"

Ruth looked at him from behind her sunglasses and something wild was going on there.

"I'd like it to be the same salt cellar *after* I'd passed it to you." He saw what she meant. He saw the subtle difference she was trying to point out; he saw crystally clear the moment of evaporation of the pure emotion, the dying of it in the moment of its being passed on. He saw it as a bright bead one minute and a dried bean the next. He wanted to say it had superb and terrifying possibilities and that, like the atom, if it could be located and harnessed it would merge their two personalities into one. It had infinite possibilities, this dark gap of hers. And where *did* the power of an emotion go when it was exchanged for someone else's? It coupled with his own idea that you could slip between two bits of time and escape if you knew how to split the two bits.

That she had glimpsed in a salt cellar a tiny microcosm of life was also disturbing. He felt (Ruth was waiting behind her sunglasses, she was expecting something of him) if he admitted to understanding what she had said it would bridge the gap between them and then safety walls would collapse and they would be almost one and he would be deprived of . . . individuality, she would be able to see a part of him not seen before, that secret he kept to himself.

The secret was that he must not be loved. He mistrusted being loved. It made him feel like a commodity. But to *offer* love was ecstasy. To offer love was intoxicating. To see the effect of this offer on another person was beatifying (and the more unexpected the person, the more sudden the declaration out of the blue, the less likely the recipient, the more ecstatic was his feeling, his rapture; never gave a thought to whether it was returned, didn't care, it was orgasm to him, it was coming) and this was his craving, this offering, proffering, and perhaps only two people in his life had ever caught on.

But Ruth was waiting behind her sunglasses, she was expecting something of him.

He saw himself bend down and kiss her on the elbow. The gesture was painfully grandiloquent (poor Ruth, how awful) and awkward in the manner of a bad actor; it was so tragically empty and then what he said was:

"Ah, but I *found* what I wanted."

"Hmm?"

"You said the reason we don't get what we want is that it isn't there, but I'm unique, I *got* what I wanted."

Ruth had slumped imperceptibly. She was younger by now and so more easily disillusioned.

"Salt?" she asked and passed him the salt cellar.

Next thought had been about Archer so there ought to be a connection but didn't seem to be in this trivial reawakening in, yes, the old office before the team moved, when they were in the old RKO Building on Sixth Avenue, the room smelling of rich cigar smoke from the now departed network program VPs, and he seemed to be trying to recover from anger. "Oh, but you were terrific," Charlotte Custis said. "I don't think Chip Downes has ever been stood up to like that in his entire career. I don't think Manny Goldman has ever been stood up to like that in his entire career and that's my opinion." Charlotte was emotionally very gratified, her small bony breast heaved, she was thrilled by all the shouting and bad language that had been taking place and in her nervousness she had taken most of it down in shorthand. "So we've won, we've *won*," Charlotte squeaked. Her eyes were as wild as if she had been on mescaline and she had bitten every lick of paint off the network pencil. Now it was returning like a disappointment to him that it was the scene of battle with the network over "G and B Diddle," his children's show, and that this had been the time of his Custer's last stand against their encroachment with their dull complaints that "G and B Diddle" appealed mostly to adults and that therefore the makers of Whirleybuzz (which in a few years' time would be successfully exposed by Nader's Raiders as a dangerous toy and removed from the market) had every right to request such changes as the introduction of more violence and a new rock theme song which in consistently bad grammar advocated greed and slyly rewarded aggressiveness.

So George told the network VPs with archducal politeness to go get a Whirleybuzz they knew up what.

"Quack," George said.

"Oh, you were superb, magnificent," said Charlotte, clapping.

"Bravo," Andre Bouclez added.

"Quack," George said.

G and B Diddle were pintail ducks wearing little straw hats, manipulated on wires. All this uproar over two ducks. Oh, but the fight had been for much more. There he stood, proud and triumphant; the fight exemplified his professional standards, George thought, just about taking bows. He had stood up to the philistines, he had fought the battle against mediocrity, against vulgarity, *that* was the important thing. "Bravo," Andre Bouclez said. Even the typists in the outer office were terrifically impressed with the way George had stood up to the VPs. He went back into his office flooded with the good feeling of strength-through-right; he had stuck by his ducks. The following Friday "G and B Diddle" received notice of cancellation. The first anybody knew of it was that the network took back the typists from the outer office.

Nevertheless George had stuck by his ducks.

At this particular time he could not foresee that it would

be the forerunner of several Pyrrhic victories. He was cele-
brating his conquest over the Whirleybuzzers of this world
in the Piano Bar with Andre Bouclez; he could hardly see
himself now for the gilded darkness of the bar and also for
the halo he seemed to be wearing. He appeared to think he
had achieved a personal triumph; he also appeared to be
scrupulously disregarded by every single network employee
who happened to pass the banquette. He seemed to believe
there was something to celebrate in the show's being canned;
there would be no more compromising with commercial
bandits and fools; from now on it would be *his* own creation,
his unhampered work of art; My *fertility*, he kept saying to
Andre, although it was a word that often distressed him when
used by others, especially women; his fertility, he said to
Andre, had never felt lusher; he was suffering from a false
joie de vivre which was like a slight fever; he had had two
whiskey sours and foolishly allowed Andre to have six; he
kept saying that he could see the future tonight, it was all
going to be better better better (he had this queer extra-
sensory feeling of being thinner, being lighter in weight, and
passing his hands through his hair, found it thick and glossy;
he must then be in his thirties this evening) and so, fatally
convinced of his new unshakable future, he had done an
unwise thing, given Andre Bouclez a bit of a hug, nothing
much, just a mannish arm-around-the-shoulder thing guys do,
but Andre's face looked splashed in the dark gold light and
at first he thought Andre was trying to push some money into
his hand under the table and, No, no, this is on me, he kept
saying until it was all too painfully clear what Andre was
about, such squeezings and tender strokings now beginning
on his knee and, Don't be a goat, he said smartly, hoping it
was too dim in the bar for anyone else to see Andre's
splashed face looking yearningly toward him (he had never
before noticed the resemblance Andre had to a mournful

cod) and, I love you, George, poor Andre said, splashed, the tears rolling now down his cheeks and, Of course you do, George had said, and I love you but not in that way, kiddo, come off it now, kiddo, you know I'm not that way.

Sorry.

Help. "Check, *check*," he called to the waiter. A little cold air ran down his spine. Why? His élan had deflated. Why? "But I am your friend," he told Andre and pressed his elbow hard. "I am your *friend*."

"Sure," Andre said and licked at his tears.

"Listen, *always*, see? Your *friend*, Andre."

Andre sagged toward him; George was momentarily shocked to see that Andre was smiling.

"Don't worry," Andre said. "It won't go any further."

Then why had he behaved in such a way? Had gathered up his change like a maniac and fled out of the Piano Bar not even looking back to see if Andre could make it. Why had he run almost a block the wrong way toward the river? *What* needn't go any further? Why had he put on the look of an angry field marshal? What had happened? With one hand he held on his hat and he ran toward the river. Well, but of course the reason was not Andre, but because out of the corner of his eye he had begun to imagine in the dark of the banquette he could see someone he probably would never see again. And the cold feeling was not, after all, fear that Andre would try to caress him; it was the cold feeling of loss.

Already they'd nearly got a ticket near Danbury until the cop lit up with pleasure seeing who it was and closed the book with a snap and said, Take it easy, though, will you and next time you see Marilyn give her a kiss for me, and in a very short time they were speeding again because of course Archer had been late to begin with and kept George waiting in the hotel suite while he made unending telephone

calls, ordered up scrambled eggs, ordered books from
Doubleday's, sent flowers to someone named Miriam Litvinov
in Beverly Hills, interrupted George at the vulnerable points
of stories by saying, Hold the thought while I make *one* call,
so that they never achieved any continuity of dialogue; all
the time Archer walking around in leopard jockey shorts and
George said, Listen, aren't you going to get dressed, it takes
over two hours to get up there, and Archer said, What's the
hurry to see a lot of spotty-faced kids play a soccer match,
for God's sake, are you still that *anal* about time? Since
analysis Archer had had no problems with time whatever
and please to remember how compulsive he had once been
about giving gifties, couldn't be accepted for himself alone;
well, now that was all done, all over with, a new life, said
the restored Archer, being princelike to the room service
waiter but giving, George noted, a stingy tip and getting
away with it; the waiter bowed out backward as though in
the presence of royalty, bathed in a golden light of being
in the presence; George had begun to feel deflated in this
presence and he had dressed wrongly, his dark blue suit was
formal and entirely wrong for this Saturday excursion, his
formal tie shoes and polka dot bow tie reduced him to a
conventional nonentity, and Archer grew more delectable
dressed. Clothes grew on him, he ordained them with his
body: mustard cashmere, sky blue shirt, oatmeal trousers
possibly hand sewn by little court tailors and expressive
shoes (Archer had always had expressive shoes; one could
read his mood by his shoes), deep honey-color glistening
loafers; when all finished, he stood in the bathroom adjusting
his neckerchief, points tucked up just so while George leaned
in the door, patient and navy blue dull, providing the dis-
appointing contrast which was always to be the case with
Archer; had nothing to do with fame and power, merely a
prerequisite for being around him, a gift from nature that

had arranged for Archer to provide superior contrast to everyone else. It had always been so, even when they were at school, Archer was never outdistanced, never outshone; it was one thing to adore Archer, quite another to be with him. They went down in the freight elevator to avoid making crowd scenes in the lobby but having reached the main floor anonymously, Archer went immediately to the barbershop to have his loafers buffed up and sitting there in the mirrored, brightly lit shop very shortly drew a crowd of close to fifty to the window, mostly nearly hysterical middle-aged women, mooing and mawing like unmilked cows, and through this human sea he made his way gracefully, hands up in the air, saying, sorry, no time, no pencil, sorry, girls, while George fought in the wake of this grace and favor until they got safely down into the garage and into Archer's car. On the seat was *The Poems of François Villon;* he was getting into Villon these days, Archer said, Do you known him well? you ought to with your mordant mind, Archer said, and took a curve on Fifty-ninth Street that included part of the sidewalk, then nearly drove right into the Paris Theater and sped off.

It was a heady, gaseous feeling, being with Archer, as if he'd been shaken up inside a bottle of soda water, a continuously bubbling experience and also somewhat draining. He remembered now how tiring it was to be any long time with Archer, merely to be exposed to that continuous personality that spouted like a fountain, never allowed itself rest, never allowed itself a lapse into dullness in case someone might be looking; Archer's was a continuous gleaming performance. Oh, yes, this was the day they drove up to Butley School because Michael, Archer's boy, was on the team playing Kent and *some*body had to be there, Archer said to George on the phone, because he and Alice were in the throes of settlements prior to their divorce; she would not dream of leaving her lawyer at the moment, Archer said, the bitch. Now the day gathered itself together sharply in George's recollection and cut like broken glass on the fact that his handling of the situation, if he remembered rightly, was not the best and that Archer had been hurt, very hurt. One tended to forget that Archer could be hurt just like a normal human being; one tended to forget that Archer could ever need anything because (George had often said and not in envy) Archer had been worshiped by the gods, bestowed with all their gifts, not the least of which was that arising in the morning he was as handsome, as unmessed by sleep as he was in the evenings; one did not think of Archer as needing anything.

This was the day they parted for the very last time—or had there been one other time, just possibly there had been one more face-to-face meeting suddenly in a crowd coming out of something somewhere, he and Ruth meeting Archer and Miriam and Archer being greatly changed, his smile now made a bit terrifying by all those caps—but George had now forgotten about it and so only this day remained in consciousness. . . .

Not forgetting the detour without warning, turning off on a lane because someone he knew used to live around here someplace, Archer said, Mind if we take a look? as they drove farther and farther down country lanes along stone fences and then pulled up deliberately by a stone gate where a mailbox read JOHN B. PILBROCKSEN JR.; he wouldn't be more than ten minutes or so, Archer said, can you occupy yourself with Villon just for ten minutes or so, Archer said and walked up the driveway and was seen to be admitted to a stone house and for the nine hundredth time George had marveled how easy it was to be duped by Archer, to believe Archer's motives, not to have foreseen there must be something more to this than driving up to Butley to see Michael in a soccer match (which must be

well started by now) and that *he* was being used to help
make it all look legitimate. For a moment, furious at being
dumb, used, agreeable, he thought of just driving off
and stranding Archer with whomever this tryst had been
arranged, but Archer had taken the car keys so George
had to just sit dutifully, listening to silence unbroken except for pods dropping on the roof of the car and it was
like Archer to have parked him under a podding tree, some
instinct led Archer to whatever was fecund, fertile, uberous.
. . . She used to be Betty Baxter, Archer said, don't you
remember her? He had been gone thirty or forty minutes,
there was nothing to imply any impropriety had taken
place but George was accustomed to scanning Archer for
signs, noticed that his neckerchief had been retied clumsily;
she was Betty Baxter in the old days, Archer said, explaining everything, the quick furtive afternoon lay of Mrs.
Pilbrocksen, Jr. (where could Mr. Pilbrocksen have con-
veniently been, away from home on a Satudray afternoon?);
Archer explaining without saying it that an old lay was an
old lay: whether you had gone up in the world or not
made no difference; it was almost endearing the way
Archer proposed this viewpoint. But Archer had never
changed. It wasn't that Archer had achieved grandeur and
success and then not changed, it was vice versa: it was that
he had grown into it, he had grown into world fame as he
might into a skin.

Then, No no, George cried out, you've taken a left, that'll
take us into New Forks, but Archer said, Don't you want
to look in on your mother? No, not really and the game will
be half over now, George argued, because the plan was
again disrupted and because Archer was incapable of taking
a straight direction to or from anything, Archer had to
approach every situation with a systematic series of detours
and flankings and it was obvious that he was delaying as

long as possible this visit with his son (indeed it was hard
to fix Archer in the role of father) and the later he could
arrive at the school the more attention would be paid to his
lateness rather than to his more obvious failings as father;
that he was nervous of his son had never been more apparent,
George saw now as they flew along the road to New Forks.

Now Archer took over George's house, George's mother
in one dashing gesture, lunging in the front door yelling
that she had visitors, Come out, come out, wherever you
are, Jessica Wood; and she had appeared in working clothes,
distrait, delighted beyond measure to see Archer, her mouth
working desperately against showing it, just, Please don't
look at me, she said. She was in her old working clothes,
she was putting bulbs away for the winter. And here you
come like a bolt from the blue, Archie Hurst, she said, it
is just like you to come down on me like Prometheus, Jessica
said, and Archer said, Oh, you don't know how many years
fall away when I hear someone call me Archie, but let's
keep it our secret, put a fond arm around her and there
they were in the stuffy front sitting room which smelled
of floor polish mixed with a queer nutmeg scent and still
had the ferns in wicker stands and the walnut tables and a
feeling of being unused (even when he was little, sad and
unused) and now he found himself perched on one buttock
on the piano stool between his mother and Archer, who
seemed more at home here than George, one leg dangling
over the armchair. And you used to do marvelous collage
things, he was saying to Jessica, fantastic things, I remember,
all cut out of magazines and pasted onto board and onto
trays and then lacquered over; you did great fish and birds
and swans and, Oh, fancy you remembering that, she said,
pink-necked with flattery, but no, she didn't do it any more,
it required more patience than she had any more to cut out
with nail scissors a hundred tiny petals and all she'd done

was maybe give a lot of people a lot of useless trays. Oh, that isn't so, George heard himself butting in, perhaps because up to now she had not so much as turned her head in his direction, that isn't so, you did the big American eagle that hangs in the Civic Center. Oh, *that*, she said, *that* was something she hated, was a commission. Jessica turned to him and gave a humorless laugh. You certainly have picked the one piece I really *despise*, she said (as though she was glad he had blundered) and turned back to Archer to ask were his parents still living?

And what a joy, what a privilege to be Archer's parents, Jessica implied, turning her back on George. Now, if she had only had a son like *Archer*, she implied in the way she crossed her legs daintly, almost coquettishly (good legs, young legs for her age, George noticed; of course she was younger now, had not yet begun to hideously blue her hair), and Archer reacted to her familially. His folks were getting a divorce, he told her, and so was *he*, yes, he and Alice were *through*. Archer was pouring out his troubles to Jessica and so, feeling out of it, turning away, George stared at a tortoise-shell-framed photograph of himself and his father, yellowed and faded now just as Hal Wood had yellowed and faded away into memory; his large gentle father, leaning on the front of their 1928 Dodge holding baby George, who was waving a flag and squirming, bursting to get out of his father's arms and out into the future, and his father seemed to be making a consoling gesture toward him, caressing his little head in the way his father used often to do, knowing some sad thing and unable to explain to him what it was.

He was swept with a sudden emotion about his father, touched with a little terror at the sight of his baby self, reminded suddenly that he was already nearer to his youth and if he reached back far enough in consciousness would he again sit in his father's arms, and knowing now about his father's sadness, could he hug and kiss his father and say, I know, I know?

The odd thing about the baby in the photograph was its wildness, little fists stuck out, legs squirming. The baby was trying to *escape*.

Oh, but you were always a bit of a monster, Jessica was saying affectionately to Archer, and she pitied any poor female who got a case on him, and Archer agreed but said what could he do about it? Where could he find the right girl who could turn him back into a toad? So they bantered pleasantly back and forth; it took Archer to be at ease with Jessica, George was thinking; *he* had never been able to touch the right spring. She was being outgoing and deliciously easy with Archer; it took such a small step and he had missed it all through his life. George said rather sharply, Look, do you want to see the game or not? Michael is playing against Kent, he said to Jessica, and Jessica and Archer looked at him. He's so conscientious, this guy, Archer said, winking, I may adopt him as my timepiece, I may just put Georgy on a chain. Oh, well, Jessica said, getting up, ha ha, George is like that song 'Time on My Hands' only George has it on his mind; time on his *mind*, his mother said, glinting.

And she and Archer had walked ahead of him with deliberate slowness, Archer being taken with an avid interest in her plants, what was this, what was that? The afternoon was beginning to wane as they got into the car and, Goodbye, you monster, his mother said and gave Archer a very warm motherly hug. Take care of yourself; divorce or not you ought to eat nourishing food, and listen, try to cheer *him* up, will you, his mother said, leaning into the car, and her eyes glinted; try to cheer him up, said the younger Jessica and stood there waving to them as they roared off and George said nothing, for what could you say about that? about being bait for them to be funny about. A very complicated woman, Archer said. What? he said. I said a very complicated woman, a very deep woman, your mother, Archer said, which was entirely true but only grazed the surface of Jessica, who was, always had been an iceberg with two-thirds submerged.

They had reached the Butley School grounds by now and of course the soccer game was over, the crowds were wending their way from the field toward the gates, and George was too annoyed to deign to answer, it was a typical Archer Hurst snap judgment, but before he could even begin to register his peeve it was snatched away from him because, Christ almighty, Archer said, there's *Alice*; oh, Jesus, how the hell did she get to be here? And indeed without seeing them Alice Hurst was standing near the entrance to Fisher Hall; she was wearing a rather pretty dress and seemed to be waiting for Michael, she was looking around her and shading her eyes from the setting sun; Archer had swung around her, nearly knocking her down, but she did not appear to see and went on looking out for Michael, something rather touching about her all alone, unhusbanded, waiting for her son under a big tree and wearing a dress too light for Connecticut in October and, Stubborn bitch, Archer said and parked by a No Parking sign, what is she doing here? She is trying to pull something because she knows it is *my* turn to visit, devious bitch, Archer said, putting on the dark glasses that wrapped around his face and going toward Alice with what on the screen was said to be his panther grace and George, following reluctantly, saw Alice turn, saw Alice appalled, saw Alice clutch at her handbag as though to protect herself from Archer striking her; poor thing, she looked completely taken aback and alarmed, took a step backward while Archer stood over her menacingly and grinned and said, What a coincidence; who won the game?

Oh, Kent won, she was saying as George came up, but they put up a good game, hello, George, Alice said and she began fishing desperately in her handbag (for a gun?) and, Just when, Archer was asking coolly, had she got in from the Coast? Only this morning and she was going back on a ten-o'clock flight that night. She found a pack of Life Savers and began frantically to peel the paper off; she'd come because Michael had said that Archer couldn't come up for the game and so *some*one had to come to see him play on the team, Alice said, trying to keep her voice calm; will anyone have a Life Saver? Alice asked. Honestly, Archer, she said, do you think I'd come all the way from Los Angeles to sit through a cold damp soccer game if I'd known you were coming? Michael thought you were to be in North Carolina. That was last week, Archer said, and Michael *knew* it was last week and furthermore *knew* he was coming up for the game and *any*way, darling, Archer said and took Alice by the elbow as if she were now to be taken back to the violent ward, anyway you had only to pick up the phone and call me at the Plaza to have saved yourself this long and expensive flight. But how could she have known he was at the Plaza? Alice said and a hint of her scornfulness had crept back like color into her cheeks; after all, she was *not* clairvoyant, Alice said acidly, and suddenly here was Michael, sweaty, out of breath, festooned with skin outbreaks and being suspiciously innocent, Hi, Mother, Hi, Dad, and, Now, Michael, both Archer and Alice said, what is this all about and, oh, no, they were both wrong, he had never meant to do anything on purpose (Very cute, you are very cute, Archer said and gave a big bellow of a laugh and punched him playfully just in case they might be observed); Oh, no, Michael fenced around them, somebody must have just misunderstood. I would like you to meet my roommate Bob Maxley, said Michael, introducing a prototype with a broken voice who said he was pleased to meet you, Mr. Hurst, Mrs. Hurst. And you might say hello to George, Archer said and, Oh, hi, George, Michael said (Michael was a poor reproduction of Archer and Alice; all the worst in both of them had run into him like dye) and Alice handed out Life Savers and the awkwardness of the situation was saved by Dean Piggott, appearing suddenly with a great deal of handshaking, who would like them, if they didn't have to leave right away, especially like Mr. Hurst to see the new Wassbinder Theater wing and the addition of the film collection; film was now on the curriculum of fine arts (shepherding them away like an ordinary family while Michael, having achieved his little revenge, went off to shower) and, well, the dean said, if Mr. Hurst could see his way clear sometime to spare a few minutes to address the seniors taking film *about* film . . . Oh, not *my* kind of film, Archer said but that he'd send so and so, that fine director who had just made *Odd;* Archer talked about *Odd,* Archer talked about *Citizen Kane;* Archer was extraordinarily good at this sort of thing, stopping to look at everything and admiring acoustics, lighting, and saying, Look at *this*, Alice, think of *that*, Alice; they moved through this interminable tour of the Wassbinder wing like the First Family; occasionally Alice threw George a drowning-woman look and dropping behind once, pretending to examine the papier-mâché masks being made for the drama school's coming production of *Lysistrata*, she said, Oh, God, what am I to do, George? Remain calm, he said, it's not your fault. I mean about the divorce, she said. I don't want a divorce, George, I don't want to hand him over to Miriam Litvinov, she is a stone, do you know her? She is a cold marble manipulator who wants an in through him and he's too vain to see it (Yes, yes, Alice called, coming, we're just looking at these terrific masks); why should I be made to give up my marriage for her? I don't care, Alice said, if he sleeps with her on the Academy Awards *show*, but I don't see why I should have to give up my marriage for her; what do you think I ought to do, George, do you think I ought to fight it? And looking at Alice, deep in woe and love, he had thought that she was one of those women who a thousand years ago would have followed behind the man with the oxen and goats; revile her and she would still stagger behind with the bundles; something Eskimo about Alice, tough and loyal. Whoever came next, Miriam, a thousand more women, Archer would never discover another Alice. And here she was now, asking George what should she do, should she fight (turning over in her hands the elaborate golden mask) to keep the marriage? Should she fight?

But why hadn't he immediately said, Yes, fight, fight him, don't give in, he needs you and vice versa so fight it all the way up to the Supreme Court? Had there been some almost forgotten, long-ago buried resentment about Alice that had made him fail her that day? He could see himself, his face drawing up into a pitying smile and, Oh, God, Alice, he had said, there are two kinds of people in the world, givers and takers, and Archer is a born taker, he said, Archer is perhaps the Pulitzer Prize taker of all time, he said, loving Archer was probably about as unrewarding a pastime as could be imagined, rather like playing championship tennis against an ace who only returns your serve when he feels like it. Well, George said, Alice was a remarkable girl to have endured it this long and he felt (and why had he not been able to look at her as he said this, why had he been fiddling with the fringe on her bag?) that she deserved more than this, that she had a life of her own and that she ought to consider this before it was too late. Well, thanks, Alice had said, thanks, and she had given him the look of someone who has been shortchanged by a friend and George saw now that this might have been the moment of split; probably she never trusted him again from this moment; Alice had actually thought of him as a friend. Thanks, she said and gave him the first of a long line of contemptuous looks. She would like a cup of tea more than *anything*, Alice said in a despairing voice but they had to wait while Archer tried out the acoustics of the Wassbinder Theater with members of the senior drama class by giving them "Tomorrow and tomorrow and tomorrow," not absolutely faithful to the text but received with applause and a lot of handshaking and charming diffidence on Archer's part. "*Ars gratia mars*" Archer told them.

But outside he shrank a little, he seemed to deflate; in the twilight evening, the yellow windows lighting up in dormitories and in the main hall, among the shouting scurrying boys calling to each other, the first bell for dinner, he seemed suddenly depressed, whistled through his teeth as if something pained him, put on his big dark glasses and whistled through his teeth and they stood on the steps to the library. We have to meet Michael at that teashop, he has permission to meet us at the teashop, Alice said diffidently and Archer said, Yes, I heard you but let me think a minute, will you? (they then stood in the darkening evening and waited while Archer thought a minute, and had done so all their lives, George was reckoning) until Archer said, You go ahead, Alice, and we'll join you, and when she hesitated (she seemed undecided whether she should go at all) he said, Go *ahead*, Alice, George and I want to see where they buried old poopface, our headmaster, he is buried up near the chapel and we coughed up for the stone and George and I would like to see it and, OK, Alice said and went off with the oxen and goats and bundles, without looking back and wearing the only thing she had left in the world, her look of scorn.

They went up the slopes in the falling darkness toward the chapel, toward lighted stained glass windows and the big bell tower looming over them, beginning to catch a sound of choir practice; pure young voices sang with praise and certainty that sheep may safely graze, safe-ly graze, and, Pure as the driven smut, Archer said, when you think of what they'll be doing later in the shower room, measuring their octaves, and they stopped a minute and listened to the choir, Archer staring up at the darkening bell tower above them, his collar turned up now against the wind that had sprung up, and with his hair all blown over his face he looked very young and, Oh, even the smell, Archer said, that damp smell of stone and moss and crap and lichen brings it all back, like yesterday, smell it? Oh, God, Archer said, doesn't it frighten you the way time goes, doesn't it, George? It's too incredible to think how time goes.

A kind of melancholy had come over him, George noticed, one of those sharp sudden melancholies that Archer caught like colds; George recognized the symptoms, whistling through the teeth and quick little laughs, these things meant that Archer was in pain, Archer was suffering, and nothing could be done until the siege was over. Pushing now through a door marked PRIVATE and up the steps behind the organ loft and through another door out into a cloister, Archer, giving quick little laughs all the time, turned, spun around and stopped so suddenly George almost collided into him and, Remember? Archer asked. Remember what? In the light, almost gone, Archer's eyes seemed peculiarly bright. Come back with me to California, Archer said, why don't you, and George had been taken again, there had been no intention of seeing old poopface's tombstone, the reason for this detour had been to make this unlikely suggestion.

Bonnngg. The great bell boomed above them in the tower, shattering the cloister with huge iron sound; *bonnngg* and *bonnngg*; apocalyptic sound, end of the world sound. He and Archer stood face to face under this cannonade reverberating around them, enclosed in sound, and between the clangs, in the spaces between the shattering reverberations, Archer said, Why not? what's to keep you here anyway? He seemed to be daring George (as in their youth, *dare* you to do it) or daring him not to, Archer balancing on the balls of his feet in his beautiful loafers, in his handsewn clothes. There was something a little desperate about him today, scared of beginning to lose his beauty, scared of getting old, or perhaps just finding out he was only plastic merchandise. Why don't you? Why don't you? Archer kept saying and the big bell dropped great iron rings of sound around them and George could only see Archer's lips moving under the sound and it was eerie, the two of them alone in the dark cloister and covered with sound and then deafened as the bell stopped, and their outraged ears stung and throbbed and George heard Archer say pleadingly, I need a friend, friend; the words touched the heart, but had he said them? It seemed unlikely that Archer would ever say such an outright thing and so may have been the distortions of the assaulted ear.

But the whole situation seemed unlikely, Archer pleading with him to come to California; it had a certain irony; George thought to himself it was almost classic. Once in the hero-worshiping days he had offered God or the devil his soul if only Archer would at that moment telephone and now Archer was standing here asking for *him*.

When at last he thought he could now be heard he told Archer that a week from Tuesday he and Ruth Carver were going to be married.

You and *Ruth*?

Yes, he and Ruth, George said, not wanting to appear apologetic about it but that was what Archer was intending him to be. Even in this spectral light Archer's smile was mocking, his lips bunched around his teeth in a ferrety way that always indicated hurt; you and *Ruth,* Archer said, perfectly making the implication he could not think of a bigger mismatch (and this was the dark unpleasant side of Archer, this was Archer, dangerous when snubbed, vanity pricked) and, Well, well, she sure as hell wins the endurance record, does old Ruth, Archer said and began shaking George by the shoulders quite violently in a parody of affection. *Congratulations,* Archer said and whistled through his clenched teeth in pain (and had this really been the way it was, in their last moments ever together?) and, Well, Archer said, no need to worry about where your mono-grammed underwear is coming from any more, is there? That's for sure, old chum, old cock, Archer said and stepped back and made an elaborate and courtly bow and, *Arch,* George burst out (and had not called him that for God knows how many years), *listen;* but Archer was not to be kept, Archer had leaped into one of the arches and over the wall and was striding away across the little private graveyard of old headmasters and George, scrambling after him, stumbled up the incline for whatever reason he didn't know, except it seemed he'd all in a minute betrayed Archer, that was what Archer had made him feel. Almost as though it might have long ago been planned that way; as though years ago George had one day planned this exact happening as a little sweet revenge for all the times of being hurt by Archer.

Arch, George called at the top of the hill, but Archer was already just a distant flying figure, going down steps two at a time, gone. *Arch,* George called, cupping his hands, but could not scream out his feelings about wounds, about what they had done to each other; Archer was too far away, not only in the distance but in years, and George in their last moment could find nothing to say except, Arch, Arch, standing there, being eyed curiously by some passing boys; must have sounded merely like some alarmed bird going *archarch archarch.*

part two

"don't look

at your watch, now."

"I wasn't," he said. "I was looking at my *wrist*."

"If you had a watch, you'd have been looking at it; I *caught* you."

"No no, no no."

"Hope I'm not boring you, dear George."

"Oh *God* no, *God* no."

Light full in his face. So he couldn't yet make out who this was, speaking to him. She had a voice that was clearly ordained for cutting headwaiters down to size and an upper-crust New York accent; "fearst clarse," she said, she had stayed at a "fearst clarse" hotel once on Lake Geneva. At the same time the voice brooked no dispute and once he said, No, that's in Gstaad, because he knew the voice was wrong, and the voice informed him in a chilly tone that she had been to Switzerland perhaps a dozen times before he was even *born*. She handed him a dish of meringues. "No, thanks," he said; he was feeling slightly queasy as the tea was too sweet, there had been eclairs, pink iced cakes, and on a stand beside him were macaroons, chocolate leaves and crystallized orange slices; altogether there was too much sugar, he thought and stirred his tea, into which she had poured a thimbleful of multicolored crystals like little stones. The room smelled of stale ferns. "Not Gstaad," she said and crossing just behind the penumbra of yellow light, pulled down a green shade all the way to the floor and he saw that it was Kitty Carver and that she was now only in her late fifties. He had forgotten how beautiful she had been with the classic kind of Norma Shearer looks even back then (back now) gone out of date. Where was Ruth? What had he been doing having this sugary afternoon tea alone with Ruth's mother? He had on an extremely ugly brown suit he had forgotten he ever had. It had been bought in Amsterdam. He touched his face and was surprised to find he had a little pointed beard that he had grown while he was away in Europe; he had grown it in a futile attempt to feel different, to feel new, but only felt staler than ever; the whole four years away had been a disappointment.

"Have a piece of almond cake," Kitty Carver said, cutting into it with a silver slicer. "It's from Rodman's in Butley, who do fearst clarse cakes, I think." If she had been truly generous she would have given her face to Ruth instead of her personality; she had given her face to her son Tony, who had had it blown off at Bastogne. "No more cake," George said. Was she trying to poison him with all this sugar? He must have been feeling queasy for some time because he saw he'd put down his plate with a half-eaten chocolate leaf on a velvet stool. And the room was hot and stuffy (was it summer?) and what a hideous room it was with its sugary white wood carving and bric-a-brac threatening to take over and the velvet Victorian chairs so low one had to sit in the fetal position, knees in the face; bamboo, velvet ottomans and china figurines. (How could Ruth have stood it all these years without going into a decline? It was like experiencing Henry James viscerally.)

He gave a slight burp and said in reply to something she'd already asked him that he'd been a foreign correspondent for a while, stationed in Geneva (she was cutting into the soft rich cake even though he'd refused it; she was willful, she would have her cake and have him eat it, this purposeful woman), that he had done a weekly letter for *Current Affairs Digest*, which had gone under after three months and left him stranded.

"Oh, poor George," Kitty said in the way moneyed people express deep concern they don't feel. "Stranded in Geneva, which is so insular a city and the French Swiss so abominable to one." How did he manage to stay on in Europe so long then?

Oh, he managed; he had taken odd jobs, taught for a while in an American school in Rome and so forth, traveled extensively and lived in YMCAs and hostels.

"Hostels," she said. She could not imagine hostels; one only had to look at her to know that she stayed in hotels that bore the names of Beau Rivage and Majestic.

"You don't *have* to eat this but just *try* it." Sure enough she'd put the almond cake beside him and he felt his gorge rise. It was like a form of subtle punishment and he was right, the situation was Jamesian, it was all coming back to him why he was here and they were approaching in disguised dialogues the dark center of it.

"No no," he said wretchedly and he was beginning to feel more than queasy, sick.

"I suppose," Kitty said, "it was still too painful for you to think of coming home for a while."

"Yes."

"How long did you stay away?"

"A little over four years in Europe."

"I'm sure it would take that long to begin to get over . . ."

"And then I sort of sat around two years in Big Sur."

"Appalling, appalling thing, George."

"Yes, well, yes, well . . . I finally, though, began to think I might as well be lonely at home, where I could speak the language."

"Ah, poor George."

"If you're not bilingual to any degree, after a while it gets to be such a drag never knowing what they're saying, never even being able to eavesdrop in a café, and I like to eavesdrop, and then you begin to wonder all the time if maybe they're talking about *you* and maybe all that laughter is about *you*, and finally I began to get so paranoid I thought I better get right out. . . ."

"And are you more settled then, now?"

"Then, now? Which?"

"Now, I mean, at home."

"More settled, more unsettled. I don't really"—*burp*—"excuse me—know."

"Don't feel you have to eat that cake, but you must just *taste* it."

"Oh, I will, I will."

"And what do you—I mean do you have any plans for what you'd like to do now?"

"I'd like to run a lighthouse."

"What sort of house?"

"Better still, *be* a lighthouse. I'd like to turn into a lighthouse more than anything I can think of right now; gulls flying into my face, spray up my . . ."

This was not fair to someone like Kitty Carver, stiff-backed and not greatly gifted with humor.

"No, I'm joking." Far too much saliva to be swallowed, so was he really going to throw up in her Victorian drawing room and should he get out now? "No, I don't know, Kitty."

"No plans then."

"No, I'm going to mooch about for a while. I've got a little sublet walkup on Thirty-third and Lex which doesn't cost much and I like to cook a bit, I like to batch. . . ."

And he would not be allowed to much longer because with her thin Giotto-like fingers clasping and unclasping, Kitty Carver had plans for him, he remembered now, all this offering of cakes and ale was not for any frivolous reason.

"I think anything's fine as long as you can try to avoid living in the past," she said, "and start over fresh."

"Yes," he said.

"After all, you must think of yourself. My dear, years and years of roaming around. There's nothing you or anyone can do to bring Dicky back."

"Dicky?"

"Your wife."

"Ron."

"Ron? Oh, I'm sorry. Ron."

"Veronica she was."

"*I* see."

The light was fading. She crossed the room to turn on a lamp. In her long dark skirt with a silk sash and full-sleeved blouse she looked Victorian, fitted into her room like her furniture. She sat down on a small bamboo sofa closer to him.

"Accidents," she said. "I don't know which is harder to bear, the accidental or the slow gradual . . . Veronica, pretty name. Was she pretty?"

"No, not at all."

"Oh."

Kitty was coiled like a spring against the back of the sofa. Only someone unperceptive would have thought she was just lolling. George had thought she was just lolling.

"You've been remarkable, I think, George, remarkable," she said.

Burp. "Excuse me," he said.

"Have you," she now asked with extreme casualness, "had a postcard from Ruth?"

Had he? Where was Ruth?

"Yes," he said, "from Taxco."

So that was where Ruth was, Ruth was away in Mexico. That's right, and Kitty had telephoned him at his mother's. Could you come over and have tea with me, she had said; you are a regular Enoch Arden, she said.

"Do you know this friend of hers, this Wyn?"

"No," he said.

"She's not the person *I'd* pick to go on a tour with."

"No, I don't know her."

"She's *not* the person I would pick to go *anywhere* with, but Ruth seems to like her." She smoothed the silk sash, stared at her skirt. "I don't know whether she wanted to go or not."

"Ruth?"

"I don't know whether she wanted to go or not. I can never tell with her. It just came up and I said, Do you want to go to Mexico, and she said, I suppose so."

He swallowed saliva for a time. "Ah, yes," he said.

"I don't know whether she's having any sort of a good time. I can't tell from her cards; they might as well be from the laundress I hire."

"Well, I suppose she is."

"So difficult to tell with her. She never shows any . . . joy about anything. The day before they were to leave I said to her, You don't seem out of your mind with excitement about going to Mexico so would you rather not go, dear? I said, Dear, you don't *have* to go. Oh, no, she said, I'll go."

She gave a very long sigh and smoothed her silk sash. One would have thought, not knowing her well, that her eyes were almost closed in sleep.

"I am at the end of my tether, George," she said.

Ipppip. "Excuse me," he said and tried to avoid looking

at the rich cake beside him, onto which she had turned the lamplight fully; it could have been polite torture. It was all he could do just to keep his gorge from rising and . . .

"I am completely at the end of my rope," Kitty said. "As you probably know, George, I am at the end of my rope about Ruth. I have never been able to give her anything she wants, never, never in over thirty years. Never once have I given her anything that seems in any way to please her."

There was desperation in the cultured voice.

"Even when she was little, she never seemed to enjoy things like other children, parties and matinees and the circus or the horse show; *whatever* we tried she didn't seem to have any fun. I was always looking for some sign that she might be enjoying something but there was never any enthusiasm, never; she was a very odd little girl, very strange and cold really, and I just thought she'd warm up at school but she didn't; just unreachable; exasperating when you are doing your level best to . . . I mean for instance when she turned twenty-one I said to her, Now you can have the pearls your father promised you; well, you'd think *that* might amuse her. I mean when *I* was twenty-one and got my first pearls I wore them to bed for a week, it was an *event;* my mother had to quiet me with sedatives; but with Ruth, well, I can't tell you what I went through with her in Cartier's for I would think a solid hour saying, Do you like this string, that string, and after all you don't buy pearls more than once or twice in your lifetime and Mr. Petrie was bringing out the entire safe it seemed and must have thought she was extremely odd, extremely odd, and finally *we* had to choose for her and I tell you, George, candidly, candidly I don't think she would have cared whether they were pearls or not, we might as well have bought her *moonstones,* and I was really cross with her; I said, You could at *least* try to remember how pleased your father would be and she said, Well, then, I'm pleased for *him*. See?"

Urrrrp. George said, "I see."

"I don't know what to do. I'm at the end of my *rope.* I don't know what to do about her. We don't talk. You can't *talk* to her. We live in the same house and hardly say a word to each other. If you ask her anything about herself you get nothing back. She just moons around with two or three girl friends who are destined to be old maids, it's written on them already, and I'm afraid she's . . . giving up. She's so forlorn it breaks my heart. I never would have believed I'd have a forlorn child."

He was doing self-hypnosis not to be sick. Perched on the low chair, he gazed up at Kitty, swallowing hard and persuading himself his nausea was ebbing; the effort gave him the appearance of being spellbound by what she was telling him.

"It would be nice if I could do something for her."

He nodded; he found nodding helped.

"She's my only child now and she's a rather nice child."

Her eyes were wet at the corners, he noticed.

"Let me put it to you this way, let me ask you a fair question and you give me a fair answer."

Nodding, wondering if his face was turning green.

"If there was someone she *liked*—and I don't think I have to tell you there *is.*"

Nodding.

"And if he liked *her* enough—am I making myself clear?"

Nodding.

"Then need the money stand in the way?"

That had been the dark center she'd been approaching, to strip away whatever last excuse he might have been making; she was desperate, she was tapping on his knee.

"If he cared enough about her—I think you know what I'm talking about—why should the fact that she's independently well off deter him?"

Jamesian.

Pale and sweating chosen suitor in ugly cheap brown suit; lovely desperate mother; forlorn heiress. He wondered if the secret anticipation of it had made him sick-nervous and not the richness of the surrounding cakes; he saw that he was looking up at her beseechingly and pressing his napkin to his mouth.

"Why? Just because she has her own money? Is it fair she should be deprived? I want your honest answer. Is that fair?"

"No," George said and was gloriously sick.

And for the rest of his life he had thought it had been his own idea to marry Ruth.

Because Kitty had handled it well, guessed right, removed his vestigial scruples about what people might think, paved the way (he had blocked all this out, of course; just as he had blocked out the havoc in her drawing room, which she had instantly put right, the elderly maid appearing, towels and sweet-smelling eau de cologne, things whisked away, pillows put behind his head, given hot water and lemon and all accomplished in minutes with her so so cultured voice reassuring him as though it wouldn't be a proper tea without someone being ill), made the decision easy for him.

But in his weakness of wanting to give himself to Ruth he had had to think it had been his own idea. Right up to the moment when he had presented himself to Ruth with his heart beating with the excitement of it.

I'd appreciate it if you'd consider marrying me one of these days, he had said, coming up behind her and taking her by surprise at somebody's party while she was standing in a group of people and in the act of putting a stick of stuffed celery into her mouth; he had taken her by the shoulders and pulled her up against him and said into her ear, "I'd appreciate it if you'd consider marrying me," and had felt his heart thumping against her and heard the crisp crunch of her jaws chomping on celery next to his ear. "Did you hear me?" he asked over the noise of her crunching celery and she had nodded. That was all. Nodded. He was disappointed, he hoped that this would have been the supreme moment of her life and here she was munching celery; no wonder people found her cold. But when she turned to face him, he could see there was a violent change in her, she seemed to be alight. . . .

And now this is as far back as I want to go, he said. Occasionally he began seeing, in glimpses, his whole life spread out like a map below him, he flying over the countries of his life, sometimes high enough to see it all in one piece, as an entire continent streaked with rivers of time and marked with hills and valleys which were the indentations he had made of it; flying over the continent of his life, which was largely unexplored territory and mysterious forests in whose dimnesses people and things moved that he wanted to forget. In the few seconds of these excursions he looked on his entire life existing in one unbroken line; here was middle age, here was youth, here childhood and here at the farthest coast, at the dark sea, the baby.

Now this is as far back as I want to go, he said, soundlessly, like speaking in a vacuum, willing himself to arrest this flight and zoom back into the right dot on the map of his life, to be where he'd taken off from, in his comfortable bathroom, and to find Ruth, stretched out on the wicker chaise, reading, just step back through the crack is all it needs, he thought; he was trying to; there was something he wanted to tell Ruth now, something he had never said, actually never said to her in his life; he wanted to say to Ruth that

tears ran down his face and dropped onto his hand and he was groping for a handkerchief; his hands were so sunburned that he stopped groping for a moment to admire them; he couldn't remember he'd ever had such a sunburn, it was beautiful burnt siena color, dyed into him over a long period, and the hairs on his hands were snow white.

It actually was the wind making him weep so, but his black mourning armband made his tears seem official (a girl stood patiently by, waiting for him to wipe his eyes), and it must have seemed that way to passersby on Madison Avenue, that this tanned young man was in a terrible, incurable state of grief.

"George," the girl said, "it's Ruth."

She had grown up. He wouldn't have known her; they had not met for years, not since they were in their late teens probably.

"Oh, Ruth," he said. "Sure."

Sure. She had been an aloof girl, he remembered. She had been a great spoiler of fun; she tagged along, nobody remembered bringing her, there she'd be, out of the corner of your eye you'd spot her standing alone outside a group and something would have to be done about her; she was a damn nuisance was what she was; she made you feel awkward and guilty. She was always walking away alone after parties and dances and you always spotted her after you'd all got into a car to go on to somebody's fun place and there she'd be, walking off alone into the night, so you'd have to say would she like to come along or was anyone seeing her home and so on; she was a wet blanket; she had had a crush on Archer Hurst, hadn't she? Poor girl; as if she had a chance. She was always looking around doors for him.

He'd remembered all this in the fraction of a second it takes to shake someone's hand. Ruth's. She had a poor handshake; one felt if you let go of her hand it might fall to the ground.

"Oh, Ruth," he said.

He continued to shake her hand; how strange of her not to say anything about his bereavement; she seemed to be avoiding looking at his armband.

"I lost my wife," he said, prompting her.

"I know," Ruth said but she seemed unable to say she was sorry, let him continue to pump her hand desperately. She seemed incapable of expressing anything; she was going to be an old maid, it was stamped all over her; no man was ever going to want her; just as she always had to go home alone, so she would go through the rest of her life alone.

He was telling her details now, blinking away his tears, which were falling fast, and she listened with great intensity but still said nothing.

She seemed unaffected by the details, so cool that nothing might really have happened to him, he might be merely a big complainer. She said no word of pity, not a consoling gesture came from her, she just gazed at him with her unsettling serene eyes. Then she said, as if congratulating him, "*Any*way, you got through," nodded and walked away quickly up Madison Avenue. What an extraordinary thing to say, he thought, what an unrelated thing to say. As if he had passed some minor exam. Anyway, you got through. It became like a little tune he couldn't get out of his mind and the more he thought about it, the more it seemed in a funny way to lighten his heart (which all other attempts by others, consoling him drably about his not having a thing to regret in regard to Ron, what a splendid husband, et cetera, failed to do). Ruth's funny little compliment sustained him.

Until, waking one night, it came to him with that deadly 4 A.M. conviction that she had seen through layers and layers of his grief right down to where he was hiding a tiny cube of emotion (only a mote, a dot), of

Of relief.

It was, just as he dreaded, Chop Island without any doubt. Oh, but not the whole thing, not all of it from start to finish, he said. It was springing up all around him like an experience, it was shaping itself into great colored globules as bright and glaring as pictures painted on glass and lit from behind: here the wild sea cliff with the tall grass continuously bent by the wind; in the distance the harbor bay with black sand and the lobster boats, the view from his house of the distant town with the gabled roofs of big decayed summer hotels gone to seed with their sagging balconies and porches where only aged people wearing panama hats rocked in the shade; the stuffy suffocating little village of ugly shops and one or two dark cafés with plastic ferns hanging in the doorways and the windows of the shops piled high with repulsive objects of clothing and everything saturated with all-year-round salt-smelling damp. . . .

He had closed his eyes again and tried to avoid it, thrashing around with weakened wrists against this part, just as one tries to avoid being attacked in a dream. Well, anyway, George said, I will not dwell on this part, this must pass quickly, I will skip whatever and whenever I

and deep blue ponds, great thick blueberry vines and wild roses that in summertime crossed the small dusty roads and joined and you took shears and hacked away at them and even so they slashed and slapped at the jeep and at you as you drove through them; no matter how you cleared away, cut and pulled at them, they would somehow stretch out their tendrils and stalks, attempting to bar your way; they seemed to be in league against you.

The whole place was in the process of returning to nature and so plants, vines, moss, algae, mold, saltbush, blackberry, poison ivy, goldenrod, Queen Anne's lace all multiplied as never before or so it seemed, everything you didn't want nourished and grew like wildfire, possessed everything in its pathway; if they didn't drive continuously up and down the narrow dirt road to their house, it would have been swallowed up in a week; indeed it was a familiar sight to see the top of a roof, a chimney poking out of a mass of vines where a house had been digested into vegetation. The only sign left of the Bay Hotel, long abandoned, was part of the second floor's glassless windows which, gaping wide, seemed to be gasping their last breath before being choked by the vines; honeysuckle covered it from top to bottom; no one could tell where the front door might once have been but part of the word *cuisine* could be faintly made out peeping through the quivering leaves eating it away. It was all more or less like that; bored children of earlier generations had left for the mainland; old people died, no one came to summer any more; the ferry came over twice a week from Cape Janet Light with barely enough traffic to warrant it; everything slept, dozed; everything rotted, decayed into encroaching nature. The tiny red wind sock flapping at the airstrip might have been the only sign that anyone remained; it bobbed in the wind signaling for help. Pheasants, unhunted, proliferated and grew impudent, hardly bothering to scuttle unless you grabbed for their tails; they seemed to know it was only a matter of time before they'd have the island to themselves so gave you the golden glassy stare, and the gulls (the biggest on the Atlantic coast, said George) swooped down very low and were not ruffled when Jamie ran at them shooing and squawking.

It was supinely, torpidly returning to nature. The electricity frequently gave out and they would light oil lamps, throwing themselves up against the walls in gigantic shadows, and everything was tired and weak, salt-ridden; telephones only gargled, instead of ringing gave a rusty gargling sound and over the old wires came weak voices as thin as copper wire and at the movie house dim, brownish, grainy films wavered weakly on the screen; the sound system had been out of sync for years.

There were (you never referred to it or stared) just too many people with something slightly wrong with them to be all coincidence; blood had mated with blood, cousin with cousin, not bothering to have the line renewed (a nuisance to take three hours over to the mainland by the ferry, six dollars each way when you took the single-engine air taxi), so there were signs of copulative apathy; here an eyelid, there a chin or lack of it, a suspicion of a hump; in the back room through the swinging bead curtains two albino children.

They lived on what was known locally as the chop bone, where the cliffs rose up from the sea "maniacally," Ron said; she was fond of standing on the farthest edge and looking down into the boiling sea; at nights she would say if it was clear that if they had a strong telescope they could see the lights of Boston. Their house stood bold and tall on the edge of the chop bone; it was sturdy, concrete-thick against any hurricane or act of God; three stories tall and two chimneys and a shock to walk in the door and find it was no house at all, merely a fake put up by the army as a gun emplacement and to spot German submarines looming out of the Atlantic waters, just one of many such gun emplacements from Cape Hatteras to Maine disguised as houses; which accounted for the narrow slitty little windows, though they had carved out a huge window on the sheltered side which gave onto sunset; thus, entering the house you were surprised, like biting into a meringue, to find such emptiness; the house was empty from stone floor to the unceilinged roof but they had built two satisfactory bedrooms on scaffolding which were reached by a wooden stairway; otherwise they had this huge stone room, vast and churchlike, safe from wind and water, cozy against the gales, cool. . . .

He was still keeping his brain closed against it; the smell

of the sea was so all-invading to the senses, but he hoped anyway to avoid this sequence entirely. And if I can hang on to *knowing* I will *not* go through this part, I will not, George said, I can steer past it or perhaps even now I can reverse the process, I

He was in the cliff house, he was alone, the sea sucked and mumbled below, otherwise it was very quiet.

He raised his head and looked through the big window to the sunset (recalling it forever afterward in exact color) and it was a peculiar greenish yellow coming after such days of torrential rain which had lashed the island, blown in gales from the sea, the real monsoon rains. Against this green sky everything stood out in bas relief. Every tree, every saltbush and rock stood out. Nothing moved. Exhausted by days of storm, everything rested; even the gulls were silent. Everything sat still in greenish silence in a dripping calm. He looked at the big derelict house nearby on the cliff which she had been using as a studio. He looked at the dark blue sea. He looked across green wet fields and drowned hayricks away to his neighbor's distant stone farmhouse. He looked back at the derelict house nearby. It was standing out so clearly against the green sky that every one of its many once-gingerbread windows, trellises, cupolas and gables seemed cut out of black paper. The tower rose straight and perpendicular—didn't it? Or had it always had this slight lean? Now it must be, he thought, just a trick of the light that could make him swear the tower seemed a fraction out of plumb, as though it had shifted during the moment he had looked away and back, just very slightly, that the house was, come to think of it, just a shade off level, leaning with a little tipsiness toward the cliff, toward the sea; wasn't it only this peculiar green light that caused the illusion? How long did he sit there and stare at the old house (now it seemed to be an incredibly long time, sitting there gazing stupidly, sleepily) before his scream began?

Pelted up the cliff pathway screaming, Ron, Ron, come out of there, and the torn entrails of the cliff showing where the huge slice had fallen off and the house gave a shudder and all in one piece went down: not believable except for the noise. First of all he tried to believe Ron hadn't been in it (tiny figures were running across the field from the neighbors, one of them had to be her), she hadn't been in it. Only later he imagined he had seen her walking slowly across the upstairs floor carrying the child just as the earth, incredibly, gave way, grass sank away. Just at the moment it heeled tipsily over he thought he saw her walking very carefully across the upper floor; she knew what was coming, she was anxious not to precipitate it, she seemed calm in what she was doing, she carried Jamie under one arm and thought they would reach the outside before the catastrophic thing carried them and stairs, windows, everything in rains of stone and clay in a few seconds to the bottom of the sea.

Later on, much later on, he would begin to think it was true he had caught sight of her. But probably it had only been his imagination; there would have been no time to see anything; it took perhaps twelve seconds.

He had sat in his empty stone house then for days on end and was simply nothing but numb, simply nothing, neighbors brought him soup and cold meats and fish and occasionally he seemed to put something in his mouth; he slept and awoke and slept again and gradually this changed to apathy; apathy was a little better than the numbness; apathy meant a slow coming back to life, it was the way of life on Chop Island.

It helped that in an apathetic well-meaning way nobody fussed or became emotional. Nobody was even very surprised. On Chop Island old houses went into the sea with regularity; the cliffs were eroding as fast as the vegetation was spreading. They mentioned he should have had the house moved back twenty feet or so; someone said it had already been moved back once and someone older remembered in Mrs. Lavender's day there had been tennis courts in front where there was now nothing but air. It was characteristic of them to give him these bits of information rather than ask what she had been doing in there in the first place.

Apathetic also was the routine investigation and the coast guard putt-putting sluggishly around the fallen cliff in launches; now, they said, as to the possibility of—well, sending down a diver, it was obvious that tons of rock and timber and sand had come down and . . .

But even so, his mother's voice said tinnily over the telephone on the gargling wires from New Forks, even so he ought to have some kind of service. As there was no church of any kind left on Chop Island, let alone Catholic, they'd held it on the mainland and it had been then, hearing the words of the litany, that he had been able at last to take it in and to weep. It had been smart of Jessica and later he realized she had rescued him from an apathetic end-to-life he had committed himself to. After the service he drove off with her; he never went back to Chop Island. Not even to get his razor.

And now Ron was still alive and coming into their bedroom in the big army fake house on the cliffs and saying in her husky charcoal voice, "Look, my dear, what I've brought you, my dear."

Watermelon. The first of the season. She'd gone down to "town," she said, to get something (couldn't remember what now) and the Cape Janet Light boat had just come in with the watermelons and this would tempt him, she thought, all else having failed.

"Watermelon," he said and beamed on her and hoisted himself up in bed.

This was during a time he had taken to his bed. Nobody

knew what was wrong with him; it couldn't be serious because he neither ached nor pained, he had no temperature; he just seemed to feel enormously heavy and his skin was sensitive, his skin hurt. All anyone could get on Chop Island was old Dr. McQueen unless you wanted to pay through the nose to have a doctor fly over from the mainland and back, so old Dr. McQueen had come and poked and pried, said it might be this or that, or a *reaction* to something (funny he should put it that way; George remembered that part of it now), so keep him quiet, keep him on a light diet, fruit and fish. Dr. McQueen went off, forgetting his stethoscope, and didn't come back for it for two days, which was par for Chop Island, and Ron said, Thank our lucky stars you are not afflicted with anything really serious, my darling.

"I am changing into a swan," George said. "I think I am changing into a swan."

"That's nice," Ron said, cutting into the watermelon. "How's your back, my darling?" It had nothing to do with his back but she said that if she asked after something different each time it would help to pass the time for him. "How is your left buttock, my dear?" she said. "How is your pituitary gland today, my darling?" Inside their fake house with the narrow slitty windows the greenish light made her look slightly Oriental with her olive skin and black hair which she wore in braids. Her hair was full of sand, he noticed, and there were patches of hardened salt whitening on her skin, and the small hairs on the back of her neck and arms were salt white. He also was salty, even his navel felt salty; they both needed to be scoured in very hot soapy water; they needed a real bath, he needed a haircut and a tooth filled; they needed to go to the mainland; they needed to take a day in Boston. . . .

"Oh," George said weakly, "I *must* get up."

"What for?" she asked. "There's nothing to get up for, my dear, unless you want."

"Ohh," he said in gentle despair, "I can't just go on lying and lying and lying," he said, "in this bed."

It was languor, it was torpor, massive lethargy, and he felt as weak as water, as weak as the sound of the sea, which had not roused itself for over a week, susurrant, swishing away there below their cliffs, and the lapping sound of it was enough to induce sleepiness (and lately they were always dropping off; sometimes in the middle of saying something, the eyes and the mind closed down and the mouth dropped open so one or the other of them was off; just go to the kitchen for a glass and come back to find yourself alone and the other sound asleep). It was apathy taking them over gradually. In the same way as the elements advanced on them. Oh, we'll do this or that next week, next month, they said, saying they needed only each other (and the intensity of their physical love was certainly not affected by the general lethargy; if anything it became wilder), but meantime the vines had begun an assault on the house; you had to tear and yank at the screen door to get in or out, yank and curse because the wild roses had attached themselves to the frame, and just recently the first inquiring tendril of a long hairy vine had entered the bathroom window and was making for the top of the lavatory. Oh, I love a leafy john, Ron said.

So here he was only twenty-six years old and drifting; he was a would-be world-acclaimed author with a book that would now never be finished; by accident would never be finished.

It was with a contraption of memory like a zoom lens in a movie camera that he now saw himself; he was pathetically young-looking even with his scraggly beard; he was lying back against the calico pillows and his young squawlike wife was feeding him watermelon and there was something extremely precious and touching about the situation as he now saw it, something at the same time very pathetic in their relationship because they were trying to outdo each other in affirming their love and affection and in this zoom-lens clarity it was obvious to the onlooker that all they were doing was canceling each other out.

"No more, no more," George was saying, pushing the watermelon away.

"Was that fun?" she asked.

"Oh, was it fun!" he said, and they put their watermelony lips together, smeared each other's faces with pink juice, and she lay back against him like a kitten. She was so small and weightless she made no indentations on cushions and people kept a hold on her in strong winds and yet out of this cage of breast, this birdlike thorax came this deep husky voice, a dark wine-colored velvet voice.

Sexy, he told her over and over again. Sexy. It made everything she said sound marvelously carnal, George said. She had only to say "bread and butter" in that voice to make him erect, George said. "Say 'bread and butter,'" he whispered to her in the dark; when she bit his earlobe and said some real sexy thing, he said, no, it wasn't as sexy as when she just said "bread and butter."

Now she leaned against him as light as a palm leaf. "I was going down to get you a lobster," she croaked, "but I couldn't manage a live lobster and a watermelon and a child all rolling around in a jeep and watch out for jackrabbits too, especially as you tell me I am a road hazard."

"You *are* a road hazard," he said and crushed her in the way he liked to crush her because it made him feel Neanderthal; she was so tiny and easily crushable; wouldn't be surprising to hear the crunch of little bones, he told her, and so throw her away. He would come into the house, yanking and cursing at the screen door, and she would be standing at the sink and he would embrace her, crushing her in front of him, lifting her up in the air and nuzzling her neck and saying, Oh, oh, oh, oh, oh, God, God, God, what you *do* to me. After he had put her down she would say in her dark sexy voice, "Did you remember to bring lettuce?"

So small and vulnerable that it brought out the incipient child-rapist in some men, who became infected with the desire to place her upon their knees, pat and pet her with their big hands, their hands going around all over her, having to restrain themselves from calling her baby doll and little girl and cutie pie; she frequently replied to their advances with both acute and searching intelligence in her husky croak; she put them down not savagely but with a quiet dignity and a crystalline common sense that shattered their fantasies. And with her small hands she made great papier-mâché images of horses and dolphins and toads three times her own size. It might have had to do with some disproportionment in her character. She, who could hit the nail on the head when other people frequently could not even find the nail, could never see far ahead, never see the road ahead or what was coming, and just as she was a nightmare to drive with, never seeing the ditch, the motorcyclist almost onto her, busy regarding the sunset, catching sight of an albatross, likewise she never saw the risk in her own life.

"You are my little bush baby," he told her and folded her against him and felt her slight heartbeat (*actually* said "my bush baby"; in horrible zoom lens it came back, young George Wood performing such idiocy, such perfunctory patronizing gestures of love upon her that afternoon a few weeks before her sudden death; and saw that she seemed weary of it, she seemed to be merely tolerant; she sighed, she looked up at the ceiling unelated at this gratuitous information). "My darling," he added and thumbed her nose like a clothespin. She got up suddenly and went to the window and looked out. Oh, there it is, she said, the thing she and Jamie had seen while they were driving home, either a whale or a submarine. "I hope for Jamie's sake it's a whale," she said. "It's one of those days when the light is so clear that if the sun's in a certain position they say you can see to the bottom of the sea and you can see old wrecks."

She hummed a little tune. She had a way sometimes of postponing coming to the point if something was troubling her.

"Does your skin still hurt?" she asked.

"Doesn't hurt exactly, just feels sensitive."

"Like you're aware of it all the time?"

"Yes, just as though I had sunburn."

"A sort of inner sunburn?"

"Exactly."

Now she peered at her little pointed face in their spotted tarnished mirror which gave to the face the appearance of fungus or leprosy; she stared first at her elvish face and then said to him in the mirror, "Do you think it's because you want to get out of it?"

"Out of what?"

"Your skin."

"That I want to get out of it?"

"Yes."

"Ron, don't be oblique today; it's too hot and I feel . . . sea-weedy."

"No, but I'm not being oblique, my dear," she said. "I'm wondering if you want to get out of yourself and that's why your skin hurts."

"Oh, don't be deep, will you?"

"I think you're sick of all this."

"All what?"

"This. The island. Us."

"Why do you say such a thing, make a statement like that which requires *energy* to deny, which I haven't *got* today; why do you *do* that, Ron?"

"Don't have to deny it."

"Don't *you* be unfair either. Explain."

She continued to look at him through the boils and mercury spots in the mirror. It was about something he had said in his sleep, she said, a few nights ago.

"What?"

"You said, 'I've got to get out of myself.'"

"I did?"

"You called out. You woke me up. I thought you were awake, you were so insistent about it, and I said, 'What's the matter?' and you were asleep but you answered me and said, 'I've got to get out of myself.'"

"Oh, pet, baby, are you going to start getting sensitive about what I say when I'm asleep *too*? I go through all kinds of nonsense in my sleep; don't you?"

She perched weightlessly on the bed.

"Yes, my dear," she said in her basso.

"So," he groaned, "don't tell me it has anything to do with my skin hurting."

"Yesterday," she said, "I had this vision. I was in the vegetable garden and I looked up and I saw you standing naked on the edge of the cliff and you were getting out of your skin."

It was his recurring dream. "God," he said.

"You were stepping out of your body."

"How? Describe."

"Oh, I couldn't now. It was only a flash, only a second or two. Quite casual, picking tomatoes, and out of the corner of my eye, oh, there's George stepping out of his body. Just a flash and it was gone, no one by the cliff, and *then* the double take, you know: my *God*, I thought I saw George getting out of his body, and laughing. But then I had this terrible feeling. . . ."

"What?"

"I had this terrible feeling: What if I went into the house and found it empty?"

They had stared at each other in silence; had she noticed at the time that he had gooseflesh?

"Empty," he said, gooseflesh at the idea.

"And that that would be the last trace of you ever."

"Ever," he repeated and shivered.

The sea muttered and slapped distantly below them. The air was still and hot but he was gooseflesh. "Vanished," he said and the word sounded like a very distant gong softly struck. It would be something he would think about again and again, her vision of him on the cliffs getting out of his body; he saw himself peeling it off like a rubber wet suit; an invisible man stepped out of it, the color of white light; then was gone.

"Vanished," he said again.

"Just for a second I had this appalling feeling of being left totally abandoned, the feeling a child has of being left totally abandoned, you know?" She looked very defenseless; she was too thin and her voice sounded tubercular and looking at her wasting away there and being abandoned, left with Jamie to the winds and gulls, all alone with the creaks and groans of night, he felt himself growing delightfully strong again.

"Oh, come here, come here," he said, opening his arms wide as she came closer and pulling her down on the bed with him. "Oh, but where would I go to?" he asked, crunching her bones to him, cuddling her to him. "Oh, why would I ever think of leaving my baby? Who would take care of my bush baby, eh?"

Who would protect her? he asked over and over again and

she said, I know, my darling, but it was just a thought and, Oh, he said, how could you even think a thing like that, that he would ever want to leave her and Jamie and . . .

Later, with his face turned to the wall, he slept with his thumb in his mouth and as she passed soundlessly around the room and as she put a blanket gently over his naked legs, it was with the touch of the mother; this girl that no bad thing could happen to while he was there to protect and they would go on living here on the cliff for years and years and

"Being in the wrong classroom." What was she croaking about now? Time had skipped (but then he had been determined to skip, he could not face reliving all this thing with Ron; too painful, too . . .). What was she talking about that had made him rigid? They were sitting in their canvas yacht chairs in the yellow oil lamp light, in the smell of kerosene; she was knitting and he was holding Jamie in his lap.

"In the wrong classroom," she repeated, "so that whatever you do you can't seem to make it, you're taking the wrong course from the wrong teacher. . . ."

Whatever had made him sit up and watch her so narrow-eyed and hold Jamie so tightly? Criticism?

"How can you expect to get grades? Now, if somebody came along and took you by the hand and said, Oh, cookie, you're in the wrong classroom, come along, you belong in here with Miss Martindale—"

"Who's Miss Martindale?"

"I just made her up, I thought she sounded right for you —took you by the hand and into Miss Martindale's class *because* that was your absolute *right* course which you would be brilliant at and right off you would dig it, you know? And so, my dear, you would be the most brilliant, my dear."

"Is this all directed at me?" he asked, smiling, and the smile very drawn back, like a dog about to snap at her.

"Not entirely," she said. "It just occurred to me while I was cleaning the fish that it is a sad thing about people who get into doing the wrong thing and flail around in it and knock their heads against brick walls for years and get so discouraged and if only they could find out in time they were doing the wrong thing and that there was a right thing for them to do which would be like falling off the proverbial log."

Why he'd gone rigid was that she was obviously referring to his lost novel. She was trying in the most delicate way she knew how to absolve him of the loss of it by insinuating it was no loss. She had been through her period of penitence over what had happened and now she was ready to bring him around to face the fact he'd been doing the wrong thing.

"Go on," he said, "about me and Miss Martindale and getting to be brilliant."

"That's all; it was just an idea I had."

"If I were in the wrong class, would you come and get me and take me by the hand into Miss Martindale's class?"

"Oh, darling, yes, of course, if I could. . . ."

Therefore had what happened been entirely accidental? The loss of his book had stunned him at first but in the months that had passed the anguish had given way to acceptance and acceptance led to apathy and (this was his secret, the reason he refused to try to start it over again or even talk about it) relief. And she had pleaded with him, begged him to try to start again, said she would take it all down in a peculiar shorthand she'd invented. No, no, it would not come back, he'd said wildly and tramped up and down the cliffs alone while she watched him, he knew, from the window with a stricken face. No, it would not come back, he said flatly, he would try something else, and all the time he'd kept back from her this feeling of relief and she never guessed that the reason he could not be angry with her for long was that she'd given him the excuse not to go on with it.

Anyway, you could not be angry with her for long about anything. She was too vulnerable, too sweet. You could not stay angry long with someone who looked always as though she might not live out the month, was so thin that you could be surprised she was able to cast a shadow. And her accidents. There were accidents of varying degrees all the time. "Just one of your accidents," he had said finally about the loss of his manuscript. "I'm prone," she said huskily in her shame and grief. You couldn't or shouldn't let her out of your sight. One day last spring something nearly fatal had happened. She and Jamie had been going to the mainland. He had come down to see them off on the early morning ferry. They waited for some time at the ferry slip. The ferry was late. Go home, she said, I know you want to get to work, so he had kissed her and Jamie but as he was getting into his jeep she called out. Wait, George, wait, she called and got out of the convertible she'd borrowed and came running; forgotten, she panted, to tell you something. Clasped him and murmured, Love you, love you, love you, and, Crazy, he said, you are crazy, and this pleasant idyll then interrupted by screams and they saw that she had left the brake off in the other car and that with Jamie seated contentedly in it, it had just begun to slip slowly forward down the stone ramp where the ferry docked and where for years of laxity nothing had been between ramp and deep water save a thin rusty chain and sparkles, speckles of sweat and horror and literally diving onto the car and squashing the child under him to reach the brake and, Crazy, crazy, he repeated to her in a different tone, shaking on rubber legs, Ron, you are *crazy*. I know, was all she said; looked terribly pinched; might not live through the month.

Would outlive them all, George often said when people asked about her in the troubled tones people always assumed when asking about her. Whenever he went down to town without her it was incredible the number of Chop Islanders who inquired about her, hoped she wasn't sick or anything, implied they hoped George took great care of her because she was popular, had a bright word for everyone when she came down shopping or to get a lobster; everyone was glad to see Ron, especially the damaged ones with the humps or the ones who moved in jerks.

Now watching her bent over knitting in the lamplight he thought he was here to protect her; she was a thin little Indian-looking girl whose mouth fell open when she knitted and who moved her lips when she counted the stitches and then came out suddenly with her notions about people being in wrong classrooms. Which he knew applied to him. Which made him uneasy. Because if the book thing hadn't been a stupid accident, then had she been trying to protect him?

He shivered although it was a warmish night, a goose walking over his grave.

"I'll put Jamie to bed," he said.

Went upstairs and tucked Jamie into the cot on the shelf over the kitchen and thought what if she had protected him from going on and on for years with a hopeless book? What if she had thought, which he had suspected, that his book was so bad that—

No, it had been one of her usual accidents, together with help from dim-witted Ruby Lark, whom they had had to fire.

Just an ironic accident, that's all.

He lay down on the bed in the dark and downstairs he heard Ron singing to herself in her strange husky basso. She seemed to be fond of mournful ballads. "*Oh, don't deceive me,*" she sang, "*oh, never leave me.*" He hoped for once she would remember to put out the lamp in the john so he wouldn't have to tramp downstairs in the middle of the night.

Again the thought: just supposing he had been deceived by her? Just supposing he was not the stronger one after all? Why then his marriage would be—

Such an idea couldn't be borne, couldn't be borne.

"Oh, don't deceive me, oh, never leave me," she sang, and he put the pillow over his head to stifle her singing and smother the thought. But it was this very night he'd waked up sweating with what had been the first signs of the baffling illness no one could diagnose.

Every two minutes regularly there was the mournful sound of the foghorn from the lighthouse; it was a long-drawn-out *blaaaaaaaat* like a sheep in pain and from the distant harbor the melancholy buoy bells clanged. They were buried in fog. A real Chop Island fog had closed in on a Thursday without warning and consequently they'd had to put up Ruby Lark because Thursday was her day to come to "help" (though what she did to "help" was not entirely clear) and now nobody could get to the town or back; the fog was so thick that cliffs, ponds, fences and roads all vanished. They lived in cloud, lived after the second day on cheese and bacon sandwiches sitting in the damp house and trying to coax up damp fires and whenever one turned around one ran onto Ruby Lark. It was impossible to get away from Ruby Lark, George thought. He found her distressing with her great white legs that reminded him of lard. She had an incessant sunny smile and her eyes focused in different directions at the same time. It took her five minutes to wipe a dish and then it was often necessary to take it from her and put another in her hands. But, as Ron said, it stayed wiped and Ron encouraged Ruby and praised her. You are a *pearl*, Ruby, Ron said and this sally could be repeated five or six times a day, it so delighted Ruby. Only Ruby with her ox strength could have hauled a heavy tin tub all the way up the cliff path to the derelict house so Ron could mix her paste for her papier-mâché in the studio she had made there. Only Ruby would never tire of bringing pail after pail of water. Ruby and Ron got along in the manner of King Kong and Fay Wray, George said, but Ron frowned and said not to say things like that and made a little rose of parsley and put it on Ruby's sandwich but not on George's. The fog stayed and Ruby stayed and as she read nothing and did nothing the long white evenings when she sat with them smiling and smiling it began to make George impatient and (in the very maw of his pride in his talent for beguiling *anyone*, even the weak-minded) he became too dashing, too jocular, with, Hi there, Ruby, when he came in or met her bulk on the stairs and, Hey there, Ruby. Some fog you brought with you, Ruby, he said until she drew back with some suspicion or memory of being put on (and she's been made fun of, Ron said, don't forget, and backward people can be very acute, my dear), so George was made to feel a failure with Ruby and also left out when Ron and Ruby sat for hours over the giant jigsaw Ron was doing and big Ruby would hold out a piece, a misfit, and Ron would pretend to try to fit it in and then say no but it was just the piece she'd need for later on, try to find another one, Ruby. Hi there, Ruby, George would say, and she would give him her frightened smile and edge a little closer to Ron and George would then make the pretense of going out to see if the fog was lifting and stand for a long time on the cliff not knowing in which direction he was looking.

Then at last they woke to a dazzling morning. "I'll drive Ruby home after breakfast," he said but Ron said, Not until evening, please, I need her today, I'm so behind in work, please. Ron had got an assignment to do six giant papier-mâché birds for Filene's in Boston and because of the fog had not been able to get up to the derelict house and she needed Ruby to fetch the heavy pails of water and help her to mix the paste and cart around the clumsy wire meshing she used for armatures.

So he had driven into town and sick of being cooped up for four days, lingered, bought groceries, had scrod at the café, found to his satisfaction he was popular, stopped in at the hardware and bought Ron flowerpots and a bright table-cloth, got the mail, lingered, which was unusual for him, leaning on a pier rail and watching the boats and assuaging his usual feeling of insufficiency, and drove slowly home over the long coast road that rose toward the cliffs with an immense view of the island.

It was twilight when he got back and there was no one in the house and looking up toward the derelict house he saw that she had lit a lamp in the upstairs room where she had the studio and when he'd pleaded with her never to do that again, an oil lamp knocked over in that sun-dried thirsty old saltbox would mean an inferno in minutes, and there she was upstairs in this dried hulk of a house with a child and a nice encouraging wind blowing in from the sea and huge clumsy Ruby and a ton or so of paper. "God damn," he said aloud and hit himself on the forehead, "what can you *do* with her!" Slammed out of the house, "because I married a child," he explained to himself and hurried down the path and saw that as well as that (ought not to leave her a whole day alone because, shit, you didn't know what you'd come home to) she or Ruby had left the door to the toolshed open which was *his* writing room and so very likely half his manuscript was blown on the floor. Then fire and violent death had been forgotten in a moment and he was staring down in a dull-witted way not able quite to comprehend, staring down at the kitchen table which was his desk and which was completely bare except for his old Royal typewriter and some odds and ends and envelopes and a postcard of Lake Como. Not absolutely certain yet, just beginning to feel sick, the probability creeping up his spine as though he were wading into very cold water, and then hunting in drawers, on the floor under piles of old maga-zines feeling his heart beating quicker and quicker and then running, panting up the cliff path in the darkening light to the derelict house and up the rotting banisterless stairs and in the dull lamplight a scene from Daumier, Ron very pasty arms and Ruby bending over the tin tub with paste and paper everywhere in the flickering light and the enormous all-but-finished ostrich gleaming stickily in papier-mâché beginning to dry with the sickly smell and his voice, just as sick, asked a question and, Are you mad, my dear, she said, are you mad? But in the dim light in the enormous mass of newspaper, old telephone books, paper towels all torn into strips to make ostrich feathers there were the bits and pieces of his manuscript, more and more as he frantically threw paper left and right and *ently Griselda was moving toward her own apoca* he read dumbly from his own typing and Ron was saying, Now do not panic, do not panic; paper was sticking to her pasty arms and her face was paste white and, Oh, Christ, oh, Christ, he said when she gulpingly said in a despairing voice, Here are some pages not torn, darling, oh, my dear, look, and she was holding out a gummy pathetic little wad of manuscript all stuck together and trying delicately to unstick it and saying, Don't panic, don't panic; YOU ARE AS STUPID AS HER, he got out in a shriek and blundered down the rotten stairs and outside and stood on the cliff looking out at the sea and his body felt as though it were falling, as though the cliff were giving way underneath him, and in the whitish dark she had followed him out of the house and was standing there apparently trying to say something; some rigmarole she was muttering like a nun saying a penance in a low toneless voice, it had to do with the fog and that her paper supplies had not come from the mainland and she had said to Ruby when it was getting dark to go over and get more paper, anything would do, there was paper in the toolshed. She had meant, she whispered, there were old magazines and never looked at what Ruby was tearing into strips. Then she had dropped onto her knees beside him and put her arms around his legs and she was saying about no matter how long it took, she would restore it to him somehow, she would type all day and night if he would just, and, Oh, don't, he said, don't, Ron, do you mind, just don't do anything, just get up, would you, and don't touch me, just don't touch me, he said because if she touched him again he would do something violent, if she tried to touch him he could go completely berserk and he could just as easily push her over the cliff. So she got up off her knees and stayed standing just behind him waiting and he just looked out over the sea and it seemed forever and then he said, Get *her* out of here, and had the feeling in the dark that she was struggling to resist him, turned on her and barked, Get that halfwit out of here, do you hear me? and she said in a throttled but bitter voice, I see, shoot the *horse*. Get her out of here, he shouted, there are too many children, he shouted, I can't take any more *children* around here, he yelled at her retreating silhouette going through the long salt grass toward the flickering lamplit empty house where Ruby's outline loomed in the glassless window watching for her and seeing her coming raised an arm in delight. . . .

It moved across like a big dark shadow moves across a screen and as it moved cliff and sea disappeared so George felt relief that he was not to review the rest of that night, the supper scene in the silence and her hardly able to say, Cake? Tea or coffee? I've got both made, and how she had gone upstairs like a wraith and he had heard the weeping and then how he had savagely forgiven her with a kind of rape. . . .

Much worse to him was watching him being a writer; a view of himself spread now, spread itself in the glass walls of the toolshed typing away with a fierce but attractive (he thought or must have thought at the time) look of desperately sincere concentration; he had even arranged a lock of hair to fall over one eye and he was typing away with the awful sincerity of youthful confidence as though he might be watched, young author in a glass greenhouse, he almost should have had a pipe clenched in his teeth; he was the conceptualized stereotype of a writer. He evidently had had no trouble with his novel, it seemed to be falling out of the typewriter by itself and building up in a pile on each side and there he was, George Wood, in this earlier state of innocence and the combination of innocence and confidence was endearing but troubling; to come across himself writing a book on a sunlit windy afternoon near the edge of a cliff and so absolutely sure, so bound to succeed beyond what he had thought then were his wildest dreams.

In the evenings he read aloud to Ron. She knitted and he read aloud what he had written that day; more often than not she was treated to it twice as he would say, Listen to it once more before you tell me what you think; she seemed to pay a great deal of rapt attention to it though she rarely looked up from her knitting and so he read on and on, page after page to her, with little bubbles forming at the corners of his mouth and his voice getting clotted with the excitement of his own words and then Ron would say, Wow, and, My God! and often she would think for a long time tapping her teeth with her knitting needle and scratching her ankle and then she would say she particularly liked such and such a bit. It sometimes seemed that the bits she liked best were the least important passages, descriptions of what people wore or how a room was arranged, and he felt vaguely disappointed that she never once praised the theme or action of his book, always the irrelevant. Oh, my dear, she said, the way you write about a peach I can taste it, my dear.

One evening he glanced up in the middle of a page, saw she was bent over and holding herself as if she'd had a sudden violent jab of pain. What's the matter? he said, and she leaned back in the canvas chair and in the gingery electric light, which happened to be working that night, her face looked drawn and yellow and she kept her eyes closed and finally she said in a very low voice, No, it's good, it's good. You think it's good? he said, delighted she was moved almost to pain, and she answered huskily with her eyes closed, Yes, it's good. Now I want to ask you something, she said another time and this was the shocker, unprepared for this; I want to ask you something, she said, but you don't *have* to tell me. What? Well, she said, has this book, has starting this book anything to do with the time you blew up at me over that poet? What poet? he asked and felt his flesh tingle because he knew damn well. John Citadel, she said and again he felt the tingle right up into his scalp because of course Ron knew nothing, it was the one thing he'd told her nothing about, and he stood up and said, Of course not, why would you associate the two things? and, I wish you'd forget about how stupid I was that night—it was the *beer;* but what it would have to do with my book I can't see; honestly you are a crazy bush baby. What *possible* connection could there be between *my book* and *Citadel?* he asked her.

He was very frightened by the perception of her connection.

George said, "Now how about the story of the piebald pussycat and the terribly tidy tinsmith?"

"Want Grinman," Jamie said.

"Want Green Man?"

"Want Grinman, Grinman," Jamie insisted, wriggling in George's lap; Jamie smelled of sun and washed flannel.

"Once upon a time right here in Chop Island, right outside that very window—"

"Grinman. Grinman," Jamie screamed, anticipating the glorious horror. Jamie was infatuated with monsters, Jamie relished stories about twilight and peril, and so George had created the Green Man. Green Man was extremely nasty; Green Man was made all of long raw string bean legs and arms and had a cabbage for a head and peas for eyes; Green Man was always lurking in the tall grass, in the salt bushes, and Green Man was a vegetarian who ate little boys.

"And it looks like a tree, it stands still like a tree, it *is* a tree, isn't it? But then just as tiny Jamie comes along the path tippy-toe in the green twi-light the tree moves just one teen-y green eye and then *allofasudden* snatches Jamie up *krrrupphhh* because it isn't a tree, it's dreadful, horrible Green Man!"

"Grinman *got* me. Grinman *got* me!" Jamie shrieked and hid in George's chest, gurgling with delicious fright and safety.

"You have a *flair*, my dear," Ron said, passing.

"What's that mean?"

"Just that with children you have a flair, my dear."

So he must have had a pair of brown and white saddle shoes all scuffed up because he had them on, neatly laced, and he had on old dungarees and a faded blue sweatshirt with BUTLEY on it. He turned around, finding himself at a loss, in the bedroom of the fake house with its continuous green-bottle light. He leaned on Ron's makeshift dressing table and looked in the mirror. Oh, my God.

He must now be about twenty-four. Oh, Christ.

That young man.

Heartbreaking. In the leprous blotches of the scarred mirror he saw this young man, this tender foolish young man; he saw the then much blonder hair combed and pomaded up into a pretentious pompadour and cut into a duck's tail at the back, intended to be, he supposed, cute; his dimple was too apparent, his cleft not yet advanced enough into his chin to make him look decisive; he had a melting, yearning look. Oh, Christ. His eyelashes were quite something; his mouth, fuller, tended to be sensual. He parted his lips and the young man presented him with teeth uncapped and undrilled as yet, perfect teeth. But the worst thing of all was the expression of assurance, bland confidence; the confident look was almost brutal.

Oh, God, what you don't know, you and your pompadour, what you don't know would fill a book, what you don't know, you poor dumb fink. Don't know what's ahead of you and perhaps worse, what is *not*. He put his fist to the mirror. If he could have smashed the reflection could he have made himself a different man? But this young man had been sincere, believing he was judicious, compassionate and kind and, God help him, with a mission. To love.

Oh, that sincere look. That young man was dangerous.

I know who you love, you bastard, he said to this glimpse of himself in passing, as they passed, he and himself going different ways

banging open the screen door, loping into the house, calling out to Ron that Jack Lavender was here, got a beer? Yelling, Come on down, I have a surprise for you, and Ron coming down with the baby in one arm and diapers. Oh, hello, Jack, how are you, my dear? She had not long had the baby. Guess what, he said, you can have the old house, I've arranged with Jack for you to have the old derelict house. She put the baby down and ran and jumped up on him, her legs around his waist, and kissing him and nothing, nothing in the world could give her more utter delight, she said. Well, it wasn't anything, really only property rights, the house wasn't worth anything, nobody had lived in it since Jack Lavender's grandmother died twenty years ago. She sat down and told Jack Lavender how they had made up stories about the people who had lived there, looking up at the glassless windows and crumbling chimneys and pieces of sky seen through the remains of Victorian ceilings and how she liked to think about people moving softly around with lamps and closing out winter twilights and calling children to suppers and gathered around a piano with old songs and in bed together and all taking place where now only wind and sea blew in and sea gulls nested.

Jack Lavender had rarely been off the island, Jack Lavender was brawny and balding and stained with sun and sea to permanent honey and he repaired and rented boats at the rotting marina; he smelled of tar and wiped his hands on a red cotton handkerchief and sat sipping his Schlitz, shy and tentative about being asked in, smiled a lot. It was nice to have a nice young couple around, Jack Lavender said, hardly anyone came over any more, let alone to live; you want those vines cut away? he asked. I would be glad to come over any time; they can slash your face real bad; how are your drains? he asked and looked at George a lot; smiled at George and finally with effort remarked that somebody had said young Mr. Wood was a writer. True? Well, George said, he was hoping to be, trying to be, and then Jack Lavender's secret came out. He read. He put it in the way a man among friends might admit to a secret vice. He *read.* The kind of reading Jack Lavender did, secretly at night, was not highly thought of on the island, too classy; he read Hardy, Jane Austen, George Eliot, had waded through the Waverley novels, the Brontës, even *Gorki,* he said, his blue eyes glittering (no wonder they had got the property for a song), and he thought that *De Profundis* was a pretty good piece of writing. He grew red with pleasure and the excitement of being able to admit this; that he couldn't get through Henry James, try as he might; but was it OK (he seemed to be asking them) to admire "Hiawatha"? He leaned toward them, sweating, his big hands trembling with joy at being able to unload all this, this big man who calked boats with his secret passion; had no one to share it with, had tried to interest his children but they cared for nothing but comic books. He would have another beer, he said, if he wasn't keeping them.

So George discoursed and seeing that he had been mistaken for a pundit, blossomed, became authoritarian, damned a host of good writers with faint praise; don't bother now with Wolfe, he advised Jack Lavender, and that he thought probably Hemingway would not make it to the end of the century. Jack Lavender was intoxicated but not by beer. He was following George's every move, walking here, walking there with burning eyes, and would have followed George outside and over the cliffs into the sea if that was where they could go on discussing books. It's extremely unwise, George told him, to go into Faulkner haphazardly. If only Jack Lavender had brought a pencil; he must try to remember all this wisdom and knowledge of literature, these pearls and rubies, and the effort of trying to screw them into his salty mind had made a deep furrow in his red pleasant face; he nodded obediently to everything George told him; it would be a sacred thing to him from now on that in Mr. Wood's opinion *Howards End* was superior to *A Passage to India*.

George had been sweating too. It was like having an unexpected spotlight turned on him; he should not and could not drink anything, even beer, and he was drunk with the attention being paid to him. To have a boatman who was ready to drop to his knees before him like Bernadette before the Vision just because he, George Wood, had once been to a lecture by and talked *to* Irwin Shaw. Jack Lavender breathed this in rapturously. Ahhhhh, Jack Lavender said, Ahhhhh. And is Irwin Shaw a writer?

Wait, George said in the delight of finding Jack Lavender had not heard of Salinger, I have to pee.

now whenever they saw him it would remind them of it, so he wouldn't be welcome for long book chats around the fire, not if he brought a dozen lobsters. All this was written plainly on Jack Lavender's wide simple face for George to read and George read it, surprised at how sensitive the slow-witted can be; it was true they had no cause to see Jack Lavender again; So come back soon, George said, *any* time, just give us a call and come on up; OK, thanks, thanks a million, Jack Lavender said and drove off back to his shrew wife and dullard children.

Why? Ron asked when he came back into the house. Why? He breathed softly through his teeth for a while on the razor's edge of indecision (to tell or not to tell), nearly succeeded and then failed. Well, he lied, a girl he knew, a girl he was sort of stuck on years ago and who had died, a girl named Clytie Bundock who died very tragically, she used to quote John Citadel all the time and now it made him sad. I see, Ron said. Ron washed and sliced cucumbers. I see, she said. (And that was that for the rest of their lives.) Do you want oil and vinegar or would you rather have a hollandaise if I make it specially; what would you like, my dear?

She had been his wife and he had not told her; he saw what he did next, he went and hid behind a magazine; and why had he not told her? Because he was afraid of pity (even from her) or of horror or both; terrified she might have pitied him.

Lied.

Missed the chance to be bigger. Like the acrobat misses the rope and plunges down. He was so stupidly young and prideful about his untouchability, he was constipated with stiff virtues and all pinned up with safety devices left over from childhood. One honest little admission to her now while she sliced cucumbers might have given their marriage an ounce of significance; he saw now it had never had any real significance any more than their house was a real house, only a lookout to spot submarines, empty inside.

It was as if Ron had now looked up and said to him, "If you had said *one* sincere thing, *one* truthful thing about yourself, it would have meant more love than *all* the caresses and lovemaking and bush baby crap and I wouldn't have minded my death so much if there had been *one* time you had truly loved me."

Oh, Ron, he said to himself now, but I *did* love you, I truly loved you, Ron. Well, at least I tried, I made the *effort* of loving you. She moved slowly across the screen of memory in closeup now, she was quiet and patient and amusing with him, resigned to everything he had been determined to do for her; what a load she had had to carry; she had pretended great peace of mind. He saw her patiently agreeing she was happy; yes, yes, I'm happy, she said in all the ways she could think of, growing nasturtiums on the windowsill, making bread, anything she could think of, yes, yes, don't worry, I'm happy thanks to you, my dear.

Then, after he had made such perfect arrangements when the baby was coming, she threw everything out of sync by having Jamie nearly three weeks early; awoke him at daybreak.

"But you couldn't be, it's still April."

"I think I am."

"Couldn't have been *that* far off, could we?"

Must have been. She couldn't be absolutely exact about dates, she said in a whisper, so better be got over to the mainland hospital. She looked pinched and scared. He rushed to the telephone to get Jim Lark at the airport. They hadn't prepared a bag for her and he behaved like a movie husband, tearing around and putting things in a suitcase while she took them out again, had the jeep engine running just in case, told her not to hurry, not to dilly-dally, not to be scared, they had oceans of time, but why the hell was she taking so long; went in and out of the house with his heart beating wildly, thanking God or someone that there was no fog because there were dark and shuddery stories about babies being born in the little Chop Island hospital; got her at last into the jeep surrounded by pillows and holding in her lap her pet little fern in a pot; nobody would remember to water it, she said, her pet fern, she said, and off they went in the early morning light with him driving as fast as he dared over the deep ruts and mounds and with the fierce blackberry and honeysuckle vines hitting at them, swaying wildly side to side, bumping all the way to the airport, and Jim Lark said, after they got her buckled into the plane holding her fern, he hoped George knew what to do if she started it in midflight because *he* didn't happen to have three hands.

But nobody needed to have worried about this possibility; she was eleven hours in labor.

"You have a nice little boy," the nurse said.

He was shown Jamie through the window.

Ron seemed to have shrunk or else they'd put her in an enormous bed.

Now at all costs he must do this bit well.

Leaned down and kissed her; she smelled of iodoform.

"Hello, sweet," he said, "how're you doing?"

"Groggy," she croaked.

"That's good, you'll have a nice long sleep now."

"What's the time?"

"Little after eleven."

"Eleven? At *night?*"

"Yes."

"Little monster took forever."

"I know."

"Did you see him?"

"Yes, just a peek."

"He's blond as hell."

"Yes."

"Ridiculous."

"Yes."

"Pretty cute though."

"Think he'll do," he said.

Then it came, plop, plop, he couldn't stop, great bloody blobs of tears on her, gushing out, had tried his best not to, had to muffle it in the pillow, shook and heaved and sobbed. "Oh, now, don't, don't," she said, "it's only you've had such a goddam long *wait*," she said, putting her weak little arms around him.

"Sorry," he said, gasping, snuffling, turning away to blow. "Just . . ."

"Just what?" she asked.

"Just . . . wish he was *mine*."

"So don't be upset, please don't be offended," he said.

"Oh, I'm not offended," his mother said.

The telephone was sweating as much as he was.

"Just a friend of mine and a friend of hers to be witnesses, so please don't be offended."

"Oh, I'm not offended," his mother said.

"We thought at first of having a church thing and then it all got too complicated because she's born a Catholic and I thought maybe you wouldn't care for the idea of me being married in a Cath—"

"Oh, *me*." His mother laughed. "Goodness, I don't have anything to do with it. Goodness, ha, ha, ha, what would it have to do with *me?*"

"Only, well, we'd like you to, you know, be pleased."

"Oh, goodness, it's nothing to do with *me*," his mother said.

"So in the end we thought anyway better just do it this way and have it over with, no fuss, so please do understand."

"Oh, I understand. Oh, I think you know I'd *die* rather than be anywhere I'd be making a nuisance."

"Oh, Jessica, you'd never be a *nuisance*."

"I'd rather anything, ha, ha, ha, than that," his mother said. "I'd rather stay a hermit than be pandered to, goodness *me*," she said.

"Well . . ."

downstairs to Ron's little basement apartment; it always smelled of old ferns too long in their pots; she had dozens hanging in the musty recess outside her front door, watered them with loving care, but their roots stank so, he held his breath waiting for her to buzz him in and once inside her apartment it smelled of papier-mâché paste, old carpet and lemons. She had switched on the outside light to see who was there and he came into the dimly lit basement and seemed to be lugging something heavy on this suffocating New York night, a mirror, a great Victorian dresser mirror. He had stolen it. Later they had it in their bedroom on Chop Island, after they had got married.

"I stole it for you off the set," he said.

"I love it even more," she said and gazed into the whorls of golden tarnished boils and outbreaks; it was like looking into the Venusberg grotto, she said.

He took it when they were striking the set tonight, George said, as an act of vengeance. He had just that night quit his job on the best show on television then, the "Showcase Theatre," which everyone once watched on Sunday nights; they did fragile little plays all about loneliness; now they were feeling the pinch of loneliness themselves, deserted by viewers. So Mr. Sweets, the producer, was being replaced and . . .

George went sputtering on about what they had done to him while Ron cooked him a cheese omelet. She had been having a big glass of red wine, it stood half full on the kitchen dresser next to an uncorked bottle; this was highly unusual for her, it should have prompted him perhaps to ask her was anything wrong, but he was too burning all over with his own rancor and hurt to take more than a fleeting glance at it, let alone think it had any significance. He sprawled in her big woolly armchair and boiled with his indignation while she brought him his omelet on a tray and tied a napkin around his neck because he was a known spiller and had on his fairly new blue seersucker suit; brought him his endive salad, spiced iced tea; she sat at his feet Odalisque-like while he repetitiously explained how Bob Sweets had been heave-ho'd and how he, George, who had been floor manager eighteen months, practically ran the show, had been passed over for promotion up to assistant director.

She said huskily when he allowed her a word in, "Television. What do you expect, reward?"

She let him go over it all again though she cared nothing about Mr. Sweets or the "Showcase" or any of it. She fetched her big glass of red wine and sipped it. She sat in the circle of yellow light from the one lamp and told George he had done right; there's no end to what you can do, my dear, out of that rut, she said. Anyone less totally concerned with himself that night might have realized by this time that she'd drunk a great deal of red wine and that all the time she listened she was frantically chipping the enamel off her nails, faster and faster as though she were furious about what they'd done to him. He finally ran down. Silence. She lifted her wineglass up to the light so that her face was suffused in glowing wine light. "I want to tell you something," she said. "I am pregnant."

In the five seconds it took for this to sink in, he thought about how they'd met.

With Dudley in the Old Heidelberg and she had . . .

Jarred, he felt the words sink in.

"Oh, God," he said, "and you let me run on and on about *myself.*"

About a year ago he had come into the Old Heidelberg for late dinner with one of the directors of the show and there under huge stags' heads sat Dudley Rivers, the English playwright, and about eleven people, and the director, who knew Dudley slightly and who was a climber, succeeded in getting them asked to the table. Dudley Rivers was pink-complexioned and a little like the younger Duke of Windsor; professionally sad. Dudley Rivers had had a big hit on Broadway about five years ago but it was rumored he was having trouble trying to follow it, a victim of the one-hit jinx, and he sat up till all hours picking up the tab for anyone who would keep him company till the bars closed and who would listen to his stories about Noel and Ivor and Vivien and Emlyn and Boo and Binky; on and on he went into the night while waiters sagged and yawned and his audience hooted and roared and sometimes became almost prostrate with laughter at his tales. Then there was this odd girl who did not laugh at the stories, merely smiled in a patient way, obviously had heard them all a dozen times. She was small and Indian-looking and she had on a strange unreliable string crochet dress that looked as though at any moment it might unravel. "And what do *you* do?" she asked him. "I'm floor manager on 'Showcase,'" he told her. Something very agreeable about her. She had pretty hands. She seemed to be suffering with a bad cold and it made everything she said seem as though she were confiding in him and, in her extreme frailness (her tiny bones showed through the crochet dress), as though she might surreptitiously be asking for his help. His one beer had gone to his head. "You are very nice," he said thickly, swelling up with the pleasure of telling her this. "There is something very—ummmmmmmmmm—nice about you."

Felt he would like to take this girl on his lap, cuddle and pet her; something fiercely caveman pulsed in him that he didn't know he had. Timid George Wood from New Forks, overeager and with sweaty palms, had a *drive*, was adult after all. Now, *now*, if Archer Hurst could only see him now (so he had been putting his arm around the girl and fantasizing that Archer had just come into the restaurant and seen them) that he was so bold he was about to caress this strange girl in front of all these people, why not?

"Ronald," he said, confused about her name at three in the morning, helping her get staggering Dudley Rivers into a wavering taxi which would not stand still for them so that George had to steady it by holding onto the taxi's roof, "Ronald, I hope to God we see each other again, are you in the book?"

So they phoned each other a lot; often Ron would call him late at night and they would talk until one or two in the morning; so they had movies together, sometimes dinner when she was free. She was very definite about her affair with Dudley; any plans she made were concomitant with sudden cancellation if Dudley wanted her. "Talk about good," she said, "now there is the *good* one, my dear." Once in a while, if Dudley permitted, she had George to the dinners she cooked for Dudley. Dudley drank and became sweet and then bitter, gave George tortured smiles, a dying lieutenant smile, told stories of the London theater and went so far as to read George's old play and say in a shattered way it wasn't bad. "You'll very likely make good, old dear, you have it in you."

"Praise from Caesar, my dear," Ron said and kissed Dudley, then seeing Dudley's unhappiness, steered the talk away from writing. Sometimes the three of them played the Ouija board but once it had become possessed and sped around spelling MARRIED over and over and then DEATH. Oh, what do *you* know, she said, and put it away. Long late summer dinners in her little yard, movies and walks together. Once when they were standing in the garden of the Museum of Modern Art looking down at the fallen Maillol woman, she said, "I never told anyone this but I hated my parents, both of them, and I'm *glad* they're dead; I never told anyone that but you, George." He was choking with importance, and could only squeeze her, and so it was that he gradually felt himself to be in love and not with the disastrous destructive elements of love he had experienced in his late teens, not those fires, thank God, not *that* kind again, but in love, and the persistence of it throbbed in him like a tune. Outwardly she treated him like a sister. He grew heavy with pining for her, had all the sweet painful symptoms, slept badly, was miffed if she didn't phone exactly when she'd said she would, sulked if she decided it wasn't his business where she'd been the last couple of days; often he behaved like an opera diva. He began to think deliciously of Dudley run over suddenly by a Mack truck, Dudley deported for contributing to the delinquency of a minor; convinced that it only needed the right circumstances, a change in the structure of their emotional lives, to make her turn to *him*, awaken to *him*. He began willing something to happen; his willpower had always been strong; ever since childhood he had willed things to happen by strong concentration in a mirror so he stood at the bathroom mirror and stared into his own pupils until the penumbra around his head was grape-colored against orange and he felt slightly dazed and willed over and over that she was to be his, be his, be his. The following Tuesday she found she'd lost her keys at two in the morning outside her door and nothing could awaken her landlord so she had to accept, had to come back to his walkup with him; he was shivering with excitement and elation. He went through the elaborate pretense of making up the sofa for himself and then tried to get into the bed with her but she pulled the blankets up around her and looked at him like a cornered animal with pleading eyes and said, "Oh, but there's *only* Dudley, don't you see? Oh, there's only *only* Dudley, George."

Always protective of Dudley, Dudley's things, Dudley's moods (and one day almost twenty years from now he would take a girl away from Dudley; it would be poetic justice), sacrosanct Dudley, the pink-skinned blue-eyed sensitive egomaniac. And now *she* needed help, so why shouldn't Prince Dudley be told she was pregnant?

"Because it's an impossible situation," she said.

"Would you like *me* to tell him?"

She stared for some time into the depths of her wineglass. "If you did that, George, it would be the finish of you and me," she said and had a face of stone.

"Even if he *didn't* have his dreary wife in England," she said.

"*His* fault, *his* child."

"Shut up, George."

"Are you sure?"

"Oh, yes, I'm sure all right."

"Well, then, what about it?"

"I don't know."

"Well, then, what about a doctor?"

"What *about* a doctor?"

"Do you know of one?"

"I want to have it."

"Why? Because of the Church?"

"No, because of me."

"Oh, Ron, I don't know—"

"I do."

"I see."

"I'm going to have it. I'm going away to Sacramento, California, and have it."

"Who's there?"

"Someone I trust."

"You don't trust *me?*"

"Trust you with all my heart, my dear, confiding in you's *why* I trust you to never say a word about it to Dudley as long—"

"Will you marry me, Ron?"

She snapped the stem of her wineglass and blood and wine ran over her hand; busy looking for glass splinters in her fingers at the sink, he had never seen how she looked; it had been the ultimate moment of his life up to this point, it was the apogee of gallantry, it was Jamesian with stiff-necked honor; he could scarcely unstick the Band-Aid, he was shaking so with emotion; he had three thousand dollars from a distant (he paused) relative; he thought they might get a little house on down payment; some out-of-the-way place where he could write his novel; he could already visualize them in some down-payment cottage on a hill or by the sea, him, her and her baby; he could have got down and kissed her feet in gratitude; he was Lochinvar, he felt himself to be shining with light.

Had he only seen her face then; but he had never looked up so how could he have known what a peculiar thing was on her face; a stricken thing. "Bathroom—scusi," she said and went into the bathroom for a long time and he stood there surrounded by all her papier-mâché masks and animals and he was exultant; astonished at the success of his sorcery, for here was the ultimate of situations coming around to his advantage. He could scarcely breathe.

When she came back she had taken hold of herself, she had taken herself back, as it were; she had had her weep and was over it, she was calm and her voice contained no hint of whatever she had been feeling that had made her push at him and rush from him in such a way, so how could he ever have known that it was just as if he had lifted an iron from the stove and scorched her.

But he had not remembered her voice being so very cool and determined; why, she sounded like a schoolteacher bidding a pupil good-bye forever; "I love you, my dear," she said, "for that. I love you for that, my love."

I can't be doing with gallantry, she said. I can't be doing with obligations. I'm not the girl for that, she said. I'm not able to cope with generosity like that, generosity like that is out of all proportion and the terrible thing is I know you mean it. I just couldn't, she said. I just couldn't begin to. It would *kill* me, she said.

"Oh, but, George," she said and kissed him on the mouth, "I will so love you for that for the rest of my life. . . ."

part three

it was like

turning a corner and coming face to face with yourself and being both shocked and enchanted, the heart melting at the comicality of it, the piteous sincerity of yourself, your faith in the shapes and substances of your world, your ox-blood Thom McAn shoes with the extra-large welts, your blue serge suit, your white handkerchief worn square as an envelope, the look in your eye, your wariness, the alarm of your youth.

And Rodman's in Butley sent the wrong cake and had closed before anybody discovered it. *Happy Birthday Enid* it said in whorls of pink icing. Well, his mother said, maybe it'll give everyone a laugh. Said it as though, with her talent for the mordant, laughs might very well be badly needed, as though, because they both knew that circumstances frequently contrived against him, this party was going to be a death's feast from the start. The table for twenty-one guests was decorated with dusty paper roses and the little ballroom of the Butley Arms Inn hung with balloons and yellow paper lanterns. But the stiff Austrian chairs arranged themselves around the wall with hostility; the leader of the little jazz combo had a port wine birthmark across one whole side of his face and made it clear they came up from Danbury and didn't play a note more after midnight. George was twenty-one today.

He stood in the hall of the Butley Arms Inn to greet his guests. He wore his new wristwatch, Jessica's gift, a repulsive steel watch which might have been designed for a submarine commander, with a steel band that bit into his wrist. She had seemed to be ashamed to even mention the event, laid the wristwatch on his breakfast plate and said, "So this is the day, is it?" "Oh, thanks, thanks, that is absolutely great, just right," he said, and she gave her vinegary titter and said, "Oh, well, ha ha, just tried to get you something useful," and they then attempted the motions of kissing, their mouths chomped the air and they turned away in opposite directions both thinking the same thing. She had arranged the mandatory celebration of coming of age; the mandatory joyless celebration which must be got over, the last of the matriarchal obligations. They both felt it was going to be a deception at best and when they saw the two frumpy waitresses putting a dish of stale faded-looking salad at each place their predictions had been confirmed. Jessica stood with him in the hall to receive his guests; she wore a brown lace dress and carried a fan and gave her little deprecating smile. Happy birthday, George, the girls said and kissed his cheek and, Hey there, George, the boys said and pinched or punched him; they were so young, these forgotten people gradually lost touch with long ago, those pretty girls with their then fashionable short hairdos and bell-shaped dresses and he standing in the place of honor shaking hands and saying something pleasant to each one in turn, Hazel, Dicky, June, Deedee, all vanished away now, never heard from again. And Ruth Carver (why had *she* been asked? She'd been given that old one about her invitation going astray in the mail when Judy Coker had had to drop out at the last minute), who gave him a beautiful glass paperweight with pale green coral inside it, the most opulent gift. "Gosh, that's fantastic, Ruth, gosh, how nice of you." Ruth looked at him in that cool way of hers (she knew she was a last-minute ring-in) and said, "I hope it'll bring you good luck and deserved fame and fortune." Ruth was capable of saying things like that with a straight face, she was as solemn as a bishop. Now he was stuck with her for the first dance and led her onto the floor and stepped on her with his wide-welt shoes and they had no conversation. The combo played things from *Finian's Rainbow*. His guests danced mechanically. A sense of duty seemed to be weighing them down. There was no feeling of revelry, only the fact that everyone has to get to be twenty-one and everyone has to help celebrate it, like it or not. People burst out laughing at nothing whatever, the girls flashed extravagant smiles, the boys were roguish. Around and around they dutifully danced; the ones having the least good time hummed as they danced. The punch was very weak and looked and tasted like pink mouthwash and everyone praised it and toasted George whenever they caught his eye. The two frowzy waitresses handed around trays of canapés so damp they might have been brought up from a sunken schooner; sodden cheese expiring on clammy crackers and greenish stuffed eggs: few people dared take one. Up and off and around they danced again, their faces stretched into strenuous smiles, some holding each other in attitudes of great carnal desire to camouflage their lassitude. Then in one of the breaks between dances someone asked him to do his party thing, his imitation of Richard Widmark as the psychopath killer reciting "The quality of mercy"; he should have protested it was not the kind of thing to do cold in a ballroom; of *course* it went badly, hardly anyone laughed, just tittered, and of *course* who would walk in while he was thus making an ass of himself but Archer; after their bitter parting, after nearly two years of silence between them, Archer *would* pick this moment to stroll in accompanied by some strange haughty girl.

"Hello, chump," Archer said. "How are you, dummy?"

But of *course* Archer had been invited, his mother said. A surprise. Archer brought out a rare quality of mother in Jessica. She smiled at him fondly and pressed his arm. To anyone else Jessica would have had something fairly cutting to say about the way he came dressed for a party (slacks and not even a jacket, a blue cashmere cardigan and loafers, all probably calculated to show his indifference, managing to make the other boys in their blue suits look merely slick while, in his relaxed clothes, he was the most graceful thing in the room and at the same time managed to imply he was here very slightly against his will), but Jessica contentedly pressed his arm. All the time the unintroduced girl stood nearby protecting herself with a haughty look as though she couldn't care less. Archer put his hands on George's shoulders and drew him into a chesty, stony, unloving embrace so George knew the gulf was still between them, the dark wounds were still there.

"Chump," Archer said.

They were, they both knew it, contemplating the division between them. If only they could speak to each other.

"Did you drive up from New York?"

Archer nodded pleasantly. Even then, before his fame, he had the royal graciousness thing down pat.

"This is Alice," Archer said, airily defining the stern, composed but good-looking girl who had been standing there waiting to be introduced. She came forward and shook hands with them briskly as if she were afraid she might

pick up germs; she had a haughty peacock kind of walk
and a long arched neck which gave her an air of persistent
disdain; she stood in the pose models assume, with one
foot forward, her weight on the other and feet turned
outward in elegant brocade pointed shoes. "She is a wry
girl," Archer said or perhaps Archer meant "She is a Rye
girl"; it wasn't the kind of thing you bothered to clarify.
George merely smiled at her and Alice gave him back a
stony look with just a hint of the scornfulness he was to
know over the years; interesting now to see them meeting
for the first time, him and Alice. Riggs? "Did you say
Riggs?" he asked.

"Gibbs," she said.

"May I?"

"Oh, well . . ." Alice said and let him put his arm around
her, for it seemed only polite to ask her to dance. The band
played "Laura" and this then was the start of a lifetime
of mutual dislike.

"This is only a local band, ha ha, as you can probably
tell."

Alice Gibbs said nothing, let him turn her around this
and that way and all the time giving him the stony peacock
stare as much as to say, So *you* are the best friend; what's a
little crumb like *you* doing being Archer Hurst's best friend?

"This is so great," George had said, to be nice, "you
coming."

"*Me* coming?"

"Archer and you."

"I just happen to be along, that's all."

"Well, nice, Alice, of you."

"What?"

"To be along."

Arched neck suggesting a cormorant, asking, Why is it
nice?

"Glad you could come."

"Oh, I never know where I'm going. *I* don't know where I am. I don't know anybody here."

"You're in the Butley Arms Inn at my twenty-first birthday party."

"Oh, am I? Happy birthday."

"Thanks. Have you known him long?"

"Some time."

"I thought I was seeing things, I thought they must have put something in the punch besides Madeira."

"I beg your pardon?"

"When you both walked in. You and Archer."

"Oh?"

"Did he tell you anything?"

"What about?"

"About the *surprise?*"

"No, I don't know what surprise you're talking about."

"Well, you see, my mother didn't tell me he was coming. Didn't he tell *you* either?"

"Tell me what?"

"That you were coming here?"

"No, we were just driving along," she said. "I *supposed* to dinner somewhere in Connecticut."

"Oho, that's like Archer exactly. But nice of him to make the whole thing a surprise. You see, we haven't seen each other for nearly two years, did he tell you?"

"No."

"Oh, I thought maybe he'd of told you. Didn't he mention that we'd had a kind of falling out?"

"He didn't mention anything."

"Well, he's— *Sorry, sorry,* did I step on you?"

"OK."

"Well, he's—he's like that, he can be very private about things and I like that, don't you? Not even to mention to you about we'd had a falling out. Good old Arch."

"No."

"What did he tell you about me?"

"You have to excuse me but I don't know who you are."

"You—oh, for God's sake—I thought—oh, how crazy, oh, that's just the craziest thing, Alice, you must think I am completely utterly bonkers going on and on like that. Oh, that's too much. Do forgive me, Alice. I'm George."

"Well, how do you do?"

"I'm *George*."

"Ummmm?"

"George *Wood*. I'm *George*."

"Should that mean something? Am I supposed to *know* you?"

"Only that—I'm his best friend, that's all. He never mentioned me? Once? Ever?"

He and Alice Gibbs circling at arms' length to the music of Lennie Onnix and the Danbury Dukes playing "Zip-a-dee-do-dah" and she had never heard of him, the best friend, and he despised her right off, in her expensive brocade velvet Jacques Fath with her brocade shoes very pointed like the look she gave, her arched neck and the look she gave you which Archer later called Alice's terrible white scorn, said you could use it with a magnifying glass to start fire. And in not so many years she would be calling in the dead of night to say, George, this is Alice, I'm locked upstairs in the guest room because he is smashed and he has a loaded gun; for God's sake help me, George, call him and keep him on the phone as long as you can while I get out the back door. Alice, who would call in the middle of the night and say, George, did I wake you, he's been gone for four days and I don't know what to do, should I call the police, George, what should I do? George, I am frantic, can you find him? Sometimes crying; later in a bone-dry voice she would say she wished he was dead.

"*Oh, Zip-a-dee-do-dah*," he now sang at Alice so as not to speak to her.

"What a strange girl," he said to Archer when she went to the ladies' room looking to neither right nor left.

"Who, Alice? She's going for her masters in physics."

"*Int'*resting girl. Still waters."

Archer fixed George's tie.

"We're gonna be married."

"You are! Arch!"

"Yes."

"Arch."

"Yes, sir."

"Well. God. Great."

Like pain, like a small headache beginning between the eyes. George, his mother was saying, will you bring in your guests to supper now. Oh, the girl was rich and good family: it was stamped all over her; Archer the snob. Well, nothing good would come of it and the girl really ought to be warned what she was getting into, marrying an actor who was so lazy he never even got through Yale Drama School and was guaranteed not to make it. I would not bet a cent on Archer's future in the theater, George thought.

In front of each guest lay a quivering aspic that looked like poisonous jellyfish. At last came the cake with the wrong name, candles burning, and now he must stand up and act helpless with laughter. Oh, hi, Enid, one of the guys said. Blow out your candles, Enid, and so good night, said Donna Chamberlain, who was considered by some a wit.

Yes, Alice Gibbs really ought to be warned what she was getting into. For instance that Archer Hurst had probably laid every girl at this table at one time or another with the obvious exception of Ruth Carver, who nobody had laid and probably nobody ever would unless she jollied herself up a bit (she hadn't even laughed when they brought in the wrong birthday cake, just bit her lip and pulled a kind of sorry, what-a-shame look about it; boring girl she was), and that Archer would continue to lay every girl in sight who was willing and most were. Alice Gibbs really ought to be taken aside and warned; master of physics she might be but bright she was not if she hadn't yet discerned it was her money and family—for of course she was one of the *Rye* Gibbses and her older sister was married to a Topping— that was the honeypot that was attracting Archer, not herself. As he had warned Clytie Bundock, George thought, and at that moment Archer must have caught the thought.

"Now, ladies and gentlemen," Archer said, very tall, very graceful at the end of the table, tapping his wineglass with a spoon for silence. "Now, ladies and gentlemen, we're here tonight to drink a toast to George and it seems only appropriate to say a word or two on the great occasion of his coming of age, so I've elected myself to say a few words about him because . . ."

So this was going to be Archer's gift to him, this was why Archer had shown up.

". . . longer than anyone else and I would certainly boast I know him better than anyone else and . . ."

It was going to be Archer's way of getting back at him.

". . . among other things, the finest chum a guy could have. . . ."

So this was it; this was going to be for pure spite. Nobody else there would know that the speech, garlanded with pat compliments, was nothing but withering sarcasm. Indeed the faces turned up to Archer wore the vapid smiles put on for such eulogies; nobody but George knew the glass Archer held up for a toast held pure vinegar.

"A guy who will go to *any* lengths in the name of friendship and I *mean* it."

A truly fine fella, a great guy, I mean it, I want to say

humbly and sincerely, old George, old chump, it is my very very singular honor not only to be your friend, your best pal, but also to be able to be here tonight to raise a . . .

Ah, don't, Arch, he said silently, closing his eyes to the anger of Archer, don't, please. Unfair, unfair. Or at least not *entirely* fair, no matter what I did to you, Arch

"Hello? Is that Mrs. Mendoza?"

"Yes."

"Could I speak to Mr. Hurst, please?"

"I don't think he came back yet."

"Could you maybe just see?"

"Who is this?"

"This is George Wood."

"I don't think he came back since you phoned last."

"Could you just see?"

"Your message is still here from the time you called before and he hasn't picked it up, that's how I know he hasn't been back since the time you called last time. I'll give him the message when he comes in."

"Well, I wonder would you be so kind as to just maybe make quite sure he didn't come back and is in his room. I'm sorry to bother you, Mrs. Mendoza, but it's kind of important."

"Welllll . . ."

"I would be *so* gra—"

"—not a hotel, you know, where they have the staff to run up and down stairs with messages all the time."

"I realize that, Mrs. Mendoza."

"I'm not supposed to do anything but leave a message. I've got more to do than be a servant to Mr. Hurst."

"Oh, I just meant would you just call up the stairs maybe."

"Hold on a minute."

Tock, tock, tock, the solemn grandfather clock in Mrs.

Mendoza's hall, and nothing but tock, tock for as long as three or four minutes, it seemed, then suddenly, thank God, Archer's voice.

"Yes?"

"It's me."

"Yes."

"Archer, please don't hang up for a minute, please do me the favor of listening to me for a minute, will you?"

Breathing.

"Because I don't know what the hell is the matter, I don't know what the hell is going on, Archer, I mean it's obvious that you are very very upset but . . ."

No sound.

"Hello? Hello? Archer?"

"Yes."

"I thought maybe we'd been disconnected."

Breathing.

"So what I mean is I think I'm entitled to some explanation, am I not?"

"I think you know."

"Well, I don't, Archer."

"Oh, I think you do, buddy."

"I really don't."

"Oh, well, you give it a twist or two around in your mind and I think you'll come up with it."

"Something I've *done?*"

Tock, tock, tock.

"Archer? Is it something I've done?"

"Yes."

"What?"

Breathing.

"What? I swear to God I haven't got a clue so how can I be expected to—to make amends for something when I don't even know what it is? Well? Are you still there?"

"Yes."

"Well?"

Breathing.

"Aren't you going to tell me?"

"No."

"Why *not?*"

"Because you damn well know."

"Oh, God, oh, Jesus, I—how can I make you believe me that I am just about going out of my mind and have been for days wondering what the hell you are giving me this treatment *for?* Is it—has it anything to do with Clytie?"

"Yes."

"What, then?"

"What you told her."

"What?"

"You know."

Tock, tock, tock.

"Did she tell you what I said?"

"No, Rosemary did."

"*Rosemary.* Rosemary told you that Clytie told *her?*"

"Yes."

"I see. What did she say exactly?"

"What you told Clytie."

"Was she upset? Was Rosemary upset?"

"Yes. Very."

"Well . . . what did she say?"

"Just a minute . . . *Idaboggadobbadob* . . ."

"What?"

Archer had put his hand over the phone and was talking to someone. So that was it. He had been afraid that might be it. Sick now with fright. Found out. "George?" his mother called. "I'm on the phone," he called in a squeaky voice. Waited. But what had been the harm? He had not meant any harm and Archer must believe that. Surely Archer couldn't believe there could be any connection with what had happened?

Waited.

"Hello?"

"Archer, listen, I want you to believe—"

"Look, somebody wants the phone so—"

"Are you free tonight?"

"No."

"Tomorrow?"

"Tomorrow I'm going back to New Haven."

"I must talk to you even if it's only for five minutes. I absolutely have got to see you, Archer."

"I don't have the time. I told you I'm going up to Yale tomorrow and anyway what's the point? What is the point?"

"What is the *point*? The point is all this misunderstanding between us and whatever you're thinking, Archer, all of which is just—I mean—we have to *talk* about it."

"Oh, why bother?"

"What do you mean? Do you mean you can't or you won't? Are you telling me you won't give me the chance to explain?"

Long, very bored sigh into the receiver. "What's the point? I mean the harm's been done, hasn't it?"

"Archer . . . but, wait a *min*ute, Archer . . ."

"As I said, the harm's been done so I don't see any point in talking about it. I guess that's all I have to say."

Click. Dial tone.

So then, swallowing all pride, at the double to Mrs. Mendoza's rooming house, knowing that this is what he should have done in the first place instead of wasting nearly three valuable days leaving phone messages and then giving Archer the opportunity of hanging up. Found out. Oh, crap, whoever would have thought Clytie would have told Rosemary? But he had meant no harm.

Outside Mrs. Mendoza's big Dutch house he lost his

nerve. Suppose Archer refused to open his door? And that damn nuisance old Miss Wales had the room across the hall and always left her door open and was always saying things like, Oh, hello, you here again? My, you *are* a constant visitor, aren't you? To be refused admission in front of Miss Wales would be the last straw. Archer's car was parked under one of the giant elms so he could not yet have gone out and the better way, George figured, would be to hang around until he came out and then say, Look, you can give me just five minutes, can't you? That's all I'm asking, just five minutes.

Archer stayed stubbornly inside. Once he walked around the side of the house and looked up and saw that Archer's light was on and the shade pulled halfway down. He leaned against a tree and waited. Perhaps there might be something affecting in being found long-waiting under an elm. What are you doing *there?* Archer would say. Why didn't you come *in*, dummy? Oh, I knew you'd come out eventually. I only want you to give me five minutes, that's all, just five minutes. Archer couldn't refuse him that. All he needed was just five minutes to explain the whole damned unfortunate thing honestly. It was the dishonesty, the going behind Archer's back that had so infuriated Archer, the breaking of deep dark confidences that should never have been broken.

So all George needed to be was honest and humble.

Then Archer came suddenly out the front door with a girl; they were in evening dress and they walked rapidly down the path toward the car and George could only lob out dumbly from the shadows of the hydrangeas.

"Hello there," he said. Thrown now, heart beating, mouth dry.

"Hello," Archer said.

Archer's look was steely. He had never seen Archer in a

cold rage before. Typically it functioned to Archer's benefit; he was really majestic-looking in cold rage.

So, "This is Miss Atkinson," Archer said majestically. "George Wood, Doony Atkinson."

"Dyoudo."

"Hello."

Now what?

"Well, we're on our way to New York for the night," Archer said.

George said, "I wonder could I speak to you for a second," and when Archer didn't move said, "privately just for a second." When they were just out of earshot of Miss Atkinson George said, "Archer, I can never tell you how sorry I am. I truly am. But truly, Archer, I had no idea it would make you so angry, Archer. Truly. I never for a second meant to make mischief if that's what you're thinking. It was just that Clytie was a close friend of mine *too* and we were very close and I know I should not have told her but knowing about you and her I thought you wouldn't mind me taking her into my confidence and I see now I should not have *presumed* that and I am sincerely sorry, Archer. I sincerely am. Truly sorry."

"What *about* me and her?" Archer said, cold as a duke.

"Clytie and you." George's mouth was very dry now.

"I know that's who you mean but what do you mean you *knew* about me and her?"

"I mean I know—I knew about you and her."

"What about me and her?"

"Well, you and her, that's all."

"What about me and her?"

"That's all."

"What *about* it?"

"Your association."

"And what do you know about it?"

"I know you were—"

"I'll tell you what you know about it, friend—nothing. I'll tell you exactly what you know about Clytie and me, old pal—nothing. You know exactly fuck all of what went on between me and her so you are simply assuming."

"I didn't mean to."

"And with your fertile imagination and with your dirty mind it couldn't be anything else but sex because you can't get your mind up above that. How do you know what it was between Clytie and me? How dare you assume anything about it? How dare you assume anything about my private affairs? What have my private affairs got to do with you?"

"Nothing, of course."

"How dare you interfere in them? Because that's exactly what you did, George. And made mischief."

"I never never had any intention—"

"And I am about to tell you it was like your goddam nerve, you miserable little bastard."

"Now listen, listen, Archer—"

"And I hope you're satisfied with the harm you did."

Archer went toward his car.

"Archer, I am *sorry*. What more can I say?"

"Yes, well, it's a pity you can't tell *her* that."

Archer got in and started the car.

"Archer, be fair . . . I couldn't help her—"

The car zoomed off.

"—dying, could I?"

So now you were arriving in what you remembered as green times, which had been carefully edited so they had seemed all to take place in a steady hard sunlight. Things were secure then, everything promised good; at nineteen you were over the worst, all the worst had happened in your childhood and was behind you; your face in the magnifying shaving mirror reflected calmly serene eyes, no stress, no lines, all blown out with good sleep in the morning and youth, happy, loved, grown up and over the worst, master of your own destiny, pick from any number of gaudy ties, vain about putting Brylcreem on your hair, smell good of Russian Leather someone gave you and this the green times, the always sunlit times when everyone said, Here's George at last, George is here, and always greeted you with gesticulations, impatient for you to join them, and we'll do this and that, George, what do you think?

There had seemed to be much embracing then, all remembered in sunlight, speckled light under trees at picnics, Sit beside *me*, George, No, I asked him first. All in sunlight, in boats on the river that summer, and back and forth in cars and very little time between getting home and going out again, his abandoned mother saying, I made a pot roast big enough for three but I guess I'll have to eat it myself, oh, never mind, I enjoy eating alone, it gives me a chance to catch up on the New Forks *Gazette* with its thrilling news. Got to *be* somewhere, late *now*, you said, pulling on yellow or blue or green sweater and careful not to disarrange your hair; all in sunlight this was, in a place where it never rained and the only problem likely was the Ideal Cleaners sent your pants back with a double crease. This was when things sang around you, you and Archer and the others, all day and every day and people were always embracing, there was a great deal of touching and fondling and they were all at the moment crushed into a booth at the Candy Kitchen in Butley, some of the kids from the Holly and Ivy Players. This their hangout, he was remembering, the walls lighting up, the sound of the school carillon in the dusk, this was the good old Candy Kitchen and here he was crushed in a booth with them, in the middle, all knees crushing together, and they would be fearfully serious and discussing was

Strindberg relevant any more, had Strindberg ever *been* relevant or just a flash in the pan like Odets had worked out to be, *imagine* the older generation taking *Golden Boy* seriously, and lighting up, lighting up, smells and sounds, charming restaurant of the past, George was combing his hair at the table actually, Judy Bickers had one arm around his shoulder, her peasant blouse was alarmingly low, and with her other hand she was dipping into a bowl of pretzels and the tablecloth was surprisingly spotty and someone said to him, Do you know that sharp turn where Forest Road comes into Randolph Drive? That's where it happened, someone said, in the rain last night, and, Who gets the fries? the waitress interjected, big grubby waitress, stains under the armpits, who gets the mashed? Unattractive greasy café, neon lighting, bile green wallpaper. Ketchup? George was studying the fly-specked menu. Your usual? the grubby waitress asked him. I'm going crazy tonight, she told him, with Eileen off sick; you be better off with the peas, I took a look at the squash. What a crazy dowdy dated crew they now seemed, he as dated as anybody in that diamond-pattern sweater; Judy Bickers' lipstick turned eggplant color in the neon, Hazel Bruce had had white eyelashes long ago when they all sat in the Candy Kitchen this night when the carillon played and misery hung over them, not the remembered crystal clear grief they'd been supposed to feel in his mind all these years, the honor of grief, the clean grief they'd all felt at their first death outside of families, heroic grief associated in George's mind with organ music and great vaulted churches and archbishops and a massed choir singing "A Mighty Fortress Is Our God," holy, washed clean, kneeling for Clytie and feeling the sanctifying of the spirit so her death was purifying for them all; misery hung over them like a smell of gas leaking yet it never seemed to affect their appetites; they dug voraciously into their gristly steak sandwiches and their greasy french fries, asked for A.1. Sauce; and poor Rosemary, seeing it happen, they said between bites, poor Rosemary is practically in shock, can you reach the mustard? They were not being irreverent or callous, George saw now, these young people, they were beginning to find out death makes no difference, the news to them was that death makes very little outward difference; you still have to eat somewhere, go to bed and get up, decide what you'll wear, answer the phone; her glasses were wet with the rain so she was dazzled by the headlights; but Rosemary said she had had time to run back and just stood there, had time to jump out of the way but she just stood there; oh, but Rosemary loves to think the worst, it's just like Rosemary to suggest there was more to it, she is a double-dyed neurotic; where were they, at the movies? Yes, the thing was they'd missed the last bus to New Forks because it was a long movie so they were walking home and you know that sharp turn where Forest Road comes into Randolph—so it was only by chance, it only takes a little thing like that. Poor Clytie. They glanced at each other in mutual horror and asked was there peach pie on, was there walnut cake? Anyone seeing after Rosemary? Yes, well, Archer was, Archer went right over the minute he heard and is taking charge of everything. No, I can't eat anything, George found he had said, I'll just have coffee. I feel a bit faint, George said. Great *God, imagine,* I'm trying to imagine it and I can't take it in, I can't believe it.

"Years and years ago there was a huge old carp in it," Clytie said. "He was supposed to be a hundred years old and was so tame he would come up to the edge and let you feed him crumbs or so they say."

He and Clytie appeared, walking around the water lily pond near the Allerton Library building on the Butley School grounds, so he must have arranged to meet her there or maybe had run into her, as she worked part time at the library. He was walking a step behind her. "And when he died they found a golden ring on the edge of the pond or so the tale goes," she said. What was she like exactly? He couldn't put her face together but her voice came back to him now. It was a very musical voice; it reverberated around certain words like organ music in a vault. "A golden ring," Clytie said. "They thought he must have spat it out." The carp story was his and he had told it to Archer and Archer must have told it to her and now she was telling it to him and it was slightly annoying to be told your own story back.

Clytie led the way up the steps to the chapel. For a plain girl Clytie had nice legs and ankles.

"The story was," George said, "as I understand it, the ring had initials inside it and had been supposed to have been lost by some dean's wife in the pond in eighteen something so that was how they knew the carp was that old. They called the carp Horatio," he added so that she would know it had been his story she was telling around. Clytie's neat legs went up the steps ahead of him, her pleated skirt swung attractively and she had a neat bottom too and nice waist with a black velvet belt.

"Well," Clytie said, "it was probably too late for the dean's wife but I believe it, don't you? Everything's possible. Now I want you to turn and look back, George."

Then Clytie had turned and now he remembered what she had looked like. "I'm fond of this view," she said. "Someone says it is like an illustration in *A Shropshire Lad* and I agree, I agree."

She had had a thin wedge-shaped face with a long swooping Modigliani neck and thick glossy hair she plaited severely into spinsterish buns and she wore thick-lensed glasses which enlarged her already big eyes into a gaze of terror. It was unfortunate for Clytie that she began so promisingly around the ankles and then tapered off upward into a librarian.

"I'm fond of it," Clytie said. "There's not too much of it, you see, not too much of it."

On the surface she seemed as pristine and unvarnished as her nails; one thought of her spotless, ringless hands holding books, not other hands. One thought of her bare feet only in relation to pedicures. One thought of her body as nonexistent, or one thought of her body only as a means of outlining her severe spirit and her hard unalterable ethics. She belonged to the Emily Dickinson Society, the Butley Chamber Music Club, the Holly and Ivy Players; she was said to be esoterically gifted. Clytie Bundock, Professor Passmore said, is the only girl I ever knew who can whistle Boccherini. She went around with other severe-looking virgins like herself; even her name had a spinsterish sound to it. One was reminded of vellum around her. And now she had been violated.

It was hard to imagine, impossible to imagine, looking at her breasts safely enclosed under buttons and latched by a tortoise shell brooch. Yet Archer had apparently undone those buttons and loosened that plaited hair, had presumably struggled with and opened those portcullis legs.

Otherwise there couldn't have been this subtle change in Clytie that everyone had noticed and commented on, not always charitably; she was boiling inside with something she'd never known before, boiling away inside with some colossal emotion and elation which was pressing against her ribs and she was obviously finding it a burden; the necessity of the secrecy that had been put upon her was so great that from time to time she had to expel some of her excitement and emotion in great gusty sighs. "Ohhhhh," Clytie went, "Ohhhhh. Do you come up here often, George?" "No," he said. "Did you know there's a little private cemetery the other side of the chapel?" "Yes, uh huh."

So Archer had brought her up and shown her the little cemetery, and what else went on in the little cemetery? The hardest of all to understand was Archer's wanting her. Why would Archer have wanted to explore Clytie Bundock's terribly white body? The thought of it was offensive somehow, like feeling up your Sunday school teacher. Well, also it was cruel, it was the single rottenest thing Archer had done up to now, to awaken these great hopes that now pressed against poor Clytie's ribs; to betray her in front of the crowd, because that was exactly what Archer was doing with terrible deliberation; to coax those great fires in her to white heat and then, as would be his wont, walk off and leave her. Because he most certainly would leave her; the only surprise was that it had gone on for nearly five and a half weeks; this innocent librarian awakened each morning to such news, George knew, awakened to such deafening news she must have had to almost groan. She was loved by, incredibly, Archer Hurst, she thought she must be loved because another day, another morning, and Archer was on the phone sounding sincere; asking how was she; George knew the tone, George had been witness to Archer's end of the phone conversations with Clytie and Archer didn't realize the powerful things he could do to a dry stick like Clytie by saying, When will I see you? Or maybe he did.

Archer and Clytie had begun to show up together in unlikely places for one or the other, she at the basketball night game and he at the Chamber Music Club, and now they were taking Professor Kinney's series on ESP together two nights a week. So something she had had intrigued Archer, but what? There was no doubt about it, there was a definite togetherness about this Mutt and Jeff couple that tended to shut out others; even in the Candy Kitchen now they often chose to sit alone in a booth and while never holding hands or making any physical expression of delight in each other nevertheless seemed delighted, ignored the rest of the gang; the only sign of excitement in Clytie was that she occasionally took off her glasses and spent time wiping them on the napkin. She moved her head slowly around on her long neck as though she were beautiful, so perhaps she was under that cheating illusion that being in love made one beautiful, actually altered the appearance. George could have told her it didn't; for all the transport she was feeling she remained as plain as a prune.

Now Clytie was walking beside him up past the chapel, up the steep path that led up the mountain that overhung Butley School. She was nice though, Clytie; that was what he was forcing himself to think; the way she just walked along beside him was nice, never asking why they were going up to the mountain (and there was no reason except he had said he wanted to walk and she was a good sport), so they walked without any purpose (or he had *thought* without any purpose that now remembered day, but seeing it now he himself seemed very purposeful and remembering now how it had ended all of a sudden, wondered if he had not seemed the least bit threatening to her in the way he walked, hands thrust deep down into his Levi's pockets and his mouth pursed into a scowl while she flounced along like a pleasant sheep beside him); never inquiring except to ask in the most general way was he all right? How? Just all right, she said; I have thought the last week or so you've seemed out of sorts, preoccupied. Oh, no, Clytie, he said, nothing's wrong.

"Ohhhhh," she said, expelling her inner elation. "I'm out of breath. Let's sit a moment."

They sat on a dank stone bench.

"I think I get vibrations from people more now since I've

been doing the thought transference. I thought I felt an unhappy oscillation from you."

"No no."

"I get these little clicks and I thought I got a resentful click, almost hostile, from you on the phone."

"Oh, no. When I phoned today?"

"Yes."

"Oh, no."

"I could have been wrong but—"

"Hostile? What would I have to be hostile to you about?"

"I'm glad."

"Hostile?"

"Oh, it's too strong a word but you see since we've been on the Kinney tests it's astonishing how much more you receive from people."

"So?"

"Oh, yes, it's truly astonishing."

"It doesn't seem the sort of thing *you'd* take up; I find it hard to see you in all this thought projection precognition occult whatever."

"Oh, no, you're wrong."

"So practical, pragmatic."

"I?"

"Pragmatic, Clytie, feet on the ground."

"Oh, no, you're quite wrong."

"I'm?"

"Quite wrong, sorry. Quite wrong. I'm very concerned with thought and the power of it, thought waves, hypnotism."

"You are?"

"Yes; I'm a believer, George."

"I guess you are, Clytie."

"How funny, you thinking that I'm pragmatic. Gosh, that's the last thing I am; I'm a *believer*. And you would be too, if

you'd been there night before last when we did the blackboard test—"

"Who's we?"

"Archer and me."

"Oh."

"I thought you knew Archer and I were taking the Kinney
course. Anyway we did the blackboard test, which is one of
the most difficult tests in thought transference. For one
thing, the subject has to be blindfolded and kept in a room
away from the the other person—"

"Oh, Clytie, these things are *tricked*."

"No, George, because Archer and I *did* it."

"Oh, Clytie."

What a pitying smile he'd given her, how dogmatic he'd
been; *he* was the pragmatic one that day, never dreaming
that one day he would tamper with time and end up back
here on Chapel Hill with Clytie, seeing himself being majestically contemptuous (seeing that he was eaten away with
jealousy, that's what he was), seeing that what he might
like to do was push her over the edge of this steep incline.

"Oh, Clytie," he said pityingly, "oh, *hon*estly."

"Archer was astonishing, George, he got seven out of the
twelve words right the first time."

"Ummmm. Well, I hate to be a cynic but knowing Mr.
Hurst I would say he probably got a little of the information
ahead of time."

"How do you mean? What? I don't—"

"I mean I would hazard a guess Mr. Archer Hurst got a
quick sneak at the blackboard somehow."

"Oh, not possible; he was guarded all the time."

"Well, now . . ."

"Absolutely *not* possible. *George* . . ."

"Mr. Archer Hurst is aw-ful trick-y."

"George!"

"I'm sorry; OK, I believe, I believe."

"I'm not asking you to believe without coming to a session. I am only telling you transference is scientifically proven. Of course he and I seem to have the right mental communication and we keep having the most extraordinary experiences all the time, like one of us knowing the other is going to call or both of us trying to call each other at the same moment and a couple of times he has actually come downstairs because he knew I was just going to call and he has to come downstairs two flights to the phone in this rooming house where he's staying and like I've had this difficult tune in my head and he's started to hum it, but difficult, like the third movement of the 'Pathetique' and the other night I wasn't expecting anyone and I was just going to wash my hair and I stopped dead on the way to the bathroom and said to Rosemary, 'Oh, Archer's just come in the front door' and the next minute he knocked at our door. In fact I don't tell Rosemary any more because she says it frightens her, some people have the idea there's something demonic about it but of course that's nonsense, it's just scientific, that's all, you just have to be on the same plane with someone, that's all. It makes you feel intensely close to someone. You've no idea how near it makes you feel to someone."

Clytie sat silent for a while, gazing away through her giant lenses.

"Why did you say he is tricky?" she asked.

"He is, a bit."

"I don't find him so."

"Now you see him, now you don't."

"Oh, I don't find that. I find him very constant."

"Well, let me tell you he's devious; deviosity is a way of life with him."

"I think he's at great pains to make people think so."

"How so?"

"He's really a very consistent person underneath."

"Do you really think so?"

"Yes, I do. I think he's very constant. Do you know he's a very constructive person; he builds you up all the time."

"*Me?*"

"I meant people generally. Only he would hate for you to know it, so he has this front he puts on of the young rip, wild, restless. Girls."

"Well, you surely *know* about the girls, don't you?"

"Oh, yes."

"Well, then?"

"I don't see what that has to do with it. He's good-looking and girls naturally run after him and I don't see why he shouldn't reciprocate like he does. He's explained all that to me."

"He *has?*"

"In some ways it's quite a burden to him, being so physically attractive."

"Oh, Clytie, you *are* a believer; I wouldn't have dreamed you were such a gullible—"

"No, it's true, George. There are lots of things against being good-looking the way Archer is which other people who are *not* good-looking tend to just brush off. You see, in many ways it's like being rich; you can never be absolutely certain you're not being loved for your money; it's the same way with beautiful people and it's one of the reasons he cuts up and carries on with so many girls and so on—it's *his* way of protecting himself by saying, Watch out, I'm tough, I'm risky, tricky, bet you don't dare love me!"

"Did he tell you that?"

"No."

Clytie expelled a long sigh of her pent-up radiance; in the sunset light her eyes seemed froglike with terror but when he looked right into them he saw they were truly beautiful eyes and the green light in them was deeply serene with something, something secure; she had had Archer in a different way from the others.

"Oh, look," Clytie said. "There's two horseback riders down there on the river path; have you been riding this summer?"

"No, have you?"

"No."

She was hooked, hoodwinked.

"Ohhhhh."

More than just ravaged.

"Ohhhhh. It's interesting. There are a lot of things about Archer that are very real, very touching; unhappy. How interesting the unhappy parts of people are."

Maybe it was much more serious than he had thought, maybe she knew more about Archer than he did, maybe she saw right through Archer and accepted what she saw. She was inviolable. That was the clue to her which made her more than the fervent librarian; she was unshakable. Here she sat now on the damp stone parapet, her polite knees close together, holding her purse on her lap and blinking through her spectacles as though waiting patiently for a bus (she was always seen to be waiting for a bus) and ready to get up and walk with him when he gave the word, and yet she was unshakable. Maybe that fascinated Archer; this would be new to Archer, the girl he could take and shake and put down and find she had not changed fundamentally. That would really challenge him, not to be able to get past her stone inviolability; to be able to arouse her emotionally and sexually and yet not to be able to master her opinions (and all girls changed out of their opinions for Archer as fast as their panties), this rocklike librarian who was willing to go to all lengths with him except allow him the franchise of her mind.

Oh, then it was serious. It wasn't the Holloween prank

everyone thought it was, What Fun to Take Clytie out of the Filing System; it was serious. Also there was the question of suitability; it began to dawn on one that here was the perfect foil for Archer, the plain girl who would remain grateful, the plain girl who would make no trouble about other girls, the plain girl who would wait at home and provide the excuse to get back to, the perfect foil, quite beautiful in contrast when one pictured them together; her froglike ugliness gave Archer's beauty a deeper significance, their just coming into a room together would be galvanic because her plainness would give his beauty a publicly revealed astuteness; think of all the handsome men who marry plain women for this reason. Then it might conceivably be.

Archer might conceivably *marry* Clytie; well, it would be dreadful for her in the long run, she was too nice, too intelligent for it not to shatter and destroy her in the long run; to be used as that most patent of all devices, Archer's wife; she should be stopped now, she should be saved from this *now*.

"Clytie," he said, "did you know that Archer and I are lovers?"

Either she had not heard or the words just fell off her flaccidly; she continued to look down toward the school, holding her purse on her lap as though obediently waiting for him to tell her when she was to get up. The sunset had caught her glasses so he couldn't tell behind the blaze whether her eyes had this time really widened into horror.

"Did you know? Did you have any inkling?"

"No," she said.

"I'm sorry," he said.

"Well . . ." she said, looking down at the straps of her bag.

"But I thought maybe it had come to the point when you should know."

"I—er—" she said. "Yes. Well . . ." Now she got up and

straightened her skirt carefully and gave a giant shrug, shook her long neck.

"I don't know," he said, "I don't know why. Suddenly. I just thought you ought to know."

"Well, I wonder . . ."

"Just one of . . ."

" . . . that . . ."

"Pardon?"

"I—er—ummmm. Well . . ."

Sighed. She gave the longest sigh; it was the last of the air in her, the way it sounded, like a last breath before dying. The carillon in the school chapel had chosen to play "Abide with Me"; the mournful hymn boomed up into the air, leaden bells into the darkening air.

"Will we go down?" she asked, starting down the steps ahead of him.

They walked down the steps back to the school in silence; he could think of nothing to say to her. *The darkness deepens, Lord, with me abide,* tolled the discomforting message from the carillon tower. Clytie walked beside him and swung her bag just the way she had done going up and there was nothing to indicate the slightest difference in her; only an older man with a hundred times the insight of this callow George Wood could have guessed she had been told anything more unsettling than that Archer Hurst had had bridgework done and had kept it quiet; nothing about her suggested the least tension, no more than the quick shrug of the shoulders she gave now and then as though a beetle had dropped from the trees onto her neck, then a thrusting out of her long neck; nothing in the swinging walk to suggest she had been looted and rifled. This girl's deepness and her meticulous feelings and inviolable tenets were so specialized that it was as if George had broken in and entered her most private sanctuaries and looted and vandalized; some things were vandalized beyond repair but how was George to know; George doing a favor in warning her about duplicity, at his own risk, how was George to know she was specialized and so unelastic she could not stretch her beliefs to cover these new contingencies. So there was no way to inform George, not until Rosemary Dodge told him about Clytie coming home and sitting on her bed in the dark for hours, no word out of her for two days while she lay in a stupor and gazed at the wall and said merely yes or no and then poured it out to Rosemary; had it been anyone else but Archer she could have accepted it with grace, she said, but not Archer, she said. She had seen Archer differently from others, perhaps like everything else she had seen him through distorted lenses but she had not seen *this* part of him that belonged to George and she felt suddenly like a trespasser, she said; anyway she could not change her opinion of Archer, which was extremely high (her opinions were precious to her, long in the making and extremely polarized), and therefore he would have to become unreal to her from now on, he would have to become a myth.

So without thinking she walked into some headlights. Maybe on *purpose,* Rosemary said, sucking every poisonous drop of tragedy out of it she could; she could not say why she thought this, because certain things Clytie told her were told in "absolute secrecy," said Rosemary, who had fainted dramatically a couple of times in the Candy Kitchen. But then everybody knew Rosemary had neurotic needs for drama, Rosemary had a long list of hatreds including men. Nobody paid much attention to Rosemary's vapors and mysteries; it had been an accident, attested to by reliable witnesses and in due time, at long last, a stoplight had been installed at that intersection.

"There's my bus," Clytie said and they ran together, her purse flapping beside his leg.

"Do you have to go? Won't you wait and have tea or something?"

"No, thank you, George."

She was fumbling in her purse shortsightedly for change. He felt the need for some affirmation from her that he had been cruel only to be kind; he was too young to know she'd been vandalized.

"Well, Clytie, I hope you don't think that what I told you was meant in any way to be unkind to anyone."

She looked at him and then at her change.

"Oh, no. You're kind, George. You're always kind, George."

So he had squeezed her hand with the change in it.

"It's nothing *really*," he said.

"Nothing," she said and got on the bus. The last he had ever seen of her, she was blundering down the aisle peering froglike around for a seat as the bus drove off. . . .

and Archer's soapdish made of china buttocks, Archer's brush and comb, Archer's razor and (days before instant lather) shaving brush and cream. These things are poignant, ordinary though they are; they belong to Archer. George was coming to, standing at the marble washstand in the cold room; Archer's boardinghouse room was always cold even in August in this dim sunless house, the stairs turning upward toward his floor with the worn carpeting and old Miss Wales peeking from her door; it was all coming back to George now, the smell of Archer's faded blue room, blue bed, blue chenille cover; in the cheap pine wardrobe were Archer's suits and sports jackets; kicked around anywhere were Archer's slippers, Archer's old loafers which took on a look of him even when lying there because Archer had very characteristic feet which made even empty shoes look like him; all this categorizing of Archer's things was back in the time of Archer's love, the time of joy; certainly George had been happy in this cold room with the little eddies of dust in the corners and the old radiator which clanked and gave out so little heat they often lay under a blanket even on a sunny afternoon; this was the time when all of these trifles had the greatest significance to him; he could not have explained to a psychiatrist why the sight of Archer's shaving brush could produce an emotion in him close to grief or ecstasy. Well, then, this had been a time of grief and ecstasy when everything around him pulsated with constant emotion; it was emotional simply waking up in the morning with the first thought being Archer: would he see Archer today? Partly because it was so secret; what they had had to be secret and he carried it around with him like a wound that would not heal and that he didn't want to heal.

To be candid, he must have looked half-witted; certainly, seeing himself just nineteen and bearing the look of tragic introspection as he stood by Archer's washstand and picked up, one after the other, Archer's things as though he were making an inventory, certainly the sight of him was ridiculous, poor kid, poor queer, lusting so for Archer that he had to pick up and sniff his talcum powder; there he was, intelligent playwright headed for dazzle and splendor, standing there like the village idiot smelling Archer's talc; well, anyway, whatever lay in the future was not for years yet, years that would continue to be divided by college semesters, divided from Archer during these long periods, both of them now to be at different colleges, and so they had to make the most of the summer. Here he was then, young and mournful, completely in love, utterly devoted to his own kind of misery (Your face is as long as a wet week, his mother said, with her cutting laugh; none of my business but you sure look glum; can anyone do anything?). It was a time of confused emotional values, mixtures of elation and such sudden despairs he had thought of himself as a romantic, almost poetic figure.

Actually he had been, he now noticed, just an underweight young man with a not very good complexion, too much the color of putty, with too many big white teeth in front of a weakish mouth saved from effeminacy by the small cleft in his chin.

This was the time he thought of as the only truly romantic period of his life. This was the time when hearing someone say "Archer" or "Get a load of the cap Archer's got on" would make him start and look around, and to see Archer moseying into the Candy Kitchen in the deerstalker hat Midge Loomis had given him that summer would make George's heart thump, make him all in a minute pulsate with adrenaline which caused him suddenly to be funny, witty, entertaining. It was a marvel people didn't catch on because of these tidal changes of mood: one moment morose and doing the cynical young existentialist bit and the next all charged up and electrically funny at everybody's expense; partly because malicious humor was fashionable among the Holly and Ivy Players set but also because bone-meal dryness was part of the smoke screen he threw around himself and Archer; George was funny and Archer was tough and laconic. Hardly ever did they look at each other, so careful were they of each other's protection. But honestly, had nobody known? Had nobody even guessed what had been going on those years they were lovers? Had nobody noticed how George deflated when, as was his wont, Archer suddenly disappeared, was gone? George a few moments before having the table in yocks and now gone down like a pricked balloon, moodily drawing circles on the dirty tablecloth with a fork . . .

Most of the time it was more down than up, most of the time it was nonactive, Archer more absent than present, and it was pretty lonely when Archer went off on a toot with a girl, and girl followed girl followed girl followed girl. But the thing *they* had together was worth all the tiresome mechanics they had to go through; the matter-of-factness they imposed on themselves was often so tiring that when the door closed they let down with relief and zest, fronts dropping off with their clothes onto the floor, to lie there until they had to be picked up again.

But less and less often did Archer take the initiative and it had always been Archer's initiative, never George's. During the times in between George waited as wives wait for erring husbands. Otherwise he never gave a thought to the girls, he rather liked the girls, one girl was the same as another to Archer until . . .

Very cold today in Archer's bedroom at Mrs. Mendoza's; he was cold all the way through with this new thing that had only been a little suspicion like a puff of smoke from a starter's pistol but had grown until George felt himself immersed in a huge black cloud. The suspicion was so incomprehensible it had every right to be true, so outlandish as to threaten to be correct, like unbelievable headlines; he was stunned and the picture of being stunned took shape as someone rushing into the room without warning and striking him in the face with a huge cold spoon. In the midst of this perfect afternoon together, in the midst of their being together and discussing their futures in general tones but really speaking of their precious friendship, Mrs. Mendoza had called up the stairs, "Telephone, Mr. Hurst," but really calling, "Fire," "Iceberg dead ahead," and Archer had got up off the bed and gone downstairs; George was damn sure who was calling.

He hadn't thought about it as being serious until about ten days before when he was walking in Allen Park and suddenly there on the top of the hill near the World War I memorial he saw them and for some reason he decided it was perhaps best not to run into them, so he had hidden behind a tree. It wasn't the fact that they were together idling

around on a Saturday afternoon that was surprising, it was
the *way* they were together. They were walking slowly down
the hill not touching hands but in step and both looking
down at the ground and even at a distance there was a mysterious communion between them, walking in step and staring at the ground, and it was obvious they were having a
very deep discussion about something and as they came
toward the tree he saw Clytie stoop and pick something off
the grass and they stopped and examined it intently as if
it were some ancient amulet, precious jade; he could see
their delight in it, whatever it was, some piece of junk,
and he could see even yards away that Clytie's face gave off
a kind of radiance while Archer looked down at her in a
way which (unless it was a trick of the late afternoon sun
and George's suspicion) was not the way Archer ever looked
at girls, not the wily sportive cocky way Archer looked at
girls, but it was his rare unguarded look when his eyes took
on an undisguised sweetness; it was the look reserved for
George.

He began skulking around, pretending to himself he had
to pass by the movie theater just as it was letting out to spot
them in the crowd, or cutting across the school campus to
the night basketball game. It was always the same; they
never were arm in arm, never seemed intimate in any way,
but there was this odd communion; it grew dismayingly in
his mind that this, this might be . . .

Put down the soapdish as he heard Archer coming up
the stairs but he didn't turn around when Archer came into
the room.

"Listen," Archer said, "I'm not going to be able to do that
tonight." George had got seats weeks ago for them to see
the musical playing the opera house in East Haddam.

"OK," George said. Archer had pressed him into getting
the seats.

"I forgot that I have to go someplace tonight I promised someone."

"OK."

Archer was pulling fresh shirts out of the drawer and throwing them around.

"Can you get someone else?"

"Gee, I don't know; it's kind of late now."

"It's only five."

"Well . . ."

"Whyncha call Jack?"

"Jack's away, I think."

"Whyncha call Patti Jo?"

"Eeeeuch, Patti *Jo*."

"Well, Hazel or Ruth."

"Ruth *Carver?*"

"Well, she's nice and she's never doing anything."

"*That's* for sure."

"Well, you don't want to be stuck with a ticket."

"Oh, I guess I'll figure it out, thanks."

"What's the matter?"

"Nothing."

"You should get around with more different people; you mooch around too much alone."

"Well . . ."

It was no use, this kind of thing, it was no good, it never came to anything, you were only kidding yourself if you thought it would ever come to anything; you were worse off than being even the unhappiest wife, you couldn't even scream and stamp and protest.

"Well, OK," he said. "I'll get along and let you get dressed."

Archer, naked now, was hunting for jockey shorts.

"You want to look through my address book, see if there's someone—"

"No, *thanks*."

"OK. You don't have to be snooty and girly about it."

"I'm not, I'm not, I'm not. Well, I'll cut out now and I'll call you maybe."

"Oh, stick around till I have my shower and I'll drive you home."

Undeniably Clytie Bundock, and the very best black suit being taken out for *her*.

"No, I better get going if I have to find someone."

Archer came over and kissed him on the forehead.

"Sorry, chump-o."

"Oh, it's all right, can't be helped. Well, I'll give you a call."

"Bye, kid."

He might have offered, George thought, to pay for the seat, seeing it was his idea, the goddam East Haddam goddam . . .

He slammed downstairs and out. He ran so as not to think. "Snooty and girly" hurt. The one sure way Archer had of putting an end to any sign of possessiveness or claim on George's part was to suggest he was being girly or faggoty; it never seemed to occur to Archer there was anything queer in *his* side of the affair; Archer was immune from guilt, untouched by what they did together; it was as unfair as hell that Archer never thought of himself as anything but straight as a die. But the whole damnable thing was unfair, George thought.

It was no use, this kind of thing, it never came to anything. It was just stupid to have thought they had something of value together when it could be pushed aside in five minutes by the plainest girl in town. At the core of his hurt was the fact that Archer had found something of deep value hidden in Clytie which was not evident to George and consequently intimated that Archer was sharper and more discerning than George. That made him feel doubly rejected; the more he thought about it the more rejected he felt, and staring through the bus window he imagined the two of them together and sharing whatever this deep lovely secret thing was that Archer had found in her; he thought then he saw in the reflection of light in the bus window Archer taking off Clytie's glasses and kissing her once on each eye.

"Finally come to my senses," he said aloud, walking up the street to his home. "Can you use these tickets tonight?" he asked his mother. Went into his room and slammed the door. At rock bottom he most resented his trusting Archer with certain secrets; he had traded so much of himself for so little in return; in the happy moments he had ransacked his inner self for confidences to give Archer. He had given away bits and pieces of his private self to Archer in his gratitude for being loved; there was nothing he wouldn't tell Archer in order to be close to him. He had at last, after lengthy consideration, told Archer about John Citadel, the poet, the remotest star in the galaxy of his life. Archer had been very moved; it was George's ultimate gift to him and Archer had seemed genuinely moved; pulled George roughly to him and held him in a hard unmoving embrace and, "You dear bastard," Archer said. "I love you, you sweet bastard."

And now what? And now it was all superficial after all, it was a quick physical thing Archer had grown out of. Archer was a man in a hurry to get on with his life, a man who wasn't like George either emotionally or sensually; a man who had found something deeply awakening, deeply responsive in himself with a plain girl. "Oh, Christ," George said into a bed bolster. "When will I wake up and learn there's nothing to these things, these things come to nothing?" Possibly at this moment Archer was removing Clytie's glasses and kissing her gently first on one eye and then on . . .

Surprisingly, genuine thunderous applause even from a small audience can be almost as unnerving as catcalls. It went on for so long he had to just stand there with the cast behind him until Clytie very sweetly nudged him forward. "Ladies and gentlemen," George said, dry-mouthed and hollow-voiced, "I am touched much—much touched at the wonderful way in which you've received my play and—" Accidentally the curtain fell, cutting off his speech, so that the audience was deceived into thinking that on top of being talented he was endowed with brevity. It didn't matter with such a success; nobody connected with the Holly and Ivy Players had ever had a triumph like this; his own original play and it had gone like a house on fire, laughter and applause all the way through, and rumor had it the critic from the Lakeville *Journal* indicated he would give it a rave review later in the week if space permitted; a little man in a dirty raincoat with winy eyes told George he was Arthur Lubin and used to be assistant to somebody in the Shubert office back in the thirties and it was only a chance but he might be able to show it to someone he knew who was looking for a play if George would be willing to work out a fifty-fifty agreement. What the seedy wine-smelling little man was doing looking for a play deal in a rented movie house in Butley with an amateur group was not clear but George said thank you and took the little man's stained card; nothing mattered but what he had pulled off brilliantly all by himself; whatever it was, it took off and made a life of its own and for the actors in it. George was a brilliant boy, a genius perhaps, everybody said in different ways, embracing him, and there was no insincerity about it. They drank his health with beer. He was on his way, they told him, to Broadway; he was the coming-up-next Maxwell Anderson, a poet (that pleased him); he was bursting with pride out of his blue serge; his face was very red, partly because he was wearing too tight a collar and partly from elation. "Well," his mother said, stroking her gloves, "I'll tell you one thing; I'd say Archer was terrific, wouldn't you? It's only my opinion, of

course, but I'd say Archer walked away with the evening."
Oh, the cold water of her smile, her right hand cut off
rather than shake his, say he had written something promis-
ing; their eyes leveled on each other's and were like cold
windows behind which each one had just pulled shut venetian blinds; it had been almost visible for a moment, their
secret, then each one had closed the blinds. Say it, he
thought at his mother, say it, I dare you, and, Try and make
me, she said back and then aloud she said, "I thought the
little girl was good too." "Yes," he said to Jessica and realized
he had been dampened; he'd forgotten how dampened he
had been and was amazed for a moment that he'd cared. He
had actually wanted to please *her* with his play, more than
anyone.

"Now, George," Mrs. Nona Holly had said, "Deena is tall
and divinely pretty."
"I know."
Mrs. Nona Holly was dictatorial; she had directed the
Holly and Ivy Players for thirty-one years; she wore steel
combs; she had once, she would have you know, acted with
Burgess Meredith.
"Also Deena will dress the part."
"I know."
In the basement of the Congregational Church they were
having the auditions for his play; the girls and boys ranged
around the walls were all hopefuls. George's play. He felt
a thump of excitement.
"Deena was a darling Lady Windermere; everyone said
so."
"I like the strange girl with the glasses."
"Clytie Bundock? Oh, not for the lead. She's too sharp-
faced; you don't want a sharp-faced girl for Araminta; she
should be tall and eurythmic."

"Not necessarily."

He was suddenly intrigued by this odd girl who had, Mrs. Holly said, only joined up tonight; the way she sat, feet together, looking through her glasses and not expecting anything, especially the leading role; something spunky about her coming to the audition not knowing anybody, with her prim plaited hair, surrounded by all the pretty girls from around, and the calm way she sat indicated she didn't expect much to come of it but that was all right, she didn't expect too much to come of *any*thing, *ever*, but that was all right too.

"There's a quality about her," he said.

"Come here, Clytie," Mrs. Nona Holly called.

Clytie seemed neither nervous nor elated. She looked at George with her enlarged eyes as he told her not to be nervous because the others were watching but to come up on the stage and read a little of a scene with the leading man. Do you know Archer Hurst? he asked her. Hello, she said and shook hands with Archer and, Are you nuts? Archer said in a look. They performed the love scene woodenly with the scripts in their hands, they embraced in a tangle of arms and scripts, reading over each other's shoulders, stepping on each other's feet, and once her glasses got caught in his sweater and, Oh, Christ, Archer's look said as she read the passionate lines in a low voice as though she were announcing the Dow Jones averages, accidentally struck Archer in the face with her script. "I wouldn't think I'm what you want," she said but, No, go on, go on, George said, impelled with some inner youthful fantasy he was Belasco discovering a star. She has pretty legs, he said to Mrs. Nona Holly, and quality, she has awkwardness. That she has, said Mrs. Holly and, Remember that Deena's father always buys out one performance. Again, please, George called out and said (shrewd David Belasco discovering Maude Adams), Dear,

don't be embarrassed by being awkward, awkward is what
I want, your awkwardness is what it needs; you see, she's a
virgin. There was some giggling at this and Clytie said, Oh,
are virgins awkward? which somehow made Archer laugh so
much they could not get back to the scene for several minutes
and then went through the rigmarole again; she leaned
against Archer like a sack of onions but somehow her futile
little gestures of lovemaking made the scene touching, her
breathy toneless voice made the purplish dialogue seem
realer and Archer began reacting to it in a new way he had
not done before with the other girls and, Oh, you may be
right, Mrs. Holly whispered, she's ugly and touching; Deena
would not have been touching; oh, the awkwardness of her.
And the reason Archer is good, George whispered, is he isn't
attracted to her so he's working, for a change; the best love
scenes, George said, are often played by people who are not
attractive to each other in real life. I want her, George said,
watching the way she caressed Archer's face as though it
were a cantaloupe she was pricing. Art, George told Mrs.
Holly, is in the *not* doing of it.

Not noticeable to him then was that he had written a
parody; his play, without his knowing it then, was a parody
of love; he had put two mismatched people on the stage to
represent the comedy of love, what he imagined represented
the tragicomedy of heterosexual love, but it was cartooned,
and what he had represented as the comic sweet tender
gropings of young lovers had truly been designed to be
bitterly ridiculous; it was Pelleas and Melisande seen as
fumbling, stumbling dolts, figures to be pitied; Romeo and
Juliet saved only to find they had nothing in common save
sex; this kind of ruefulness ran through his writing; it was
bitterly sarcastic but no one told him so in those days, so he
never knew his play was greatly revealing to some people,
that several people were disturbed at this public admission

of his incomprehension of love; some even saw his play as one giant Freudian slip. But it was already then too late to point this out so the ones who noticed smiled and said nothing; thought it best just to fuss with their gloves.

"You're good for me, you know."

"I hope so."

"No, you are."

"I hope, I hope."

"I need these times sometimes."

"I know."

"It's like getting away, you know? It's like a better-balanced diet."

"Oh?"

"Yeah."

"Huhhhh."

"What's that 'Huhhhh' for?"

"Can you see if you can see the time without putting on the light?"

"Wait, Waiiiit—er—it's either five after eleven or five of one."

"Five after eleven."

"Yes, it's good for me every now and then."

"Has to be five after eleven, can't be five of one."

"What's it matter?"

"Have to get up and go home."

"Don't go."

"Got to face it sometime."

"It's still snowing, see? See the shadows of it on the ceiling?"

"Yes."

"So whyncha stay over?"

"No, can't."

"Why not?"

"She'll worry."

"She know you're with me?"

"Yes."

"Well, then she won't worry, your mother won't worry if you're with me."

"Funnily enough no, ha ha, funny."

"Well, stay then."

"No."

"Well, go then; I can't persuade you to stay if you don't want to."

"*No spatchitytherways.*"

"What? I don't hear you if you mumble in the pillow."

"I said it doesn't matter much either way."

"What doesn't?"

"Whether I go or stay."

"Yes, well, look—er—I would like it, George, if you would not put on that injured-girl tone."

"So sorry."

"I get that from girls, I don't need that from you, OK?"

"OK, OK."

"What began this?"

"Began what?"

"Oh, come on now, this hurt-lover-but-never-mind stuff."

"All I said was I have to go soon."

"You didn't like me saying I consider this part of a balanced diet, I think, right?"

"I just—I mean, it's not the kind of compliment, as someone said, I'd pick if I had a choice."

"Well, listen, goof, are you listening?"

"Yes."

"Well, turn around so I'm not talking to the back of your neck. It's my way of saying I enjoy what we have."

"Well, I guess I know that."

"So why can't you relax and enjoy it too? We have our

own private arrangement here which is nobody's business but ours and doesn't hurt anyone else and there's not a goddam thing in the world to be upset about, George. What do you have to bring emotion into it for? What do you have to be emotional about?"

"Yes, well . . ."

"Well? Well? What's this extremely long silence for?"

"Just thinking how funny we can be in the same bed and just thousands of miles distant from each other."

"Oh, for—"

"Archer, don't say things like 'injured-girl,' do you mind?"

"Christ—"

"Don't say things like that. I find that fairly hurtful."

"—sake, George, I say that to anybody. Look, when Johnny Mannix gets into a big froth over losing the game, I say, 'Don't be a big *girl*.'"

"Well, this is a different situation; this isn't a football game."

"I'm saying don't get emotional, emotional spoils it."

"The difference between you and me is—"

"And *talking* about it spoils it. I don't want to talk about it, George. I want to be in bed with you and have sex with you but I don't want a lot of emotional faggoty conversation."

"The difference between you and me is that as far as you're concerned we're not really doing anything."

"Not doing anything *wrong* is what."

"Just not doing *any*thing."

"No, that's not so."

"Whereas it's the opposite to me: it's everything, it's my whole life, it's my whole inner life, it's my source."

"Oh, why do we have to *talk* about it?"

"It won't ever change for me."

"Oh, you're an eighteen-year-old virgin; don't bet your heart on anything."

"Even if we never saw each other again."

"I'm here. You're here. That's all there is. Relax. Sleep."

"Even if I walked out now into the snow and never saw you again as long as we live."

"Sleep."

"I don't know why. I don't know how it happened even."

"George."

"I only remember when."

"Huuuuuuuuuuh."

"Because I was so damn raw—I don't mean green raw, I mean raw raw, inside and I was so much in need, in neeeeeeed at that moment, maybe it could have happened with anyone but it happened to be you and you were there, unbelievably there, unbelievably there and tender and strong and beautiful and there and it was like—like breaking through a wall into a—it was like being in prison and breaking through a wall. That day in the school cemetery I remember thinking I wanted to escape from everything. I was so sick of being lonely, I wanted to turn *into* something, into a bird, into a salamander, into any creature but get out of my hurting skin, get out of this hurting time but not die, go on living as something else other than George and then you touched me."

"Hmmmmmmmmm."

"I will love you all my life."

"Hmmmmmm . . . sleep."

"I will love you, only you, all my life."

Zzzzzzzzzzzzz.

"Hello."

"Oh, hi."

"I startle you? What're you doing there?"

"Well, I—is this out of bounds?"

"You look like you're just ruminating on which grave you'd like to be in."

"Oh, do I? I do? Well, no, ha ha, not contemplating *that.*"

"What's so sad?"

This is how it happened, in the school chapel graveyard; this is how it began. Here he was caught, sitting on a gravestone, like Hamlet, head in hands, springing up now alarmed, very embarrassed, flushing, could feel it again, scarlet.

"Probably I was concentrating so hard . . . it makes me *look* kinda glum; I got a math paper . . ."

"You're John Wood, aren't you?"

"George. George Wood."

"I'm Archy Hurst."

"I know."

"How'd you know?"

"I guess everyone knows who *you* are."

"Yeah?"

"Guess so."

Archer, leaning on a gravestone, smiling.

"You live in or out, George?"

"Out. In New Forks. You?"

"I'm a boarder. You come up here often?"

"No. Up here to the chapel, you mean? No."

"I do. I like it here alone. Have you read some of the inscriptions on these old gravestones? This is my favorite, over here; come on, I'll show you."

This could not be happening, him leaning over a mossy grave alone with the most sought after boy at Butley; this could not be happening was what he felt at the time, bending over the stone with a burning face and Archer Hurst leaning on *him* and them reading off the eroding stone that DEAN PYE 1878 HAD SUCKLED THE IGNORANT LAMB. Sounds pretty dirty, Archer said, don't you think? What do they call you? Georgy? George? Brilliant flicks of a future flashed in his mind, they would be pals, they would go to football games together, they would save each other seats next to one another, buy each other sodas at half time; they would become inseparable. But none of this would happen; one of his fantasies, this would all be over in a minute or two. Already a silence had fallen between them. One could not long sustain a friendship merely on a mutual interest in gravestones. Then the chapel bell began up above them thunderously.

"I gotta go," he said.

"Where are you going, George?"

"No place special."

"What's your hurry? You're a real nervous kid, you know that? What's so bad?"

"Nothing."

But he was trembling because he had been fantasizing that he had a best friend; he'd been sitting on the grave and fantasizing he had a best friend who was coming up the hill now to meet him and there suddenly was *Archer Hurst* in the *flesh*, jumping impudently over graves; Archer Hurst, now sitting chewing a stalk of grass and grinning and asking personal questions of him.

"What are you sad about?"

"Nothing."

They had to speak between the sonorous chimes above them.

"So what are you scared of then?"

"Nothing, nothing special."

"It's all the same in the end, kid, so why be scared?"

He was trembling all over because it was real, it was no fantasy, and in an eerie way he felt he had somehow brought it *about*, so now must deal with it; it was as though he had sent out a secret SOS and Archer had heard it; it was thrilling; frightening; too much to deal with. So he looked at his watch.

"I'd better be getting—"

"Don't go," Archer said and grinned again.

" 'S after five and—"

"Don't go," Archer said.

"Wellll . . ."

Light began fading, chimes gradually dissolved into air, into silence; only birdsong; something else though, pounding in his ears, what he'd brought about. And so must deal with. And so? What? He made a slight movement downhill but Archer put out a long leg across his path and gently stopped him with it. So now?

"Don't go, George," Archer said.

part four

now that he

was almost there, bumping along in the first taxi he'd ever hired, he was so nervous it was close to being thrilled and little shivers ran over him as a cold wind ruffles a pond; he was actually doing this thing he'd imagined doing for weeks; he could see his thrilled face in the driver's mirror and he looked as if he were going to laugh or cry hysterically and for the hundredth time he pursed his mouth and narrowed his eyes so as to look bored. That's quite a ways, the taxi driver said at Stockton, that'll cost you three dollars, son, the taxi driver said, and Georgy said, Could you take me as near as you can for maybe two dollars and a quarter and I'll walk the rest. Well, the taxi driver said, if I drop off two other fares first, I'll take you for two bucks, and they'd driven around to two other farms and so on top of being excited he was now concerned because this had eaten into his time schedule which he'd worked out so carefully with secret timetables in order to deceive his mother, who believed he was in New York with a group from his English class seeing Maurice Evans and Judith Anderson in *Macbeth*. You know them, they expecting you? the taxi driver asked, and

Georgy, dodging the first part of the question, muttered he wasn't sure exactly if they were expecting him. They won't see people they don't expect, the taxi driver said. I brought people out here before they didn't expect, they wouldn't open the door; you want me to wait? No, Georgy said, appearing he hoped blasé but with eyes as big as those of a frightened horse. How he was to get back to the train was another dilemma too late to worry about now; now that he was almost there in actuality (in his dream about it everything meshed, no possible hitch occurred, he must catch the three-ten back to New York to make his connection at Grand Central, he told them, and they willingly drove him to the station but in dreams there are no measures of time and distances and who was to know they lived so far from the depot?). Because, the taxi driver went on, I have to charge you both ways if I have to come out to get you; not me, the boss, you understand, the taxi driver went on, looking at him in the mirror as if he was an oddity, which he probably looked all dressed up in his best navy blue suit with a startling red tie and white socks and being so urbane and all, the way he'd said, Taxi, taxi, in a lordly way to cover his nervousness and constant swallowing and the fact he was outgrowing the suit so rapidly that when he breathed in heavily (which he had to do constantly) the zipper on his fly opened, so that if he wasn't breathing he was zipping up his fly, the frigging thing was open again now, he saw, glancing down and seeing a wide display of white underpants, and was still struggling with it when they stopped at a gate and, This is it, the driver said; sure you don't want me to wait while you see if they're going to let you in? No, thanks, he said and got out shakily. *Mudge* was the name on the gate. He paid the driver two dollars; your funeral, the driver said, and was gone in a cloud of reddish dust before Georgy remembered he'd left the little gift package on the seat containing an imitation silver pinbox and so the dream was not working out exactly smooth as silk as he'd anticipated in his splendid ambition. The house was in a little dell surrounded by seedy pine trees; a big house, it had a closed look about it as if the owners had long gone away, as if some very mournful thing had happened here, Georgy thought; it had a deeply melancholy look about it, standing in perpetual shade with its many windows staring at him sightlessly, not a sign of life from any of them, all shut tight, not a friendly dish towel hanging out from one of them even, not a potted fern, no curtain moving in a breeze, no half-seen face inquiring who was this boy in a navy suit with his fly coming open, coming down the mossy steps; the nearer he got down toward the mournful house the surer he was nobody was here and that maybe they had died (only that would have had to be in the papers) or gone away and this mad trip of his, so carefully planned, so artfully disguised, might all be in vain and in that case what would his reaction be? Disappointment? Relief? The front door was darkly recessed in a wooden porch and the doorbell was bright green with verdigris but he pushed it and heard nothing echoing inside the house (and in his dream he had prepared now for the door to open and then after a few incredulous introductions came screams and screams of incredible joy and this was followed by an enormous amount of kissing and embracing and tears running down faces), only the shivery sound of the wind in the pine trees giving off a very singing sad sound which made it seem all the more possible something very very melancholy had taken place or was taking place in this house. He rang and rang the dead bell and was so sharply divided as to how he should feel that he almost saw himself split right down the middle and his innards exposed like in those medical illustrations in encyclopedias; thought something moved in the hall so gave a tentative knock on the door but only hurt his knuckles. But someone was around. There was a distant sound of sawing wood. He walked around the corner of the house and saw wash hanging limply on a line, women's things, blouses and stockings. There was a stringy vegetable garden and somebody had left a pail of damp clothes not yet hung up. Beyond was a kitchen door and, Now you must either do it or run like hell, Georgy said to himself to control his heart rising right up through his chest into his throat, and he marched, he thought boldly, up the steps and banged on the screen door and instantly the house exploded with what seemed to be thirty-five dogs but proved to be only two small dachshunds. "Who are you looking for?" from right behind him through the barking had apparently been asked by a huge bullying kind of woman, the kind of woman Georgy thought was only in movies about women's prisons and who got the girls down on the floor and shaved off their hair for the slightest thing. "Want someone?" asked the bullying woman. "Shut up," she said to the dogs, who continued to bark and throw themselves against the wire. "What?" she demanded when he said nothing, stricken dumb for the moment partly by the terrible size of her, towering over him, her huge red arms akimbo, her big face jutting down toward him (and partly because he didn't know which name was used), but while he wet his lips a window at the side of the house opened and a man with short stubby grassy gray hair called out, "What's going on, who's there, what do you want?"

"Miss Mudge," Georgy asked, thinking better not to ask the other name yet.

"I'm Miss Mudge," the man said.

"George Wood," he said above the cacophony of barking, but the name seemed not to carry any weight at all, or perhaps the man had not heard it.

"I'll take care of it, Emma," the man said to the bullying woman.

"Wait here," the bullying woman said to Georgy, as if to say, You are in bad trouble, make no mistake about it. She went off, swinging the heavy pail of wash in her beefy arm, and in a minute or two the man appeared in the kitchen saying to the dogs, "Down, down, stop that, stop that, Bulwer, stop that, Lytton," only Georgy saw now it wasn't a man after all but a stocky woman in a tweed skirt and a blouse and wearing a lot of rings and a man's watch. "What do you want?" she asked through the screen door. "I'm George Wood," he said and waited but nothing happened except the continual barking, yet he thought Miss Mudge seemed to freeze against the screen door. "What?" she asked. "I can't hear you because of the dogs. Who are you?" "I'm George Wood," he said and now he saw Miss Mudge had certainly heard him because she sagged suddenly against the screen door in a way that suggested somebody in the dark kitchen had struck her from behind with a steel chisel and after a moment she opened the door and said, "Come in quick, I don't want the dogs to get out," and he came into the dark musty-smelling kitchen and Miss Mudge (who was about his height so they stared at each other eye to eye) leaned one arm on the kitchen table and was so still that even the dogs caught it and stopped barking; her stillness filled the whole kitchen with a weight so his name must have meant something judging by the way Miss Mudge leaned on the table with one arm and with the other made a pro-tecting gesture around her breast as though she were ready to ward off any attempt to come near her or attack her or embrace her, one hand making pawing signs in the air that she was not yet ready to believe this thing. Finally she said, "George." "Yes," he said, not sure why this was so terrible yet. "You're George," she said and took cigarettes from her pocket and lit one. Her face looked swollen and obviously there was not going to be scream after scream of incredible joy. "Sit down a minute," Miss Mudge said hoarsely and pulled out a kitchen chair, and he sat down and she pulled a chair out and sat opposite him puffing away on her cigarette and he could see she was deeply troubled; he could tell now that what he'd done was the worst thing that had ever happened.

"How did you find us?" she asked.

"Someone told me."

"Did Jessica tell you?" She sounded incredulous.

"No," he said. "She doesn't know I know."

"How did you find out, then?"

"Someone told me," he said, looking at her tweed knees. "A man told me; I don't think you'd probably know him. Mr. McLean."

"Who's he?"

"He's a friend of my mother, *used* to be a friend of my mother."

"A *friend*," Miss Mudge said. She got up and walked around the table two or three times and then sat down again. "Well, I don't know what to say," she said and chain-lit another cigarette. "I don't know what to say to you, George. You weren't ever supposed to know, you know."

"I know," he said apologetically.

"I don't know what we can do now," Miss Mudge said hoarsely.

The women's prison warden came into the kitchen and put down her pail. "Want tea?" the woman asked. Miss Mudge covered her face for a moment and then said without looking up, "Emma, find something to do outside, would you?" and the bullying woman clumped out.

"How'd you get here?" she asked.

"Train," he said.

"What, all the way from there? From Connecticut?"

"Two trains," he said. "Change at Grand Central."

"How old are you now?" she asked.

"Fourteen," he said.

"Fourteen. My God," she said. It was very like talking to a man, the way she sat with her legs splayed out and one hand on each knee. "My God, you've got a nerve," she said. "For fourteen I'd say you have a lot of nerve."

"I guess so," Georgy said.

"I suppose you want to see *her*."

"Yes."

"Why didn't you write first to ask if you might come?"

"I don't know."

"Afraid we'd say no?"

"I s'pose."

"Yes, I see."

"So I just came."

"Oh, my God," Miss Mudge said to the wall and was quiet for a while, puffing away. "My God, this has been some year. One thing after another, I want to tell you. And now this."

"I'm sorry," he said, "if I picked a bad time."

"I don't know what to do," she said. "I suppose you want to see her."

"Well, that's why I came."

"Just to show up like this without warning. How would you know what you might find here?"

"I know, I'm sorry, I had to."

"Well, I'm afraid you've come a long way for nothing."

"Isn't she here?"

"She's here but she wouldn't be able to see you; she's ill."

"Oh."

"She's been ill on and off for a long time now."

"I see."

"I couldn't put her through something like this."

"Well, but—"

"So I'm sorry you've had this long trip for nothing."

"Could you maybe ask her?"

"It's no use you being persistent about this."

"Would you just *ask* her though."

"Ask her is the same as telling her you're here; she's not up to it."

"I'll only stay five minutes."

"Not up to it; I'm sorry."

"Well, then, could I see her for a minute if you don't tell her who it is?"

"She'd know you."

"Could I just see her for a *minute?* Not even go in the room. Could I just maybe see her from the doorway?"

"My God, you're a hard one, aren't you? You'll get somewhere."

"Miss Mudge, could—"

"Nance, I'm Nance," she almost yelled.

He felt sorry for her, sucking on her butt to light another cigarette, poor mannish thing; maybe she hadn't much of a life stuck out here looking after a sick woman.

"My God, you put me in a predicament," Nance Mudge said, glaring at him. "I don't know what to do."

In a moment he could have relented, she looked so hunched up and wretched, but he was smart enough to know that somehow he'd made a chink in her armor and it seemed to him as though he *must* gain this victory, that if he let this go now, if he capitulated now, his life would be altered to some degree for the worse forever, that he would be stamped as a loser from this moment on. He took from his pocket the much marked Oxford University Press edition of the poems. Nance Mudge saw it at once and sucked her cigarette in a frenzy.

Georgy said, "If I could see her just for a minute and if she would write in her book for me that's all I'd want, I'd have something to keep."

Nance Mudge thumped the kitchen table hard twice with a round fist and then struck her forehead a blow, stood up and said, "Come," and sighed a tragic sigh that said everything about the situation that could not have been said in words. She led him through a gloomy somnolent dining room with an immense table, holding immense silver candlesticks, and then along a dark hall and opened a door. "Wait in here," she said and then as he passed into the room she said in a low voice, "This is on both our heads, do you realize?" "Yes," he said politely. "I want your promise there's not to be one word about . . . your family and so on unless she brings it up. Promise me." "I promise," he said, and she went upstairs.

The room was unaired and suffocating and smelling of flowers and some strong scented dried rose leaves in pots. The room was heavy and dark with great curtains and furniture and mirrors and cabinets crammed with china and huge lamps made of Chinese vases. It was more like a stage setting than a real room, he thought. He sat down on the edge of a giant wing chair from which Elizabeth might have struck down Essex. He held in his hot sticky hands the book of poems. Now if this were a play there would shortly be offstage voices and then a woman's voice would cry out, "George. *Here?*" then there would be the sound of someone running around upstairs and then running downstairs and then she would appear in the door and then he would get up and very slowly they would approach each other and then, then, after looking into each other's eyes for a long while, neither of them capable of speaking because of the miracle of this perfect crystal moment.

He may have blacked out part of this occasion. It seemed as if he had fallen heavily asleep for a few moments into one of those deep catnaps people have on trains and then woke with a start in this overpoweringly scented room aware that nothing was happening except that according to the grandfather clock at least twenty minutes had gone by and nothing had happened, no offstage voices, nothing. And as well as this, if he must catch the three-ten train (and he must if he was to keep his secret from Jessica), then there was hardly any time left at all. Oh, crap, oh, crap, where were they? Or had she refused to come down? He might go into the hall and call Miss Mudge but that was acting pretty silly and juvenile. Oh, shoot, maybe he was beaten after all, she wasn't coming. He was ready to call up to Miss Mudge that he was leaving when in a mirror, one of those convex mirrors which deform, he saw a figure silently descending the stairs and, turning, saw what seemed to be a young boy about his own age, fourteen or fifteen maybe, wearing a pair of dark trousers and a black velour sweater; hand on the stair rail, the boy came down very slowly but without any indication of tension, perhaps not knowing he was being watched. Then the boy turned at the foot of the stairs and came directly into the room and stood in the doorway looking at him. What it was like was looking at a poor photograph of himself or looking at an older distant cousin perhaps. Face to face with John Citadel.

"Hello," she said, because at once the voice dispelled the illusion of maleness; the soft doelike voice could not be anything but female even though the face was masculine with its strong forehead, like faces in medieval pictures with its shiny cap of brown hair, very faint blue veins at the temples; very like a young friar in a religious picture of the fourteenth century except that closer up she was not so young as you first imagined; little minute wrinkles were around the incredulous blue eyes looking into his; waiting, she waited quietly there; she didn't seem to be either appalled or elated; she was like a thin ghost, her hands were like membranes, she was in the room and yet she seemed not to be there.

"You're George, are you?" She said rather than asked the question in her faint voice.

"Yes," he said.

And they stood, these two similarities pretending one was a mirror.

At last she said, "Well, come along and sit down."

They sat down opposite each other in two huge armchairs.

"I can only stay a few minutes," he said.

"Well," she said, "I see."

"I'm supposed to be at a matinee," he said. "I'm supposed to be seeing Maurice Evans in *Macbeth*."

"Oh, yes?"

"It's my English class. Actually they *are* going to it, you see, so I have to go back with them so I have to get the three-ten from Stockton, which gets me into Penn Station with just enough time for me to get to Grand Central to get the six twenty-five for Butley, otherwise if I miss that the only one on a Saturday is a local that you have to change at Danbury and—"

"Oh, yes."

Her paper-thin hands were clenched very tight.

"So," he said, swallowing, "I can only stay a few minutes."

She crossed her little legs.

"Butley," she said.

"I—we live in New Forks."

"If I remember right it was—"

"Pardon?"

"Scuse me," she hoarsed, "frog in my throat." She coughed for a few minutes and then leaned back in the huge arm-chair, tears in her eyes from coughing.

"Well . . ." he began hopelessly.

"Pretty," she said.

"Butley?"

"Pretty."

"Oh, it's OK; it's nicer than New Forks, I guess."

Another spasm crossed her face and he waited while she coughed silently behind a handkerchief.

"There used to be, in my time," she said, wiping her eyes, "a wonderful, an absolutely wonderful cake shop in Butley."

"Oh, Rodman's," he yelled. "Oh, Rodman's is still there."

"A big shop made of dark green marble with brass—"

"Rodman's, yes, it's still there on Main Street."

"They used to make," she said with an effort, it seemed,

sighing, "a genuine Viennese Sacher torte, a very rich cake I was—excuse me—I was very partial to."

"Ah, yes? No kidding."

"And tarts. They had marvelously original tarts, little greengage tarts and tarts with molasses and pecans and tarts with mince in them and raisins, some of which looked rather"—long pause while she choked behind her handkerchief—"rather objectionable."

"Oh, I bet they still have them." His voice was so eager it rang against the glass cabinets. "Oh, I'm going to check on it when I get back."

"Meringues . . ."

"Yes?"

"They made everything in their own kitchen."

"Oh, yes, I bet they still do, uh huh."

Silence began appearing around the edges. Georgy felt the silence creeping up on them; it was like trying to keep awake in the snow to fight that silence but he must fight it if there was to be any hope she might say one personal thing, admit one thing to him.

"I bet they do," he said loudly against the silence coming up.

The clock whirred and struck something. Time to go.

"Was the Arcadia Bookshop there in your time?" he asked, hoping to lead her from cakes to books.

"I don't know if it was called that," she said.

"Right at the end of Main Street before you get to the firehouse?"

"I don't know if that was it."

"That's where I got *this*," he said and put down his ace, John Citadel's poems, on the table beside her but she only glanced at it and then glanced away out the crack of window between the heavy draperies and after leaving him to swallow his failure for a few minutes she turned back toward him and touched her boy's cap of hair. "There was a—" (How

you had to wait for everything; she was so slow, apparently
ran out of thoughts, had to begin again; all the time you
leaned forward expectantly, stupid eager smile on your face;
you were a paroxysm that day, you with your eager smile and
holding your stomach in so your fly wouldn't come undone.)
"—a Mr. Halvorsen," she said; the effort of bringing this out
seemed to leave her exhausted; she leaned her head on one
of the wings of her chair and he was about to relieve her of
the load of going on when she started up again: "who had
the bookshop; I imagine he would be dead now because he
was quite—"

"Mr. Halvorsen I don't—"

"—decrepit even then. He was a rather dirty old man."

"Oh, ha ha."

Wrong. She hadn't meant a joke; she waved her handkerchief to signal him to wait.

"Aha," he said.

"Not in the sense that con-no-ta-tion usually conveys."

"I see."

"But in the sense of bathing."

"Ohhhh."

"He had—he was a greenish gray color, the color of the
bottom sides of—"

He didn't want to turn his head to see the clock but he was
getting desperate and if he lost the train, Jessica would find
out.

"—mushrooms."

"Gosh."

"With dry dry hands so scaly and dry that when he turned
a page it set your teeth on edge."

"Well," he said, and careless with anxiety for a moment
let the word slip out: "he's probably passed away but I'll ask
my mother." The word was quite harmless really but it had
the effect of a hailstone against the glass cabinets and the
silence rose up around them and folded over them and it

seemed to grow dark in the room from the thick density there was between the two of them and he saw her stiffen and a spasm again cross her face and she hid it behind her handkerchief.

"Or *someone* will remember," he said, trying to smooth the damage. She was looking at him in a curious way halfway between horror and incredulity and he saw he had struck a chord deep within her and that whatever she was feeling (her breathing had become quite rapid) was intense and he must, even if he lost the train, wait. She was going to ask something. Would she ask about Jessica? Would she ask where they were living now? What grade he was in and how he was doing? Was he happy?

But like machinery long out of use, the rusty wheels and cogs that put speech together had to clank and rattle and connect in her brain; meanwhile she drew herself up, she drew in a deep breath as though she were going to dive into the sea from a great height.

"Can you—" she began but Nance Mudge blurted into the room like a vacuum cleaner gone berserk, like a tank bursting into a quiet glade and letting off shots so the two of them sitting there were changed into birds instantly, Georgy thought, both of them changed into birds and flew away. "Mary must go upstairs now," Nance Mudge thundered, beefy little arms akimbo and making it clear that she was the one suffering outrageous fortune, she was clearly being victimized. "No more," Miss Mudge said. "This has been some year, I tell you, and she can't take any more, nor can I because next it'll be *my* health breaking down; no more, I tell you, of you people coming here and trying to get in at her, no more, not from you, not from anyone."

Mary. It was the first time anyone had said her real name in front of him. She seemed aware of it too. She bit her lip and looked at him and her look seemed understanding of the fact that they were interrupted.

"You were just going to ask me something," he said but her eyes looked dull now and the machinery had stopped.

"Was I?" she said. "Well, I seem to have . . . lost the thread."

Nance Mudge hit pillows. "The gardener is going downtown and he'll drop you off at the station."

"Thanks," he said.

"But that means you have to go now, this very minute."

"Yes."

"And Mary has to lie down, this very minute."

He got up and took his John Citadel poems to where she sat shrunken in the big chair and took out his school fountain pen. "Would you write something in your book for me?" he asked, and she took hold of the pen and he saw she was left-handed and she opened the book and looked strangely at the frontispiece as though she might never have heard of the author in her life and then she made some quick scratchy movements across the page and closed the book and handed it back to him.

"Good-bye," she said.

"Bye," he said and followed big square-assed Nance Mudge out of the room and down the hall feeling that if he concentrated on Nance Mudge's huge ass he wouldn't be so aware of the prickling feeling behind his eyes.

Outside the day had grown gray and cold suddenly just in the short time he'd been inside; the day had grown unrecognizable. The gardener was waiting in an old Plymouth with the engine running. "Now that you've seen her," Miss Mudge said, "don't go telling people what she looks like."

"I won't," he said.

She stood there, cigarette in one hand, the other on her fat rump, between him and the windows of the house, but he thought behind her a face was at the drawing room window between the drapes. "God knows," Miss Mudge said, "you have seen a wreck, you have seen all that is left of her."

Nance Mudge gasped and bit the back of her hand savagely. "Christ," she said, "you forced your way in here but the least you can do is shut up about it."

"I will," he said.

"Do her the favor of not telling anyone how she looks."

"I won't," he said.

"Don't you go telling *Jess* how she looks."

"No," he said. "I don't plan to tell her anything."

"Go along now."

And never come back, never set foot here again was what she meant, the way she glared at him, her short stubby man's gray hair, the keeper.

"Good-bye," he said. "Thanks."

Was then driven away off the property.

On the dirty train, all the feeling wearing off until there was no feeling left at all, he finally opened the book. On the title page she had written in little chicken-feet handwriting, *To George*, and then she had drawn a line through "John Citadel" and written, *from Mary*. He may have imagined it but it looked as if she had hesitated a fraction after writing the *M*.

And, "George," she said and again, "George," not "Georgy" so it was very serious, she was very seriously wounded. He was watching himself, he was very clear to himself, his older self now watching himself sitting under the bright light wearing a green eyeshade doing his geometry homework when Jessica came into the kitchen and he saw she had the John Citadel book (so had he hidden it in his shirt drawer so that she was sure to find it?) and that her face was putty color with tiny red spots as if she were breaking out in measles and that she was breathing very fast and holding the book open against her breasts as she sat down opposite him. He bent over his geometry book and was drawing a scalene triangle with such care he had to exercise his tongue.

He'd rubbed right through the paper. She sat silent for a while; it was a funny feeling; like he was the boss and she was some poor old charlady come asking for a job and him keeping her waiting. "Oh, my sainted soul," she said to herself, one of those old-fashioned saws she used to throw around like corn to the chicks. "My sainted sainted soul," she said and then, "I always thought I'd *know* if you found out. Honor bright. Oh, well. None so blind, I guess, as those who—" She sat for a while and he drew. "So now you know," she said. "Well, anyway, it's come out. I hoped of course you'd never know, not for my sake but for yours."

Exactly as if she were some old employee caught stealing, the way she gripped the table, waiting to hear was he going to keep her on now she'd been found out. Well, she wasn't going to get a clue from him.

"What happened?" she asked after a long silence.

"Where?"

"*Where?* On the moon. Don't do that to me, *please*. I mean what happened in Pennsylvania. What did she say? Was she shocked?"

"No."

"I'd have thought she might be. Did she refer to me?"

"No."

"No? Well. What *did* she say?"

"Nothing much."

"What did you talk about?"

"Nothing much."

"Well, I'd like to know *something* she said."

"She didn't say much of anything. As a matter of fact we talked about tarts."

"*Tarts*."

"Cakes and stuff."

"Oh."

"She asked me if Rodman's was still in Butley."

"Oh, oh, it's like her; ir*rel*evancy, always."

"Anyway, there wasn't much time; I only had about ten minutes with her if you want to know."

"Well, I'm sorry then. I'm sorry if you had to go all that way and get the brush-off."

"I didn't get the brush-off. I *saw* her."

"Well, but not to say a word—"

"She talked, we *talked*."

"Did she ask you about school or anything?"

"No."

"She didn't even ask you—"

"We *talked*. Anyway, she's sick or something; she's not supposed to talk to people."

"Oh, that's always been the excuse for as long as I can—"

"Well, she *is* sick."

"Maybe."

"I was there. I ought to know."

"Oh, sure, sure. Well, maybe she was. Maybe you were too much of a shock for her. I'm sorry if you were so disappointed, Bitsy, but I could have told you to save yourself all the bother you went to, hiding it from me and getting on and off all those trains just for ten minutes with her. I could have told you, 'Save yourself the bother because when you get there, even if Nancy whatever—the watchdog—lets you past the gate you won't get any satisfaction, you won't get any kindly word out of Mary Boxer, dearie,' because she isn't *capable* of it and it has nothing to do with being *ill*. She hasn't got a drop of blood or anything in her veins. I could have *told* you that."

He was standing up, he found. He couldn't contain himself any longer. The room was rocking in a gale.

"You could have told me about *her*."

He had screamed, his voice ugly and cracked, his recently changed voice, half boy, half man.

It was like being in the boy's body and outside at the same time, having lived for twenty-nine years since this happened.

It was a terrifying thing for him now to hear the things he had called her that day, the force of his rage at her; he would not have thought himself capable of such fury at age fourteen, such boiling righteousness with which he hurled down imprecation upon imprecation on her. Spat words on her, snatched burning words and phrases he had only read in books and heard in movies and not sure of their meanings but only the terrible sounds of them and so *spinster,* he spat at her and then *harlot,* totally illogical, discrepant, *liar,* he yelled so the neighbors would be sure to hear as far as the end of the street, *vixen,* he shot at her, *bungler.*

Well, he was a victim of deception and plots and it was all her fault, she merited this. She was all the things he called her and more.

Yet it now looked to him differently, it looked ugly to him; this woman, shrunk down in the kitchen chair while the fourteen-year-old boy shrieked and spat at her, it seemed to him now that *she* had been the victim.

At length she moved. She raised her eyes to him. She was mild. He was amazed to see how mild she had been, only asking, appealing to him to let her have one moment to plead her case.

"I'll just say one thing if I'm allowed," she said. "Only this. I loved you, Bitsy, you were my little baby. You were truly all I ever had, ever. Truly."

"Well, I am not," he said. "I am not your baby, I was never your baby and I never will be. I'm not yours or hers or anybody's, I'm only myself. I am only *myself,* do you see? I belong to *me.*"

"Yes," she said.

He saw then she had cracked. He saw then she was turning into vinegar. She had got up from her chair very slowly and moved around into the beam of the overhead light and he saw now he was witnessing the very moment when Jessica Boxer Wood became what he remembered of her for the rest of her life. She smiled and it was the first of the wintry smiles she would smile at him right up to the last moment in the hospital when she would press into his hands the book of poems that lay between them on the table and smile that wintry smile and say, "I have escaped from you." But now in the kitchen all she said was, "Well, I guess I know my place from now on. I guess I know where I stand." She gave the first of those little icy titters. "I guess I don't need bifocals to see where I stand. . . ."

So when the big man stepped out from behind the tree, Georgy started and almost ran. "Don't run, Georgy, don't run, son," said Mr. McLean and had taken hold of his shoulder. "Give you a shock, did I?" Mr. McLean said and laughed. It was partly the twilight. That thick dusk of day when things and people seem larger and Mr. McLean seemed gigantic; even his hands were huge. His hands were huge and covered with soft golden hairs. "Where are you walking to?" he asked. "Home," Georgy said.

"How about a soda?"

"No, thanks."

"How about a ride home then?"

"No, thanks."

"The car's right here."

"No, thanks."

But the big soft hand was on his shoulder and though it lay there heavy and gentle he knew if he were to twist away and try to run it would clamp him in a vise, all just a bit frightening because of his absolute out-and-out dislike of Mr. McLean and Mr. McLean knowing it so what was he doing stepping out from behind a tree in the dusk and nabbing him like this? And now they were walking over the grass toward Mr. McLean's car and all the time Mr. McLean's big soft hand was on his shoulder and Georgy looked from right to left in the hope one of the kids would come along and he could hail whoever it was and rush. But nobody was in sight and the school was empty except for the old people who came in to clean and so when they got to the car he said, "No, thanks, I'd rather get the bus," but the big soft hand clenched his shoulder, pinched the bone just a fraction, and Mr. McLean gave a soft laugh and said, "Georgy, I'd just like to give you a ride home, that's all, I'm not trying to kidnap you or anything, so get in," but the hand propelled him into the car, into the front seat, and as they drove off a wildly improbable thought came to him.

"So how've you been, Georgy?" Mr. McLean asked. "How've you been, old lad?"

"OK," he said and noticed they were driving east off Allen Street away from home. "Hey," he said, "the other way."

"Oh, yes?" Mr. McLean asked. But he had to know, living in New Forks.

"The other way."

"Well, now, it's early; you're not in any rush, are you? What time's your mother expect you home?"

"Oh, right now, about now."

"Oh, well," Mr. McLean said, "a bit of a breath of fresh air's good for everybody, don't you think, old lad? I thought we'd go round the Brush Park way."

Mr. McLean steered with one hand and the other hand was on the back of Georgy's neck, not pressing or anything but there and it was a goosy feeling especially when Mr. McLean moved his big thumb up and down the little V of hair on the nape of his neck in a friendly way maybe just to reassure him he was only being friendly after the big blowup when Georgy was much younger, maybe to assure him he was not being menacing but just the same not to try to get out of the car at a stoplight; the big warm hand remained always on his neck no matter how they swung in and out of the evening traffic coming the opposite way with the headlights beginning to turn on; the big warm hand stayed on his

neck and felt around with the thumb and now, thinking about
the maybe deserted and getting dark Brush Park with all the
trees, he started feeling his heart thump because maybe Mr.
McLean did have something in mind, maybe Mr. McLean
was one of "those" they told you over and over never to get in
a car with even if you knew them and never go for a soda
with just like Bully Lynch who got lured into Allen Park
with one of them and finally got away but not before there
had been one hell of a fight and Bully had smashed the
guy's glasses into his face.

Mr. McLean was asking how was school? Was he on the
swimming team this year? Ordinary things like that but they
could very easily lead up to something. Mr. McLean's foot
on the accelerator looked as big as the foot of a dining room
table in its polished shoe and his horn-rimmed glasses were
also large and thick and unbreakable-looking, partly perhaps
because he was an optician and appeared in the advertise-
ments for his shop in the Butley *Chronicle* wearing the latest
in horn-rimmed spectacles and saying in a balloon coming
out of his mouth, WANT SOMEONE FRAMED? I'M YOUR MAN.
Occasionally Mr. McLean's sister Mabel appeared in the
ad also wearing the latest horn-rims.

Something to do with Mr. McLean's glasses, the fact that
they were almost certainly plain window glass and only
worn for business reasons, was a clue to Mr. McLean, was
part of the difficulty in liking him or believing him, and another thing was his smile, which was too bright under his
red mustache because even as a kid Georgy could tell that
Mr. McLean often didn't mean it at all when he smiled, often
meant the reverse, and it had been baffling to him why his
mother had been so taken in by Mr. McLean when a blind
person practically could have told you he was a phony.

Now, Georgy, old lad, Mr. McLean was saying, fondling
Georgy's neck, I am real sorry that we couldn't be pals. That
was the kind of fakey thing he was always saying but now

in the car, trapped, it took on a threatening tone like it was too bad that Georgy had made the mistake of not being pals with Mr. McLean and now he was going to find out why. I'm indeed sorry, Mr. McLean was saying, you didn't want me to be your papa and I think your mama was indeed sorry too for the way you felt, I think your mama felt pretty bad about it at the time.

He started to protest about this but Mr. McLean's hand tightened on the back of his neck bidding him be quiet until Mr. McLean had finished this piece of long baloney. Well, Mr. McLean said, no hard feelings, old lad, not between you and me anyhow. Not between you and me, old laddie boy, Mr. McLean said later as they swung into Brush Park under the dusky trees. Was he going to park somewhere and was this going to be the lead-up to things going on? He shrank down in the seat as near the window as possible. Now I wanted to make that perfectly clear to you, Mr. McLean said, that's the reason I wanted us to take a little ride together, Georgy, because I wanted to make you see I would have liked to be your papa, I'd have been very proud to have you as my son. But you seemed to act up very hysterical about it, didn't you, old lad? Now, of course you were much younger then, you were only a little kid of seven or eight so it's all a long time ago, all water under the bridge, but I wanted you to know there's no hard feelings.

They drove a long way down a tunnel of dark trees that met overhead. Mr. McLean seemed to have said his say and when Georgy began again to reply, quickly the hand closed over his neck again to restrain him. Now, Georgy, Mr. McLean went on after they had driven almost down to where the river ran through the park, now, lad, I am glad we have had this opportunity to straighten things out now that you are of an age to understand these things more clearly and I hope you understand that your sweet mama, your very understanding and unselfish mama, if I may say so, made a big sacrifice for you. Hmmm? Mr. McLean asked suddenly sharply when Georgy said nothing. Hmmm? I asked you a question, son, Mr. McLean said and his tone was severe. Yes, Georgy said, unsure what he was replying to. I'm glad to hear it, Mr. McLean said, and the car flew by some falling-down old summer cabins not used any more, past decaying boat sheds closed up for the coming winter. I am glad to hear it, old son, because I think you know in a way it's a double sacrifice she made, when she didn't have any responsibility to you. Hmmm? Mr. McLean asked sharply again and this time his hand firmed around Georgy's neck in quite a grip. Don't you agree? Uh huh, he said, not knowing what to agree to, feeling only panic, they were so far into the park now, almost down to the old picnic grounds where no one came once it was fall, Uh huh, he said and remembered what you do is kick them fearfully hard in the balls and then run; Mr. McLean's balls were pretty high up but he would do his best. Uh huh what? Mr. McLean asked. Just uh huh, he said. Well, then I guess you do know what I mean about making an additional sacrifice in her own life to please you, to placate you, old chap, when she really didn't have to pay you much mind at all with all your hooting and hollering.

Suddenly Mr. McLean brought the car to a screaming halt in the broken-down picnic grounds, in the lime yellow creepy light there under the trees where the cracked sign on the falling-down weatherboard shack read HOT DOGS, ICE CREAM, PEPSI. Considering she is not your mother, Mr. McLean said as if he had waited until the car was quiet so the words sprang up like foxes; it was like being bitten with little sharp teeth all over.

Mr. McLean took his hand off Georgy's neck and they stayed sitting there in the damp quiet; dripping bolls and nuts from the tree fell on top of the car roof. So he knew one thing: whatever it was they were parked here for, it wasn't sex, he wasn't going to be molested but maybe worse, the way Mr. McLean was looking at him through his clear windowpane glasses; Mr. McLean was looking at him so kindly and sorry, such a kind daddy look, that he knew something terrible was coming.

Mr. McLean licked at his red mustache and said, You *do* know, don't you, son, that Jessica's not your real mama; you know that, of course, old lad. It was so hot suddenly in the car he was perspiring right through his shirt. Did you know that, Georgy? Mr. McLean asked again in the kindest, gentlest voice, and he knew it would be useless to pretend that he *did* know because Mr. McLean *knew* he didn't know, otherwise he wouldn't be here, trapped; this was the reason for the drive, worse than being molested, he was here to be told something about himself, something quite new, quite terrifying, like being told you aren't really yourself but someone else, that that person in the mirror is not you after all. It was terrifying; whatever was coming was going to be the worst shock ever in his life; he could tell by the way Mr. McLean was being so matter-of-fact. Did you know? Mr. McLean asked and gently ruffled his hair. No, he finally said. He decided to just look ahead out at the falling light on the river. Well, that was a slip, Mr. McLean said, shaking his head sadly, that was a slip on my part, old son, wasn't it? I could bite my tongue out, old boy, I promise you. Mr. McLean put a big hand on his knee and left it there. Sorry, old lad, Mr. McLean said after a spell of hissing through his teeth the way some grown people think in that way they are expressing remorse. Well, Georgy boy, I don't know Jess's reasons for not telling you but I will tell you I think she's wrong not to have told you by now, now you're fourteen or so, big enough feller to be told by now; I don't know Jess's reasons but I think she's *wrong*. Mr. McLean hissed through his teeth to show his disapproval of Jessica and his bafflement at people and especially, he said, as you never had a daddy to tell you anything, Georgy, specially as the only one who *could* have been a daddy to you passed away when you were only a baby practically, I mean Jess's husband, Hal Wood I mean. Tch, tch, tch, what a mess, Mr. McLean said sadly and hissed a bit more. She's your aunt, Georgy, she's your aunt on your mother's side. Your real mother's older sister. You're Mary's child, old son. Hasn't she told you about Mary?

"No," Georgy finally said.

"Hasn't she even *mentioned* Mary to you?"

"No," he said.

"Holy Jesus," Mr. McLean said and took a white handkerchief and dabbed at his hairline so as not to untidy it in any way.

"Oh, boy," Mr. McLean said, "this *is* one hell of a slip, my boy."

The best thing to do was try to be as matter-of-fact as possible about it, not show any surprise or shock and therefore take the wind out of Mr. McLean's sails; also it wouldn't make it hurt and sting so much, it would help him not to feel all those thousands of little prickings on his skin all over as if thousands of little fish were nibbling at him.

Never mentioned Mary? Mr. McLean asked again, and nudged him. I don't think so; maybe she has, I forget, he said and looked out the window at the river, imagining he was far away. Well, Georgy, Mr. McLean said and shifted down in his seat to get more intimate, closer to him. It's like I said before and I meant it; I would like to have been your papa because you are truly a sweet kid, you honestly are, Georgy, I'd like to have had you as my adopted boy and so I'm telling you all this just as if I *was* your adopted daddy, OK? Understand? Uh huh, George said. You *want* to hear, don't you? Mr. McLean asked. Oh, yes, I guess, he said. Well, now we've got the worst over, Mr. McLean said, the rest isn't so bad, Georgy, you might even be *pleased* it's all coming out now.

Sounded more like it was Mr. McLean that was pleased, the way he went on telling the story and spinning it out to a great length, even going so far back as to remember Grandfather Boxer living. All the time the story spun on and on, the dry pods and bolls and twigs from the tree fell on the roof of the car so it was like sitting in a dusty rain; all the time the twilight grew thicker until he could only vaguely see Mr. McLean and all the time he listened with only part of him, holding part of it away from himself until he could be all alone and begin to take it in. But once or twice a word buzzed him like an electric shock and he automatically repeated it. Forced. "Forced?" he asked. She had been "forced" and by one of the "damn workers," Mr. McLean explained. Out along the road one of the "damn workers" got her; attacked her; you might say she'd been asking for something of the sort, crazy girl, a solitary girl, nobody ever got close to her and you couldn't get a word out of her even if you tried, Mr. McLean remembered. But she seemed to have some wild thing tearing away at her, no one knew what it was, some unhappy thing, queer, she was very queer even then and people didn't know what to make of her, her hair cut like a boy and all that, queer as hell she was and one of the stupid things she would do was go off by herself at night like a bat, nocturnal she was. Well, nineteen twenty-six, the year they were beginning to work on the big reservoir out there, some of those guys working on the dam, those dam workers, they were any kind of trash at all, on the lookout for anything that might come along so that's how it happened, Georgy. She never even saw his face, she told Jess later, never could have picked him out in a police line, she said, but that he *forced* her. Guess you know what I mean, old buddy. Know what I mean? I know, Georgy said.

It was completely dark by now and somewhere farther down along the river one light trickled on the water and he tried to imagine her, this queer nocturnal girl with a boy's haircut walking along in the dark in a lonely spot just like it was here and suddenly the dam worker rose up in front of her and grabbed her, hand over her mouth to smother her scream and tearing off her little boy's jacket and— Queer, Mr. McLean said, it seemed to send her off, send her right off, because she kept quiet about it, said nothing to Jess, just lay in her room with the shades pulled down for days and weeks and didn't want to speak to anyone, just picked at something off a tray now and then, laid on her back, Jess said, and covered her face up with the sheet the way they lay out dead people and of course Jess should have guessed by the way she was acting it out that she wanted to be dead, Jess should have got the truth out of her but, Georgy, you can't blame Jess because she was queer as a three-dollar bill, Mary was. So Jess hardly thought too much about it until it was too late. It was too late, I mean, to *do* anything about it. I guess you follow me. Jess took her way up someplace in Maine and when it was over Jess brought *you* home and Mary went down to live with some Dutch woman in Pennsylvania. I mean Jessica *had* to take you because she was so queer, Mary was so queer you couldn't have left a child with her. So there you are, old kid, and here you are.

So that's your story, old son, Mr. McLean said. And you mustn't mind about it. Grow up and make your own life, son. She's made hers, Mary has, and I guess never once asked could she see you even though she's only down there in Minton, Pa., not dead or in India someplace, and writes poetry and calls herself John Citadel and I've heard lots of people say she's a genius and they handed her that prize, whatever it is; well, maybe that's why she was so queer, maybe she *is* a genius.

*Any*way, Mr. McLean said and laughed and kneaded his shoulder, you can't really blame *either* of them for what happened; it just happened and here you are; you can't very well get yourself *unborn*.

Running. Where? He had been running away from the car
and Mr. McLean still shouting, Georgy, come back, I'll drive
you home. Running where? What, back? To be unborn? Or
running to find John Citadel and find out it wasn't true she
was queer, find out she was wonderful maybe, maybe the
ugly things Mr. McLean said about her weren't true and all
the things that ran with him in his mind the night he ran
all the way home out of Brush Park in the dusty dark but
suddenly it was day and slowing down, green grass was
under his feet wearing kid sandals and the day was hot and
blue, grass smelled and the reason everything looked so odd,
so big, was his child height, was being in his child body.

His child body now led him along, skipping, while he saw
through his middle-aged senses; thought jadedly but spoke
in the chirrupy little-boy voice. How different he was, how
different everything was, how much brighter, as if skin had
been peeled off his eyes, sky, grass, clouds blazed, why, at
nine years old the sign over the general store on Prize Street
which was for Old Dutch cleanser was delightful, all those
girls in yellow wooden shoes and their skirts so blue and
rushing about with sticks, was the kind of thing that makes
you feel glad coming home from school and you hop, skip and
jump, then make out you are a werewolf, drag one leg behind
you and opening your mouth wide give out terrific groans,
jut your jaw out as far as it will go so Mrs. Ransome coming
by said, Oh, Georgy, how you scared me. Yung yung yung,
he said to Mrs. Ransome and lifted his arms over his head in
a menacing gesture coming at her so she obliged him by
pretending she must run from him; the feeling that nothing
much in him had yet been used, his new teeth were coming
in a bit crooked, his young skin was fresh, his thick brown
hair was clean and glossy and had finally learned to part
itself on the left; funny to think he didn't know anything
about sex yet, his virgin little thing, pretty as a seashell, was
for only one purpose, pee-pee; he slept on one side without

quivering from eight until seven in serene dreamlessness or so he thought; the joys of eating were such that the perspective of a day could be said to center around a bacon and tomato sandwich; possession could mean having a new school ruler that marked both inches and centimeters and was so beautifully shellacked that it tasted of gold when you sucked it; if he thought about anything in the future it was to own a pair of Thom McAn oxblood shoes with extra-heavy welts like older boys had; the songs he learned because it pleased him to sing aloud were brand new and splendid and it rattled him to be told they were not all fresh as new-laid eggs but old as all get-out, some from way back in the twenties.

He had stopped at his house and decided to hop all the way in on one leg, supposing he had lost the other one; hopped up the kitchen steps, hopped into the kitchen and said to nothing, nobody, I'm home. Hey, I'm home, he said to nobody. I'm home, he said into the refrigerator and then because she wasn't around, gulped cold milk right from the bottle and then looked in the parlor and in the little sewing room but everything was empty, the house sat sunning itself and giving comfortable little creaks of contentment. He went upstairs singing *Ten cents a dance is what they pay me* and his mother burst out of the bedroom tidying her hair and closed the door very quickly but not before he had seen That Man sitting on her bed and tying his shoelaces. Well, you gave me a start, she said and pushed him gently downstairs, what are you doing home so early? We didn't go swimming on account of Mr. Jorgensen's mother kicked the bucket, he told her and he knew by her face she knew he'd seen. What was he doing tying his *shoelaces?* Had he taken his shoes off? Milk? she said. She had on her good lavender dress too and perfume.

Mr. McLean, she said, came by to give me a hand moving that marble washstand. She poured milk. Now, Georgy, you be nice to Mr. McLean; he has been a great help to me lately and I need his help from time to time; now you be sweet to him, Bitsy.

But the marble washstand wasn't in her bedroom and why was he lacing up his shoes? He knew and didn't know, he almost knew and the almost knowing was worse, was like telling a dirty story without understanding the point of it but *something* was going on, he knew right off by the way she was moving around the kitchen, in a quick jerky way, all dressed up in her Sunday lavender dress too and had on her pearl necklace in the middle of the day; why, she was so excited she was boiling over. How young she was; he wouldn't have remembered how young and pretty his mother was then, her soft brown hair with no gray in it parted in the middle and drawn back over her ears in the manner of Kay Francis; her legs were pretty too.

Georgy's home, she said in a breathless voice when Mr. McLean came into the kitchen. His plaid suit seemed to make him huger than ever, his great horn-rimmed glasses circled his big face like antlers growing out of his red eyebrows and his huge red mustache could have been used to brush a dog. Well, now, hel*lo*, old buddy, Mr. McLean said and put a huge hand on him and kneaded his shoulder and he saw that his mother was flashing a message to Mr. McLean; funny but her messages were so easy to read it was pathetic, she thinking she was conveying something he couldn't understand, the way she kept sliding her eyes from one side to the other in quick succession which meant, Be careful, he is on to us, I think, and then she said, Bitsy, if you have homework to do you better go do it; we are going to eat early tonight because Mr. McLean and I are going to a show down in Westport and Ginny Hancock's coming in to stay with you. And will you look after the house while we're gone, old bud-bud, Mr. McLean asked.

No, he said and ran out of the kitchen and upstairs be-

cause he'd been struck with what was going on and very
likely the walls would fall in pretty soon, the roof of the house
would cave in pretty soon because what his mother meant
with her signals and Mr. McLean meant by "we're gone"—
we are gone—was *they* were going steady. So that was
what it was all about lately; she was forever on the phone
talking to someone in a low breathy voice and then hanging
up quickly when he came into the room. That was one thing
and another was that lately they'd started going to church
again every Sunday and this was funny because she was
against the church; after his papa had died so suddenly with
his head in the pea soup at the table, after all the crying was
over she had screamed out at some of the comforters who
came around with jelly and soup and things, Don't talk God
to *me* in this house, I don't want Him here, and once when
they had been walking down Oak Street past the Presbyterian church she had stopped a minute and read out the text
"Come Unto Me All Ye Who Are Heavy Laden and I Will
Give Thee Rest" and, Well, she said, I'd have to be *pretty*
heavy laden to go to *them* for anything.

Now all of a sudden they were off to church every Sunday
morning like it was a treat or something, her in her lavender
dress and her pearl necklace and simply bathed in eau de
cologne and then coming out of church she always made
believe something was in her eye or her stockings were
crooked or something and she'd fuss away about her dress
or fumble in her purse until Mr. McLean (of course he
should have known all along this was why) came out with
his sister Mabel and then they would greet each other in
these high put-on voices adults use when they are up to
something and think, poor simps, they are throwing dust in
everybody's eyes and, Oh, Jessica, he would say, I didn't see
you in church, what a surprise, you know my sister Mabel,
and, Oh, *Bob*, his mother would cry, well, my goodness yes,
how are you, Mabel, and are you walking our way? Every

Sunday morning was the same only lately they'd begun to
drop the high-voice stuff and begun the flashing of messages
above his head accompanied by talk about the weather and
talk about Mr. Roosevelt (Mr. McLean was terribly against
Mr. Roosevelt for some reason) and gardening (Mr. McLean
was always urging his mother to get her somethingorothers
in) but all the time their eyebrows flashed signals to each
other, their eyes went up and down each other, they arched
their necks and walked like cats with tails weaving in the
air, which meant only one thing, they were in love and going
steady and maybe *even* . . . maybe even doing whatever it
was the kids hooted about and wrote about in the school
lavatory and only he and Willy Ransome didn't know the
full facts about but pretended they did.

Now supposing Bob McLean with the big hands, awful
hands, covered with golden hair, was going to *move in* and
stay in his mother's bedroom. Well, he'd rather be dead,
that's what, dead like his papa than see that happen. Mr.
McLean was the kind of man who in the movies you knew
right off not to trust, like Monroe Owsley, and yet his mother
didn't seem to see this, she was behaving like a young girl,
always swooning around, always putting her hands up to
touch her hair and breathing rapidly as if something were
wrong with her heartbeat. But what was going to happen?
He took a crayon and destroyed the face of Babe Ruth while
he thought about it. Something desperate needed to be done.

Then he knew, all of a sudden, what to do.

It took them a while to notice, of course, they were always
so taken up with each other even handing the vegetables
around, and the way Mr. McLean spooned turnip you would
have thought it was *his* spoon, *his* turnip, the way Mr.
McLean served you peas was as though it were a terrific
privilege to be served by him; he was so uppity that he kind
of *bequeathed* you the bread and never noticed whether you
had said thanks or up your ass but at last he *began* to notice

and leaned over and said, "You're very thoughtful tonight, old buddy," and his mother said, "Cat got your tongue, Bitsy?" and later when they were leaving for Westport Mr. McLean said loudly, "I think we have a case of the sulks here, Jess," and his mother said, "Now, Bitsy, maybe you need an old-fashioned dose of castor oil; we'll see tomorrow."

It was hard not to crack at times when he felt a bit sorry for the way she began to look and the little ways she tried to trick him into speaking by being very sweet. "Bitsy, I wish you would say *something, anything*," or, "Maybe you could just give me a hint what's wrong?" and then she would storm and say, "You're behaving like a silly fool and I've had enough of it," and she would flare around the kitchen banging pots on the stove and threatening there would be no movies this Saturday, no allowance, no reading in bed, *nothing* if he didn't stop this. But after the storm had subsided and he was still pretending he didn't exist (that was how he thought of it, as if he were air, invisible; it was easier to keep silent if he pretended he had vanished into thin air, and he saw himself turning into vapor) she would begin to look very tired and she would begin again to wheedle. "Are you going to keep this up forever?" or, "What is it you want from me?" "Would you give me just a hint, would you nod or shake your head?" and when he remained just air, not in the room, silent while the clocks ticked around his now desperate mother, she would get up and push her hands against her temples and say, "All right, all right, you can't keep this up forever; nobody could keep it up forever."

But days went by.

Then at times she would be very quiet for hours, wiping dishes, making pastry, and then try to catch him off guard. "WHAT WAS THAT?" she would yell and once or twice he almost fell for it, or suddenly she would swing around on him holding a cookie and say, "Want a cookie, yes or no?" or she would come rushing in on him from outside calling, "Was that the phone?" He almost bit his tongue through one day not to say no, it wasn't. At times she became faint and sweet and sank down in a chair next to him and put her arm along the back of his chair and leaned her face down to him and said, "What is it, Bitsy? What is it, baby? Please tell Mama, oh, please don't go on like this for another day, baby, you are making Mama sick; I can't sleep or eat or anything, Bitsy; this is cruel, baby. Is it just because you don't like Mr. McLean very much, huh? is that why, Bitsy?" and then her waspy stinging-bee side would take over her voice like a locomotive whistle and she would shriek, "I mean it, if you don't stop this immediately I am going TO TAKE STEPS, YOU HEAR ME?"

His cold childish heart knew it wouldn't be too much longer. How cold his childish heart had been, how it had gradually warmed over the years so that it could give in in situations, so it could lose; but not now, not then; it was as cold as the heart of the little boy in "The Snow Queen" with the sliver of ice in his heart.

They grew awkward in his silent presence and began making chat; you could tell it was chat because it was not interesting to either of them. Then Mr. McLean began leaving earlier and earlier, he always had a very big day tomorrow, and then he began staying away and all they had were long conversations on the telephone. "I don't know what to do," he heard his mother say. "I don't want to take him to a doctor but . . ." and then she would say, "Of *course* it will pass, it's just childish jealousy, that's all," and he knew his heart must stay as cold as ice because this was the testing time and if he felt a drop of sorrow and pity for her now he would lose the battle she was waging with her slumped shoulders, her sorrowful accusing eyes (and he watched for her little traps; she set traps to make him utter a word; she hid all his underpants expecting he would have to ask for a clean pair, so he went to school in just his pants; she apple-pied his bed, so he slept on the floor; she took his chair from the table and he ate standing up until she brought it back), and now she fought with the only thing she had left, by not speaking to *him* either; the house was silent as the public library.

But when she broke it was different than he'd imagined; she just came upstairs and leaned into his room and flicked a duster and said in a flat voice, "George, Mr. McLean is not coming to the house any more, at least for a while so you can have your tongue back," and then she turned away and as she was going she said a peculiar thing, or rather she had begun to say a peculiar thing and stopped. "You are *exactly like*—"

Then she had gone downstairs and far away slammed a door as if to put an exclamation point to it.

How very cold he was, had been, cold-blooded, that was, heartless as could be; he had merely picked up again his *Swiss Family Robinson* and gone on reading; how cold he had been; he could hardly believe it, he could not recognize this child on the bed calmly reading after this thing he'd done so deliberately, not even getting up and calling out after her something, anything; how could this child have been he? Was this little boy, now brushing one piece of hair out of his eye and putting a licorice drop into his mouth while he read, going to grow into likable George Wood, friend to all? But of course he had been only nine, he did not know then that she was not his mother and therefore he had even less right to interfere in her plans for herself; he had been too young to consider that even though Mr. McLean might be odious, he was what she fancied and he had come between them and spoiled that for her and she had never mentioned his name again (stopped going to church from that day), which was extremely fair of her, but this child sucking licorice on the bed was not concerned with fairness, this child was cold as ice, loved no one but himself and didn't know it and no one would have guessed it in the photographs that later remained of this child with the big eyes half shadowed in lashes; nobody would have guessed the secret that this child was as cool-headed as any thug; the child killer with a stone heart who later would become the biggest mouther of warm sweet nothings so that he would be known as "sweet George"; he observed his child self with consternation; he would have liked to be able to split the moment here and, tearing the atoms of time apart, step into the room and shake the child of himself and say, Go on down now and say something comforting to her and make some sort of amends, for if you don't you will be the worse off for it in twenty or thirty or forty years, I promise you; you are hardening at this moment into something so distasteful I cannot tell you, I see it beginning at this very minute, the beginning of some kind of stasis of the heart; do you know what that means, a cessation of feeling which will gradually make you impotent emotionally; go on now, Georgy, quick, run. This moment could decide against you becoming a fraud about love for the rest of your life, immune to any real feeling, not willing to be bloodied, but only safe and faking passion, making out with getting people's undying affection, rewarding them with garlands of pretty compliments for the rest of

very quickly changing, walls running liquidly down into floors and what was running hot and wet down his legs? why, he had peed his pants, he had pee-peed; why, then he was only practically a
Baby.
Baby, his papa said, sit up at the table with papa, but he wasn't quite high enough yet and they sat him on the telephone book to reach his mug and dish; she was at the stove and his papa was playing a game with him, his papa, he adored his papa, his big papa who smelled so nice always,

smelled of lemons, clean; this was very hazy indeed because it was practically beyond memory; he was entering the final zone of reexperience before darkness, before actual birth, he was already in the outskirts of the time no one remembers; they were at the table playing a game and they took turns being things, each had to guess what the other was; Hal had been his name, this man he still thought of as his papa (had preserved a photograph of him from which every sign of character had been removed by genteel retouching); his face had been enormously creased as if he had been sleeping on it too long, it was crushed and lined and great fissures appeared in the cheeks when he grinned and it was easy to see they had an intense regard for each other but in his baby state he had not recognized it as love; his papa was tying on his bib and he was in a fit of giggles because his papa had very cleverly impersonated the water pitcher pouring itself out; now it's your turn, Bits, his papa said, and he became an orange by closing his eyes and puffing out his cheeks and thinking very orangy. What I am? You are a big fat pig? You are a big fat basketball? Now, Hal, his mama said from behind putting their big plates of steaming pea soup in front of them, now, Hal, don't distract him, let him eat his dinner, please, Hal, let him have his soup while it's hot. You are a *huge snowball,* his papa guessed but no, no, no. Well, I give up, his papa said. I'm an orange, he said, and heard the baby say, I's an onnnge, but his papa, unlike his mama, always knew what he meant. Oh, you're a terrific orange, his papa said and lovingly covered his little head with a great hand. Now it was Papa's turn. Oh, don't distract him from his soup, Hal, his mama said. What you be? he asked his papa; his papa had sat up very high suddenly and opened his mouth and eyes very wide being something and then pitched forward face down into the hot pea soup. Oh, how he shrieked with glee and clapped his hands; this was the best thing Papa had ever pretended to be, lying with his face right in the pea soup, oh, he was almost sick laughing, it was so funny, but maybe it was not quite so funny, a bit frightening when his mother began calling, Hal, Hal, a bit frightening when she managed to lift Papa up in his chair and then the way the thick green soup slowly dripped down his papa's face with the eyes wide open, staring. . . .

It isn't that I hold any enmity toward Mary, it's just that she always seemed to be in my way, his mother was saying outside on the porch to his father.

And he was in his bed, earlier again, on a hot night, the faint light on the ceiling showing the plaster fruit where the gas lamp once had hung when she was young and at the time of babyhood when this was going on he had been awake but he could not make out the adult words, just as he could not then read but in his old mind now the words she had said that night slowly formed in smoky syllables to become understandable and what she said was:

I felt I was always working my way to some point of my life and when I got there Mary was already there, do you know what I mean? I was always cruelly shy and had to work *so* hard to make friends and Mary would do nothing and yet they would invariably be more interested in her and that sort of thing. I wanted so much to be a concert pianist and worked and worked to get my scholarship and she did nothing, lazed around, and then she wrote that first long verse in two days and people are still reading it. Well, she was a genius even then and of course I wasn't and funnily enough it wasn't her success I envied, it was her effortless nature, the way she just drifted through her life and everything came to her and I thought—forgive me, Hal—that I'd got the better of her when I got married; oh, don't misunderstand me, my dear, I couldn't help feeling I had at last trumped her ace and then when that woman friend of hers explained to me about what she *was*, what *they* were to each other, I suppose I should have felt sorry for her but you know all I could think was she'd got the better of me again because —and again don't misunderstand me, dear—even if I had married the president of the United States it wouldn't have mattered to her, and now that I no longer have to compete with her, at a time when we are finally parted in our separate lives, now I've even got her *child* instead of one of my own, like the cuckoo in the nest.

Shhhhh, his father said. Jess, you must never say that; I want you never to say that again, hear?

Don't be silly, Hal. You don't think I meant I don't care, do you? Of course I love him and I'll always love, do my best to love him, in my own way of course, but it's not going to be easy and I won't pretend it is, ever to forget whose baby he is; you can't rewrite the past and what I'm saying is —and, Hal, don't misunderstand me that I don't adore and cherish Bitsy just as if he was mine, ours; but don't you see what the ironic thing is?—the ironic thing is that every time I want to put my arms around him and hug him it comes over me that he's Mary's and you see she has managed to spoil it again for me, she has got the better of me again.

With a great effort he had turned in his bed, hot with shame for the years he would misunderstand her, had misunderstood her efforts at affection that left her weak sometimes.

Don't be sorry, he called out through the window. It's I that ought to be sorry.

Was that the baby? she cried, coming running.

Whatsamatter? Did he have a bad dream? Whatsamatter? Want a drink of water?

He was blubbering for her, poor woman, stuck with him until she would die over seventy, free of him at last, duty done, her best; blew on cold fires in herself to heat warmth and affection for him, and her constancy through all those

years, unwilling, disappointed, but plodding along hiding all
this under simulated sarcasm, broke his heart now, touched
his heart with the splinter of ice in it: she was deserving of
some respect from him.

He cried about it.

Are you hot, baby? It's a terrible hot night; wait till I slip
the sheets down a bit; there now, poor baby.

He said between sobs, I wish I could have become just a
little solicitous for you.

What, Bitsy? she asked. What is it? Want your teddy?
Let's see can we find your teddy. Wheeere's teddy?

He put an affectionate hand to her face but to her it was
only a baby's paw sticking in her eye and she removed it
firmly.

Here's teddy, she said. Now lie down and go to sleep.
You're a good boy now, such a good boy, such a good baby
he is, poor baby all made out of lit-tle bitsand*pieces*, lit-tle
bitsandpieces of this and that and pudding and pie.

Tucked in, he said, I wish I could have read you better,
Jess, but it made no sense in baby talk and only made her
irritable with him.

Now go to sleep, Bitsy, that's enough now. You've got your
teddy and you had your drink; now I don't want another
peep out of you tonight. Go to sleep now, Georgy.

Was this the end? His dimming consciousness had begun
to expect some blacking out as the point of actual birth ap-
proached, had begun to long for the anesthesia of being
senseless to anything tangible going on around for certainly
that would happen soon, he was quite beyond the remote
shores of anything but subconscious memory now; his body,
growing smaller by the hour now as the acceleration of the
ingrowing counteracting inversion of his flesh reduced chro-
mosomes, bones softening, weighing less and less, his vision
paling so he was conscious only of vivid colors now, of the
primary colors, could no longer see gray or pale blue or pink,

but when would the actual moment come when he was entirely superseded by air into fetus and then drowned in placenta and from that into egg into ovum into sperm of an unknown dam worker (and he could still remember that, so part of the memory chain worked) and into wind then, he imagined it, just the wind of outer darkness that blows above us around the silent constellation but

Poon, he gurgled, poon. Goo-goo.

Poon was spoon, goo-goo was egg, he remembered, lovely salty egg and spit running down his chin into his bib, banged poon on goo-goo, must be breakfast, in his high chair with little yellow ducks on the tray. Spooge, he said; his older mind could not translate all that he said; he was talking aloud to himself alone in the kitchen. Spidge, he said, doo doo. He was fascinated for a long time with his thumb, what a thing it was with a little pink nail on it; into the mouth it went with goo-goo all over it; it was comforting, like something missed.

Not wind and darkness yet, then, but something was changing, he felt as if his self, his body and what was left of consciousness, was being atomized now into two separate entities, one going one way and one the other as if the baby were being drawn away from him or him from the baby and looking up through the baby's gauzy eyes he saw what was the most terrifying sight of anyone's life: there he was outside the window, grown to middle-age, the tape measure of his life had been finally paid out end to end, it stretched from the baby to the man at the window and the man at the window already knew it; was tapping on the glass to get the attention of the baby, the man wore a Sherlock Holmes cap and a blue woolen muffler and had a big ridiculous mustache and worst of all a hopeful look as if life still might hold something for him when even a baby could see he was a hopeless loser at everything: no talent, no depth, no originality, no

passion, no gallantry, purpose, courage, honesty; only a talent
for mild compliments and a talent for being liked; why, the
man was fatigued beyond his capacity with the search for
approval—he even wanted the baby's approval; he tapped
on the glass and waved to the baby.

i don't want to be *that*, the baby screamed; the baby threw
down his spoon, shrieked until his mother's voice called, stop
that, bitsy, i've had all i can stand of you today, naughty

darkness was beginning and he could faintly hear the sound
of wind and in the redness coming down color of blood
around him he sucked in breath, he made the last great effort
to put man and baby together; man's strength into infant
body, stop the process for the few seconds before disappearing; he hung onto a rock, searched in his life for a rock to
hold onto a second while his river swirled around him, the
rock ruth, ruth was the rock, plain as clear glass ruth, the
best of everybody, unchanging ruth, and now he had to say
a word, he summoned every last remaining breath of willpower pushing against the current and got the baby out of
the high chair onto the floor and got the baby's feet tottering
to the kitchen table and climbed the baby at last onto the
chair where in reach of the phone he held together the two
ends of life with enormous effort before vanishing, now if
you could scream loud enough as a baby could you be heard
at the other end of your life? now it was prayer for time
enough to remember that all time, his past-future, was just
this tape measure, all the same time, same time, the baby's
fingers forced by the man terribly hard to do keep awake
remember ruth was still there somewhere ages it took to remember figures dial receiver weighed a ton could kill you if
it fell on you years light light years ago ahead or back didn't
matter all the same ringing ringing and then from another
star he felt ruth said hello and ruth he thought he said I am
dying of extreme youth can you hear me, hello, ruth said, I

set everything going back and am going ruth, what did you want, ruth asked, who is it, I have only time to tell you, he said, that I didn't know I loved you

She was in the garden cutting back some of the honeysuckle vines that had begun choking the roses when she was startled by the ringing of the telephone.

Startled because it was now so rare. But also as she went indoors, taking off her gardening gloves, because she was shaken with the feeling that it was news of him; without any doubt the telephone had a shrill insistency, come-quick ring to it, so much so that she let it ring several more times to quieten her heartbeats with several deep breaths before she picked it up.

"Hello."

And now whose voice?

But to her disappointment it was a child with a wrong number. Or it seemed to be a child. Ruth could make no sense of the voice, coming through the static, perhaps long distance.

"Who did you want?" she asked. "What number are you calling?"

The indistinct babbling continued. "Who is it?" she asked once more.

After a little while she hung up.

72 73 74 75 10 9 8 7 6 5 4 3 2 1